DIARY OF INDIGNITIES

DIARY OF INDIGNITIES

BY **PATRICK HUGHES**

PRESS™

MILWAUKIE

 # DIARY OF INDIGNITIES

Publication design by Jon Resh/Undaunted.

M Press
10956 SE Main Street
Milwaukie OR 97222

mpressbooks.com

badnewshughes.blogspot.com

First Edition: May 2007
ISBN-10: 1-59582-103-1
ISBN 13: 978-1-59582-103-4

1 3 5 7 9 10 8 6 4 2

Printed in the United States of America

INTRODUCTION AND ACKNOWLEDGMENTS

Many moons ago, or I guess just several moons ago, I came home from my dead-end job to a cramped, empty apartment, clicked on the TV so it wouldn't seem so damn lonely and started inhaling supper. I was constantly depressed, and food was one of my few comforts. Somehow, though, while trying to take off my tie and vigorously eat at the same time, I smashed a fish taco into my forehead.

Goddamn, I thought, sitting there with cabbage bits and sauce dripping off my face. My life sucks. Something stupid like this happens to me every day. And I really, really was looking forward to eating that taco.

Convinced I had been singled out by fate for special attention, I started cataloging these small, daily indignities, hoping to eventually assemble enough proof to take my case before, um, the gods, I guess, and have my grievances addressed. I mean, I was only slightly more awful a person than average, and yet horrible things were visited upon me, body and mind, on an all-too-regular basis, something I felt I did not deserve.

I used a thing on the Internet called a blog to collect this evidence, and people started reading it. Many seemed to find my stupid life simply funny, but I suspect I touched a few people as well, people who didn't really find that shit funny at all but were aghast at the openness with which I addressed issues concerning my butt and pee-hole and such, and, fixated with disgust, couldn't turn away.

Now, an indeterminate number of moons later, I'm still depressed, alone and in the same bleak little apartment, but I sit naked on a throne of human skulls, drinking warm blood while surveying my blog empire of pain. Dozens, if not several, semi-literate people make it a point to read my site on a regular basis, and, obviously, a carefully calibrated combination of bribery and extortion has enabled me to convince the otherwise ambivalent dudes at *Hustler* to publish a collection of juicy select indignities, freshly lacquered with an enticing sheen of copy edit. You now hold this in your hands. What? It's M Press? Look, whatever.

Anyway, I guess this is all an improvement over where I was back on sad taco-face day, so I'm obligated by society's demands to acknowledge the following people for their support, kindness and assistance in getting me to this point:

Thanks to Brian Doherty, Chris Warner and all at M Press, Jon Resh, Neil Hughes, David Cassidy, Scott Adams, Todd Campisi, Sean Bonner, Greg Ceton, Chris Edmundson, Tracey at Sweetney.com, Caitlin at StyrofoamKitty.com, Maud Newton, Mimi Smartypants, the *Boing Boing* people, the Metafilter people, Dana at the sadly defunct NumberOneHitSong.com, Kim du Toit and everyone who ever bothered to link, read and comment over at http://badnewshughes.blogspot.com. Thanks to all the ex-girlfriends, roommates and cronies I wrote about who didn't get mad and played along. Thanks, too, go to all the shitty jobs and petty bosses of my adult life, both for the computer access as well as for ensuring I was idle and unhappy enough to type this stuff out in the first place. Finally, I'd like to give heaps of thanks to my beloved family for being such a big, sociopathic draw, and single out Mom and Dad for special credit, because where would all this come from if it wasn't for their special approach to parenting? All y'all are good sports.

Oh, and to my current boss: please don't fire me, assuming I can't hide this book from you. I like *you,* and wrote all this stuff on other people's dimes, I swear.

DIARY OF INDIGNITIES

KISS ME, YOU RETARD

1981

Oh, I just remembered—one time I made out with this retarded kid in church.

Ah, shit. I, uh . . . You know, I actually shouldn't say "retarded." I should say "Down Syndrome."

You see, like your average low-grade racist, everyday homophobe or commonplace hypocrite, I employ a double standard when it comes to certain types of pejorative language. For example, I distinguish between Down Syndrome and retarded. This is chiefly so I can go around applying the latter term to everything around me with only minor flashes of guilt, mind you, instead of an attempt to remain in the good graces of polite society.

I know from personal experience how few things are as delightful as watching some dickhead squirm his way out of a semantic dead end, so allow me to explain in detail: in my stupid brain, Down Syndrome describes a medical condition. Like other—let's face it—less than ideal medical conditions, such as having a gross hairy unibrow or being Irish, that's something only a real creep would mock or deride.

Conversely, retarded, at least to me and my labored justifications, is not a condition but rather something implying choice—deliberate, willful action. Like that time Sean Atwater looked up from his sandwich and said, "Hey, you know what they say? They say if you took your intestines and stretched them from end to end they would reach all the way to the moon."

Ha ha, the moon. He really said that. There were like eleven guys in the room, all sitting around eating food and watching the NFL draft, nodding and going, "Oh, really, I didn't know that, how interesting," while I sat there dumbfounded for a minute before blurting out, "Motherfuckers, do you know how *far away* the *fucking moon* is?!"

You're in deep shit when I'm the voice of reason.

Anyway, retardation can be activated or exacerbated by outside forces such as marijuana, a license to drive or the Bible, but ultimately the responsibility for that shit lies with . . . well, the retard who propagated it.

I'm not saying people with Down Syndrome can't be retarded, just that in my little world the two things aren't necessarily tied together as cause and effect. Shit, it'd be almost disrespectful to say they can't—people with Down Syndrome can be just as retarded as anyone else. They can also be just as boring, petty, sheeplike or surly as you ~~or me~~, and nobody can take that away from them.

Oh, and even though I don't want to appear insensitive, even though I sort of am, and I swear I got nothing against folks with the Down Syndrome, I'm not afraid of them either, and I'd totally fight a guy who has Down Syndrome, no problem, unless he's big and mean or one of those Special Olympics dudes who's in particularly good physical condition.

You know, I just realized—I don't *want* to fight anyone with Down Syndrome. I don't really hang around anyone with Down Syndrome, but thinking back, most of my interactions with people who have the condition have been pretty positive. This is more than I can say for just about any other group out there. And hell, no bullshit rationalization would be complete without an analogue to a Some of My Best Friends Are Black story, so allow me to share an example: two years ago I was in the checkout line at a grocery store, wearing my Four Horsemen T-shirt, a cherished artifact from the bygone days when professional wrestling wasn't so lowbrow.

Anyway, the guy bagging my stuff, a dude who pretty obviously had a touch of the Down Syndrome, glanced over at me and did a brilliant double take before fixating on my shirt, staring at it with unblinking, wide eyes like I had a set of big juicy titties under there.

"The Four Horsemen!" he yelled.

"Yup," I said.

"I love the Four Horsemen!" he said. You could tell he was excited. The cashier looked nervous and started exchanging looks with the other cashiers and bag boys.

"Me too," I replied. I was getting a little excited as well.

"The original Four Horsemen was Ric Flair, Ole Anderson, Arn Anderson and Tully Blanchard!"

"I know," I said.

"But the *best* Four Horsemen was when they had Ric Flair, Arn Anderson, Tully Blanchard and Barry Windham!" He was practically yelling.

"I know!" I said. I guess I was kind of yelling, too.

"Luger sucked! He was a bad Four Horseman!" he yelled.

"Paul Roma, too!" I yelled back. Before he could yell another reply, though, some douche bag assistant manager with a child-molester mustache commandeered two burly stock guys to grab my new friend under his arms and drag him away.

I gazed after him, sadly, maintaining eye contact as long as possible. The look he gave me said, "It's alright. You and me, maybe we're not made for grocery society. But you can still run—go, save yourself. We dared to soar today, and they can never take that away from us. These stock boys, these petty managers and cashiers—they'll never quench the fire in our hearts." They got around a big pyramid of soup or canned pumpkin or some shit and he was gone.

The cashier tilted her head at me in a way that invited punches and said, "We're sorry about that, sir."

Sorry for what? For dragging away the only guy in the store capable of having an interesting conversation? I doubt it. Reluctantly, I gathered up my grocery bags and left. A better man than me would have beheaded the assistant manager with a clothesline, sprinted to the back of the store, put a couple of piledrivers on those two stock-boy meatheads and freed Four Horsemen Guy from the walk-in cooler or wherever they hide people too awesome to conform to their safe little square-ass grocery regulations. And then we would run out of the store with a giant bag of money. And go on to have adventures.

I think about that guy every time I go to the store and some lame white guy with too much gel in his hair gets all fake-buddy on me while bagging my groceries: "Heyyyyy! Noodles! I've been meaning to try some noodles! What do you think of *these* noodles, sir?!"

"What? Uh, they're, um, good," I say, while in my head I'm like, "I think you've been instructed to say that by some assistant manager, probably the one who took my pal away, and instead of pretending to care about noodles you need to shuck the fut up. I mean fuck the shut . . . Aw, forget it." Goddamn it, I get so upset I can't even mount an effectively snappy comeback in my own fantasy.

Wait, where was I? Oh yeah, the making out. No, I never really got the opportunity to make out with the guy at the grocery store. The make-out session was with the kid in church and—okay, well, technically I didn't really *make out* with the kid in church, either. It was more like he made out with me, and I kind of just let him.

Growing up, did you have these weird churches that would get buses to drive around and kidnap kids during the summer and lure them in with ice cream and stuff so they'd love Jesus? We did.

One of those buses came around one summer day when I was about eleven. They were pimping the free ice cream, so I went ahead and hopped on. Plus, back then I believed in all that kinda stuff, and even though I knew I was going to have to sit through an hour or two of boring churchy talk before getting a crack at the goodies, I felt like it was a healthy way to spend a hot-ass Wednesday afternoon.

Mom, of course, being crazy and a lesbian, was always sprucing up the house with Wicca and spells and crystals and the Goddess and shit, so I was on the lookout for opportunities to get a little Jesus infusion and inoculate myself against the hippie paganism that was always hanging around trying to drag me down to Hell.

Sometimes if I was careless about inquiring after denomination during these little bus rides, I'd get kidnapped off to a Baptist day camp, where the church ladies and clean-cut regular kids pretty much made you feel like a grain of dirt just by their shiny all-American existence. Plenty of sweet tea at those things, but there's nothing like hanging around well-adjusted normal people who have all their teeth and wear recently laundered pants and stuff to reinforce just exactly what rung of society's ladder you're on. Kind of made me uncomfortable.

This time, though, the ice cream landed me the jackpot. I was so excited when the kidnap bus pulled up to the church, because it was this terrifying renegade non-denominational church that had intrigued me for years. At night the church would shine this megawatt giant black light on itself, I guess to make it look all holy and impressive and full of cosmic Jesus radiation, but really it just made it look all haunted and creepy as fuck. My sister and I would actually bug Mom to drive us by it if we were anywhere near that part of town at night, chanting and calling for the Spooky Light Church like other kids do for Dairy Queen.

It was almost as good in the daytime. An unearthly, eldritch glow didn't seep out of it or anything, but it was run-down and plenty seedy. I felt right at home.

I don't really remember what all kinds of heretical made-up stuff they indoctrinated me in for the first part of the day. They would collect kids from all over the city, so like everyone else I was busy sizing up all the unfamiliar faces. Gradually us kids began to relax, after we all realized they had only culled from the dirty, poor and weird neighborhoods, and no Baptists were going to come along to make us feel inferior.

I shuffled from one classroom to another for a few hours with the other loser kids, listening to various pastors and ministers and cantors and such drone on about how listening to the Beatles was going to send us all to burn in a lake of fire or how we'll need to know how to field-strip and clean these surplus M1 carbines when the race war comes, blah blah blah. They kept taunting us with that ice cream, promising us cold creamy treats and eternal salvation if we sat through two more filmstrips about how the Bible says it'll be our duty to someday beat our wives or whatever.

Eventually they rounded us all up and herded us into a large auditorium for a little final brainwash. I got sat in the very front row, right in front of the podium or altar or whatever it was. Next to me was a kid with Down Syndrome.

This kid noticed my fancy digital watch right as the church folks started up their little lecture. Now, these days you couldn't impress a backwoods Yanomami with that thing (and don't think I haven't tried), but at the time its sleek, biscuit-sized, red Light Emitting Diode face was at the cutting edge of new technology. The kid stared at it with interest while I looked straight ahead and acted like I was listening, trying my best to impress God with my ability to pay attention to things that are boring.

I felt a tapping on my watch and looked down. The kid was poking at it, curious. He looked at me with his eyebrows raised, and I guessed he was curious why the watch wasn't showing the time. I returned my gaze to the front of the room but, happy to show off a little, quietly pressed the button that activated the display.

Man, that kid broke into a big smile, so I thought I'd *really* show him something, and slyly pressed the button again to show the date. His eyes got wide. I pushed that bitch again, and the seconds popped up. My new buddy was transfixed, like I had a set of big juicy titties under there. I ran through that sequence of technological marvels for him a few times, staring straight ahead all the while, before noticing that the guy up there in front of me giving the sermon was starting to wise up and disapprove.

Not wanting them to make an example out of me and zap me with their eerie nighttime holy ray, I quit fooling around and concentrated my efforts on the business at hand. Something about the glory of becoming a child bride of The Leader, I don't exactly remember. This didn't sit well with the kid, though. He wanted more sweet watch action.

He started tapping at the watch and pulling at my sleeve, but I was unmoved. After a couple seconds he figured out the button trick, using it to access the endless amusements of the time, date and electronically ticking seconds. I was confident in my battery's reserves and happy to let the guy mash away. I was even proud of myself, seeing as how I was the only one there with the foresight to bring along a gadget to occupy the restless Down Syndrome kid.

A few more minutes of preachifyin' and button mashing went by before I noticed that people were starting to stare at me. Pretty sure of what might be causing that, I glanced over to my left and was startled to see the kid bent over in his seat and kissing my watch. He was really going for it, no tongue or anything, but definitely generating some impressive smacking noises. I sat there frozen—I mean, I was a man of the world and everything, but having a kid with Down Syndrome go nuts and fellate my fancy watch in church was kind of a new experience.

Shock quickly turned to horror as the kid started kissing my wrist. Then, like Pugsley getting bonked on the head and confusing himself with Gomez, he began working his way up my arm, leaving a little trail of drool behind and making a big loud kissy noise each time he planted one on me. I didn't know what to do. Punching him in the head and screaming presented itself as the first option, but somehow doing that seemed unfair, not to mention the kind of thing you want to avoid in church, where Jesus watches from above, blistering lightning bolts of godly vengeance clutched in each meaty hand, just waiting for you to screw up.

He was up to about my shoulder (not Jesus, the kid with the Down Syndrome) and my mind was racing. What could I do? Politely ask him to stop? Throw my watch to the other side of the room and hope he chases it? Maybe pray? People were starting to mutter. I didn't want to make a fuss.

He paused at my shoulder, nuzzled it for a moment, then reared his head up and grinned as I turned to look at him. The entire auditorium paused, waiting to see what would happen. He lunged forward before I could react and kissed me, rather wetly, right on my eyeball.

The pastor roared in anger. The entire place went nuts, completely outraged. Kids pointed and shouted while church ladies fell to their knees in prayer. A couple of adults grabbed the kid, one on each arm and I think one around his neck, and hauled him out of the room.

"Please, everyone, please!" someone yelled. "Stay in your seats! There will be ice cream, ice cream for everyone! We'll get through this!"

As everyone settled down I just sat there, a little moist, and wondered why this kind of shit always happened to me. Maybe I was too prideful in my LED watch and God wanted to teach me a lesson about folly or something, who knows. Ew, do you think my watch gave him a boner? Until just now I didn't think to check. I mean the kid with Down Syndrome, not God.

Anyway, the main church guy struggled through the rest of the sermon, but nobody was paying attention. They were all glaring at the back of my neck. I simply went blank, sending my mind far, far away.

They wrapped shit up and marched us out to some courtyard, where we all stood around glumly eating our ice cream. The kid with the Down Syndrome was nowhere to be seen.

The various deacons and church ladies rationed me out a tablespoon-sized dollop, treating me with an attitude somewhere between suspicion and faint disgust. All of the other kids stood around in little groups, staring at me with open hatred and refusing to talk to me. But I was pretty much used to all that.

MAGIC ANAL ROOTIN' AROUND

1995

About ten years ago I dated a sexually liberated girl who was a little too interested in the human butthole.

. . . And that's it. That's it, diary, that's the entry for this week! "About ten years ago I dated a sexually liberated girl who was a little too interested in the human butthole." Thanks for stopping by, diary, and have a safe drive home.

No, no . . . Just kidding. If only that was the end of it. No, this was one of those women who'll publicly endorse all sorts of kinky, alternative-sexuality mores, but who in my experience turns out to be about as fun to hunch as a pile of compost. (No offense to you compost fuckers.)

Now, I admit that it's certainly within the bounds of possibility that the simple exhibition of my naked body is dampening the carnal fires in these situations—in fact, my parole officer hinted as much to me after that one incident in the mall. (Not to get off-topic, but can I just say that I really think

America would be a better place if society was a little more open to public art and expressing our feelings through dance? Thanks.)

I have a theory about all this, in the unlikely event these unsatisfying sexual situations aren't actually the fault of my doughy, scarred physique. I think it's part of a psychological need to deal with intimacy and sex in a safe, controlled environment. This frequently manifests itself during the college years, when a final personal identity is being formed. In the process of exploring these complex feelings and testing the boundaries of individual sexuality, displayed behavior might run contrary to a person's true comfort level with certain kinds of bedroom activities.

Or it might not even be that complex—maybe this kind of behavior is just a simple survival tactic, a way to armor-plate emotions or divert attention from vulnerable parts of the psyche.

But who knows? I never bring it up. God knows I don't want to hear about feelings and emotions and psychological crap from a girlfriend, or anyone else. Ultimately these issues are for people who, unlike me, care about the happiness and well-being of others.

Anyway, I was dating one of these girls, and she was always talking about the butthole. One time she even recommended some book with a title like *Healthy Butthole Lifestyles* or *Your Stinky Gateway to Fun* or *Magic Anal Rootin' Around*. However, this didn't have much of an impact on me. We had a long-distance relationship, so it's not like I was faced with any actual buttholes on a day-to-day basis, and when we were on the phone I was usually pretty distracted by the fact that I wasn't paying any attention to whatever it was she was saying. In fact, I was so dense that the vibrating buttplug she sent me on Valentine's Day didn't even register as a possible clue as to the seriousness of her rectal proclivities.

The actual plug on this gizmo was a small, silver lozenge with a pronounced seam. It had a flimsy remote control attached to it by a few feet of plastic cord, and the entire apparatus generated a disagreeable buzzing noise when switched on. Fact was, the thing was so chintzy that I thought it was a gag. I did manage to find some uses for it that deviated from its intended purpose, though . . . Chiefly, turning it on and whirling it around like a set of nunchucks while screaming and chasing houseguests.

It went on like this for a few months, with me occasionally wearing the clumsy thing like a bolo tie or using it to mix drinks. Then one day I happened to be visiting friends, a heavily pierced and laboriously transgressive married couple who had a few sex-toy catalogs on their coffee table. Leafing through this stuff in hopes of spying a titty I could "save for later," I noticed my buttplug.

Holy moley! The thing cost forty bucks! I couldn't believe something that was so cheaply made and dinky (not to mention specifically designed to be befouled by the human ass) would be so expensive.

I gasped and my friends, no doubt really hoping I was shocked by something other than a price tag, came running to see what was the matter. "My . . . My . . . It's my buttplug," I said, pointing at the catalog.

"Ohh, that's a good one," they said, almost in unison. "Don't you just love it?"

Hmmm . . . I sure did love horrifying people with it. But was it possible someone would actually stick this kind of thing in their butt on purpose? And enjoy it? I mean, the place where the poo comes out? I wasn't exactly thrilled with the primary function of the butt and in general monkeyed around with it as little as possible . . . A few embarrassed swabs with toilet paper here and there, just to keep my somewhat tenuous membership in civilization active . . . That was it. Could it be that fetid hole might do double-duty as a source of sexual pleasure?

"Dude," I asked, addressing the husband. "You stick this doohickey in your ass?"

"I love it," he said.

"It feels good?"

"It feels GREAT."

"Huh. Well. I reckon maybe I'll give it a try then."

So I went home and called up the ol' bunghole queen. Sure enough, she had always intended that I use her gift for sexy good times, rather than assaulting my friends. She even told me she was getting kind of hot then and there just thinking about me cramming the device up my pooper (perhaps not her exact words). That was enough for me. I made the decision right then—I was going to get it on with myself in a forbidden, anal fashion. Awwww yeah.

As I made preparations, a thousand thoughts shot through my head. What if it hurts? What if it feels really, really good? What if it feels so good that I freak out? Hey! . . . What if I turn gay? I already had a Bronski Beat album, but if the buttplug turned me gay I'd pretty much have to start over from scratch in every other area of my life. That'd be a lot of work. Is it worth the risk? Will my girlfriend break up with me if her buttplug turns me gay? And when I go through with the actual deed, should I put on the Bronski Beat album to, you know, give the place a little atmosphere?

I have to admit that, all doubts aside, I was pretty excited. I mean, I was fixin' to open myself up to a rear-end roller coaster of mind-bending, ass-blasting erotic thrills. Skin flush with anticipation, I stripped down and got on the bed. After a moment's reflection, I wrapped the plug in a condom, to protect it from poop. Lying on my back, I got down to business. After a few minutes of whacking it, I was ready. I leaned to one side, lifted a cheek and started easing it in . . .

Oh, there . . . There it goes . . . Hmmm. Is it in yet? Never thought I'd be asking myself that question . . . So far so good, though . . . No discomfort . . . Don't feel gay yet.

In fact, I didn't feel much of anything. I very gingerly activated the vibration . . . Nothing. Primed for an explosion of sensual ass-fireworks, I upped the ante a bit. Nothing. Anxious to generate any kind of sensation at all, I cranked it, really putting the pedal to the metal.

Nothing. Not even a tingle.

The luster began to fade. I noticed the faint buzzing noise coming from deep within my crotch, like a sad, degenerate bee had flown down there. The only discernible sensation was a slight pressure, pretty much identical to the feeling I get when I have to take a dump. I glanced down and saw myself: a naked man . . . with a cheap, plastic remote control coming out of his ass. A wave of self-awareness shocked me . . . I was a failed libertine, a battery-powered pervert . . . An unadulterated square too vanilla to get off even with the assistance of the latest in advanced butthole technology.

The room suddenly seemed dark and cold. I was very alone.

ADVICE FOR CHILDREN

Don't use one of those little Handi-Vac things to empty an ashtray. Because the inrush of air could potentially reignite any fading embers. And, uh, a big jet of flame might shoot out of the thing, surprising you and making you scream like a ten-year-old girl. And you might knock over your beer.

If you're ever fishing, and a poisonous water moccasin swims up to try and eat one of the fish on your stringer, and you think that maybe flipping the snake out of the water and onto, say, me is a good idea, please reconsider.

Just because you can stick toothpicks in your forehead and they'll stay there and it doesn't really hurt all that bad doesn't mean you should go ahead and do it, at Denny's or any other restaurant.

All those skinheads over there? They'll beat your ass.

Yes, popping a paper bag in the mall makes a very loud noise. Yes, you can hear that shit echoing all through the place. Yes, rent-a-cops are all dicks.

Don't try to pee and ride a bicycle at the same time, even if Jim Marburger can do it. Not that you were watching or anything.

The rash won't go away on its own.

Should you ever decide to use bamboo sticks and stretchy, decorative string that's designed to wrap presents to make a bow and arrow, and should you decide to wad up a bunch of duct tape on the end of your arrow and soak it with WD-40 so it'll, you know, burn better, I would recommend not shooting the flaming arrow onto the roof of a house or into the lap of your friend's cousin. Even by accident.

There are no secrets when it comes to fucking. Everyone will eventually find out about it, and probably a lot sooner than you want them to.

God created assistant managers when he was in a really shitty mood.

Knife wounds inflicted on bodily extremities, such as hands, should receive firm pressure with a clean, dry towel or cloth. Elevate if possible. Remember, dry is the key. The wet washcloth is a poor choice for staunching blood flow, no matter what you've heard.

Be careful of what you headbutt. Some doors are not as sturdy as they might first look, and it can be hard to estimate your own strength immediately after inhaling nitrous oxide.

Wear the condom. No, for the love of Pete, not the mint-flavored one. Jesus, that thing burns.

Here's a helpful tip for job interviews: try not to stab your future boss in the arm with a freshly sharpened pencil. If you must stab someone with a pencil, have the common sense to dull the point to a state where you can be sure it won't easily break the skin.

Burt Reynolds? Nope. Tom Selleck? Uh uh. Try Chile D. Molester. Shave that fucking mustache.

If someone passes out on the couch and you want to put them in a figure-four leglock, ensure that the hold is correctly applied before they wake and fuck your goddamn knee all up.

Head wounds do tend to bleed a lot. Don't panic.

Pajamas are indeed comfy, but society dictates we not wear them to school, work or the bowling alley.

For that matter, be aware that bowling-alley employees may have a limited tolerance for other non-pajama-related behaviors, such as getting all loaded and pretending to be Godzilla and stomping on that windmill over there in the indoor miniature golf course.

You better ask before you try and stick your finger up there.

Socks should match your pants, and your belt should match your shoes. After that, if anyone complains, tell 'em they should be happy you're wearing any clothes at all.

If you suspect someone likes to do a lot of cocaine, don't let them "borrow" your CDs.

Try not to get too depressed. There's always something to look forward to. Keep alert, and sooner or later you'll see someone slip and hurt themselves.

Beat off enough and eventually someone will walk in on you while you're doing it. When this happens, the best way to handle it is to pause, look them directly in the eye and say, "You done ruined the romance, so go ahead and say whatever it is you want to say." Hold their gaze until they leave. Alternately, you could run over there and put your hands on their face.

You should never put a string of lit Black Cat firecrackers in someone's back pocket while they're on stage playing bass guitar with their band. Even if they fucked your knee up by reversing the figure-four on you that one time. And even if you crack up at just the idea of someone with their pants on fire jumping up and down and spinning around and around like a dog chasing its tail while trying to figure out what's going on. Yup, someone could get their ass burned, so it's wrong. Despite the fact that shit is really, really funny.

You can whoop those two guys easy enough. But what if they come back with a friend who's big enough to lift you off the ground and pin you to the wall with one hand? What then, slugger? (You're going to feel like a fucking idiot, that's what.)

If, while chugging a beer, the phrase, "I bet this is going to be the last coherent thought I have tonight," runs through your head, get someone to take you home. Now.

The cops never think it's as funny as you do.

THE BRUTAL
Q-TIP
OF DESTINY

1989

One time a doctor stuck a Q-Tip in the pee-hole of my wing-wang. By Q-Tip, I refer to the cotton-tipped swab, not the pleasant fellow rapping on the TV who all you kids seem to like so much these days. Still, it was mighty uncomfortable.

It all started with one of those rare bouts of sexual intercourse that included participation from both myself and a living, female human being. And, happily, I did not render myself unconscious at any point during the brief consummation of the act. Though I did get a little distracted wondering why girls who act all liberated and dirty and sexually adventurous with their clothes on always turn out to have so many uptight rules when it's naked time: "What are you doing?! Sorry, I don't do *that*. Don't touch me there! Don't look at me! Just what do you think you're going to do with THAT thing?! Untie these ropes right now! I'm allergic to dogs!" Etc.

Anyway, I lay there as instructed, flat on my back with my arms at my sides, staring at the ceiling while my partner ground away, satisfying her sadly pedestrian urges. The television was on at the other end of the room, and at one point I got kinky and sneakily tried to watch the video for Big Audio Dynamite's "C'mon Every Beatbox" (which is a bad jam) over her shoulder, but her stupid hair got in the way.

A week or so later my nether regions developed a mild itch. Now, this was hardly unprecedented. My groin area was (and is) a thing of mysterious, uncomfortable functions. And, biologically speaking, the male crotch is as unpleasant as, well, the word *crotch* itself, and is considered by leading scientists to be the source of much that is evil in this world. Many men routinely experience itchiness and mild groin discomfort, as evidenced by my personal observations during the years before I had a real job and was forced to live with dudes:

"Christ, do I ever got me a case of the man-itch. I've been putting ice cubes on my balls all day."

"No shit? My red-ass was so bad yesterday I scratched it with the cheese grater."

Etc.

Despite the prevalence in society of this sort of relatively benign male itchiness, I nonetheless heroically summoned my full powers of neuroses and convinced myself that my discomfort was the direct result of those recent romantic fumblings. "Great," I thought. "Chlamydia. My reward for an awkward orgasm that was just slightly less satisfying than a good sneeze."

I didn't want it to fester too long so, being unemployed and destitute, I made an appointment to go see the fine doctors at the free clinic. Where I had this delightful exchange:

"What are your symptoms, Mr. Hughes?"

"Well, doctor, I did it with a girl who's considered to be kind of slutty though, frankly, her performance didn't live up to her reputation. And now my ding-a-ling is itchy."

"Hmm. Have you experienced any discharge?"

"Uhhh . . . Discharge? Ew. Thankfully, no."

"Can you milk up some discharge?"

"Can . . . I . . . *milk* . . . up . . . some . . . *discharge*?!"

The doctor unwrapped a Q-Tip that was about three feet long. "If you can't milk up some discharge for us to test, I'm going to have to painfully ream out your pee-tunnel with this bad motherfucker," he said. (Those might not have been his exact words.)

"Fuck! I'm milking! I'm milking!" But it was to no avail. I sat there frantically yanking and tugging on my peener for a full minute, but my sad little pee-hole was as dry as the desert sands. It coughed up a miniature tumbleweed and a few grains of dust, and the doctor smiled as a malignant gleam crept into his eyes.

"No discharge, eh? Taste the brutal Q-Tip of destiny, pee-hole!" (Again, those might not have been his exact words.) He held that fucking thing waaaaay back at one end and with a sniper's accuracy plunged that thing down a pipe which had until now been an exit-only orifice. My scream, which cracked the glass on his framed diploma, was cut short by a choking cough as the cotton end of the swab made its way up my throat and out my mouth.

He twisted and worked that thing around like he was churning butter then, after what seemed like an eternity, withdrew it with a sickening "plop." When I was done crying he had me fill out a few forms and handed me a bottle of antibiotic pills.

"The lab will contact you with the results in two weeks, Mr. Hughes," he said. "In the meantime, take two of these a day on an empty stomach, and stay away from dairy products. And, um . . . call me sometime, okay?"

The clinic called two weeks later. Turned out nothing was wrong with me. Or with my pee-hole, anyway. Except for a lingering soreness.

INDIGNITIES THROUGH THE AGES

Age eight: I develop the bad habit of picking my nose and absent-mindedly flicking the boogers away while lying on my bed and reading. I more or less unconsciously continue this grotesque behavior until the day my dad pulls me into my room and angrily demands an explanation as to why there are six or seven huge, bloody, dried snot-wads stuck to the wall. The room seems to spin and recede and I am dimly aware, somewhere at the back of my mind, that making up a lie to cover this is beyond even my awesome powers. "Maybe I'm doing it in my sleep?" is the best I can come up with. My dad stares at me in disgust for a few moments and then walks away. Later, upon noticing that the booger wall is a good twelve feet from my bed, I'm quietly impressed that I managed that kind of range.

Age nine: Digging through my mom's old albums, I discover *Freak Out!*, the first record by Frank Zappa and the Mothers of Invention. I become enamored of side four, titled "The Return of the Son of Monster

Magnet," which features one twenty-minute song consisting of little more than drumming and hippie yelling. I bring it to school on "music day," exciting the other members of my class, who see the words "freak out" and assume it's the then-popular disco-pop hit of the same title by the band Chic. We make it through about six minutes before the teacher takes it off. Everyone just stares at me.

Age ten: I discover that I can very proficiently burp and talk at the same time. One day in science class, my teacher (the hated Mrs. Cruickshank, who a year later narced to the cops on me and Matt Krogh for making and detonating homemade bombs in the woods next to her house) asks me for my folder. I burp out the words, "I left it at home," and am sent to the office for the first time in my life. On the verge of tears, I wait to see the school principal and receive my inevitable paddling. He calls me in, and I sit quivering with fear across from him at his desk while he reads the slip detailing my transgression against society. He eventually looks up and starts to stare at me with a blank expression on his face. We sit there for a long time. He hands me back the slip and goes back to work, ignoring me. After a few minutes, I go back to class. He never says a word.

Age sixteen: Go to see D.C. hardcore band Scream at one of the local city-run recreation centers. Visiting the bathroom, I walk in on a conversation between a relatively friendly local skinhead and some out-of-town baldies. I overhear one of 'em complaining about unwanted participants in "the scene" and ask, "What, you guys have to put up with a lot of rednecks and Nazis?" It suddenly becomes very quiet. Four large, bald and tattooed men turn to face me. The local skinhead looks a bit uncomfortable. I notice the Confederate flags and swastikas. "Ha ha," I say, in a very small voice. "Just . . . kidding?"

Age seventeen: Some magical combination of booze and luck lands me in bed with two gorgeous young women, my exceptionally tall, busty, blonde girlfriend and the petite, athletic redhead hosting the party happening outside her parents' bedroom door. Actually, I was in bed with three women, but one was making out with my buddy Jon way over on the other side of the mattress, and the two of them split when they saw things kinda starting to heat up on my side.

I can't get my girlfriend to fool around with the other girl, but have no complaints: I'm drunk, horny and on my way to experiencing my first-ever two-girl, one-me threesome, an event that's obviously pretty much the Holy Grail for every idiot seventeen-year-old creep (not to mention every idiot thirty-seven-year-old creep) the world over.

Things start to progress farther than I had ever dreamed possible (outside of various masturbatory fantasies), and when the time is right I climb over and kneel between the tender legs of my gorgeous girlfriend. The redhead strokes my hair and looks on, mouth open and wet with expectation . . . "You do have a condom, right?" my girlfriend asks.

I stand up, rip the sheets off the bed to wrap myself and venture out into the party in search of a rubber while the girls giggle and await my return. I'm drunker'n Cooter Brown, ass hanging out of my makeshift toga and blind without my glasses, staggering around this wretched party and bumping into groups of disgusted jocks while desperately bellowing for birth control. Someone takes pity on me and hands me a rubber, so I make haste back to the bedroom.

Once again kneeling between those magical, silky thighs, I bring out the prophylactic, my key to Nirvana, and begin making preparations. The wrapping on the thing had been ripped, half drying it out, but this would not dissuade me.

My excited, inexperienced (yeah, like I was Burt Reynolds in the sack department) two girlfriends grabbing the condom and excitedly unrolling it before it could be properly applied didn't help, nor did the case of whiskey-dick that had started to set in . . . After a few minutes of drunken, frantic attempts to cram this sticky, useless wad of plastic onto my half-hard dick, I keel over unconscious and start snoring, thereby ruining my one and only chance to ever make it into *Penthouse Forum.*

Age twenty: Putting the plastic-wrapped candy canes in the microwave at my boss' Christmas party? It was a bad idea.

Age twenty-one: I get off from work at noon and spend the day drinking and throwing knives into the wall with two guys named Weasel and Chuck From Hell. After Chuck leaves, me and Weasel get into an argument. I spray him with some oven cleaner or something, and he spits on me in retaliation. I respond in kind and the next thing I know am engaged in a bona fide spitting war. About a half-hour later I am completely drunk and, for the first and only time in my life (as far as I know), covered from head to toe in another man's saliva. Saliva from a man named Weasel. I have a date with a heart-stoppingly pretty girl that night, so I hop on my bike to go home and clean up. While riding into my yard at high speed, a steel support cable attached to a telephone pole catches me across the head and clotheslines me off of my bike. I dust myself off, laugh and proceed to making myself as presentable as possible. Later, after a few glasses of wine, my intelligent, delightful, sexy date and I recline on the grass at a private little spot in a local park and stare up at the full moon. She looks over, smiles and asks me how I got the red welt across my forehead. Laughing, I tell her the whole story, spittle and all. Suffice to say I do not get laid that night. Days later, when I call her at work, I'm told she's not there. I can hear her and her coworkers in the background, laughing at me.

Age twenty-three: If you're going to fire a bottle rocket into a full can of beer, don't do it in the house.

Age twenty-four: I stumble in the door at three in the morning, drunk, and find four or five friends and roommates watching a porno video. Bleary and off-balance, I brace myself on the wall and glance at the screen, which features an attractive young lady coughing and choking as she forces a big, lumpy weiner all the way down her throat, and boast, "Aw, I can do that!" before passing out. I wake up with no memory of this incident. My roommates, however, recall it in great detail. And often.

Age twenty-six: Planning to fry up some okra, I put a bunch of oil in a pan, throw it on the stove and crank the heat to "high." The phone rings and I get into this extended long-distance conversation, no doubt on a really important topic like how awesome Black Flag was in '84 or some such. I totally forget about the stove until some time later, when I walk back to the front of the apartment and am bathed in a thick, black smoke. Through it I can see the pan, which is glowing red-hot and beginning to sag. The oil has totally evaporated, generating the foul, clinging fog that's coating my kitchen with soot. I somehow manage to take care of the situation before my apartment bursts into flame and kills everyone on the block, and I spend a little time trying to clean the oily muck off of my kitchen cabinets. The pan is half-melted and totally fucked. After a while, I decide dealing with the mess isn't worth the effort and ride my bike to the market to buy some replacement supper. Walking around, I notice a cute girl glance at me, do a double take and then give me a big smile. I smile back, nod and continue to shop, swaggering around and grinning at everyone, convinced I'm the stud of the supermarket. I shuck and jive over to produce, which has mirrors on the walls above the various vegetables, and catch my reflection. My hair is standing on end and my face is completely covered in greasy, black ash.

Age twenty-seven: I spend a lot of time holding up the bar at local Irish pub Durty Nelly's. I didn't think I was spending THAT much time there until one late afternoon, when the phone rings. Sadly, it's for me. And it's long-distance.

Ages twenty-eight to thirty-seven: Nothing but smooth sailing through the calm, pleasant seas of social propriety. I am accepted for who I am and respected.

THE ASSBREAK OF PSORIASIS

2004

In addition to guilt, shame, a generally comical appearance, low I.Q. scores, a receding hairline, a grumpy temperament, chronic flatulence, failing eyesight, a third nipple and a propensity for boozy mayhem, my parents have bequeathed a gift to me through the magic of genetics—a symbol of their parenting skills made flesh, if you will. Yes, match two sets of malformed chromosomes under the right conditions and nine months later you get a kid who's going to go through life afflicted with fucking psoriasis.

Fucking psoriasis? It's a rash. A red and crusty rash. A chronic, persistent rash for which there is no cure . . . It's neither contagious nor fatal; in fact, it's superficial by nature. But to a certain extent it can determine personality and outlook, if not destiny. Think of it as the icing on a cake, a cake made of crippled emotions. Yup, that sounds about right. The red, crusty, cracked and bleeding icing on a rotten cake made of crippled emotions. That was baked by, ummm . . . monsters! Monsters and Nazis. You don't want a slice of this dry, scabby cake, my friend. No way.

Its cause? Well, those affected usually suffer from having to carry around a huge and constantly erect, diamond-hard penis. The stress of wielding such mighty genitalia causes the immune system to . . . No, I don't know what the damn cause is, other than the lack of a law preventing booze and sick, bestial urges from causing two people who should be kept apart by forcing them to live in deep, separate wells to inexplicably meet, decide they like each other and copulate. Shit, from what I've heard, my dad accidentally brushed his teeth with some of my mom's psoriasis cream after the first night they spent together. What is it you need, Pop, God to throw up a neon sign reading THAT WAS AN OMEN. AN OMEN OF ILL TIDINGS. RUN! GET OUT NOW!

Actually, while faulty DNA is its origin, the actual psoriasis rash is the result of a profound deficiency in tiny, nimble teenage Asian girls frolicking around in sexy anime costumes. Some dubious group of scam-artists calling itself the National Psoriasis Foundation says the rash is caused by a wonky immune-system response that makes the body generate skin cells faster than it can shed them, but, uh . . . fuck those guys.

The delightful affliction can show up pretty much anywhere but prefers to make its appearance on the scalp and various stretchy extensor surfaces of the body, such as the knees and elbows. Of course, it wouldn't be fulfilling the complete scope of its rashly duties if it didn't declare a little manifest destiny on other, sometimes more sensitive body parts. Hence the title of this entry.

You know, people occasionally comment on the presumption I hold nothing back in the *Diary of Indignities*. Well, guess what? There are, in fact, indignities I do hold back, both for society's sake (and by that I mean "restraining order") and because, unless your name is H.P. Lovecraft, they resist description. Like the indignity of getting a heaping dose of psoriasis lodged in your ass-crack.

Now, as I've mentioned before, youthful experimentation aside, I monkey around with the pooper as little as possible. An embarrassed post-crap dab or two with some toilet paper to comply with the rules of society (and by that I mean "the Eighth Judicial Circuit Court in and for Alachua County, Florida") and I'm done with the whole gizmo. But there are a surprising number of sensitive nerve endings living it up in your ass-crack. For the most part they spend their time enjoying the warmth and doing their jobs, sensing the proximity of the opposite ass-cheek or whatever, but get 'em all riled up on psoriasis and shift in your chair wrong and I swear by all that is fucking right and proper it feels like you just got zapped in the shitter by a lightning bolt made out of mentholated scorpions.

Don't even get me started on when the skin gets so dry and cracked it starts bleeding. Just don't. Because I will break down and start sobbing. Despite evidence to the contrary, I really do try to keep as much of my blood as possible inside my skin, no matter the point of origin. But losing precious ass blood . . . well, frankly, it's extra disconcerting.

Dry, cracked and bleeding skin is no good on your ding-dong either. You can quote me on that: no good. Not only does having a flaky, crimson rash on your weiner put a crimp in the ol' social life, but experiencing this problem can also make it difficult to hit your regular masturbation quota. And if your goal is, like mine, to run off a batch by hand anywhere from four to seventy-three times a day . . . don't get thrifty on the lube, my friend. Turns out they don't make ding-dong-shaped bandages, and that's all I'm going to say about that.

Okay, let's see . . . Libeling my parents, check . . . Ass blood, check . . . Rash dick, check . . . What else sucks about psoriasis? Getting it on your face and having people treat you like you picked up some new atomic kind of AIDS that's only caught by molesting animal corpses; that sucks. Spending money on dermatologists and creams and shit and just having to waste time on maintenance so people don't scream and shoot you in the face with Lysol when you leave the house; that sucks. Dropping five hundred clams on the wrong kind of medicine because some quack from a walk-in clinic thought you had a skin fungus; that sucks. Oh, and the cockamamie home-brewed hippie remedies everyone tries to foist on you. They suck as well.

Just in case any hippies end up here by accident, I'd like to say a few things about your sham alternative-medicine hokum: Herbs don't cure shit. Herbs go in quiche, yes. They are not medicine. Sure, cavemen used herbs to try and cure shit, but that was before we had science and stuff. Your commie, repellent herbs and garnishes might've been in common medicinal use for two thousand years or whatever, but the average life span for people living during those two thousand years was, like, fifteen. I mean, I have nothing against the Indians, and think them getting shafted so much and stuff sucks, but they tried to cure shit with Echinacea . . . And, ah . . . well . . . they died. I'm sorry, and I'm not happy about it, but it's true.

I've had a few pinkos suggest that I might try fasting to clear up the occasional out-of-control patch. "It'll cleanse your body of the toxins," they say in that dreamy, annoying self-righteous hippie voice they affect whenever passing on some spurious wisdom-of-the-ancients type bullhonky. Well, you fucking hippies, listen up: your phantom toxins aren't the problem. It's that overactive skin-cell doohickey or whatever. But fasting *could* be a solution to one of my problems, at least. All hippies reading this please start a program of total abstinence from all food and water for . . . oh, I reckon thirty days ought to be sufficient to totally cleanse your mind, body and spirit of all those nasty toxins. There, problem solved! And also please give me all of your cool stuff, since you hate capitalism and private property and America so goddamn much.

Mmm, on second thought you can keep your dirty hippie stuff. I don't want it. I'd hate private property too if all my private property was, like, filthy tie-dyes and Phish bootlegs. Get a job, buy some cool stuff and see how you feel about private property then, Tofu Joe.

Alright, my work here is done. If anyone needs me I'll be over in the corner, scratching my elbows.

BUTTERFLY-KNIFE ROMANCE

1984

Jennifer Testa was the first girl I ever really loved.

She looked a little like Jane Wiedlin, bassist for popular, crappy new-wave band the Go Go's, and had transferred to Tarpon High shortly into my freshman school year. She sat in the back of my science class, catching my attention with her short, curly black hair and stylish, offbeat clothing.

I adored her at first sight and spent weeks watching for an opportunity to talk to her. I found it the day we were slated to dissect crayfish.

She seemed a little reluctant to chop into her specimen, and who could blame her? The crayfish were preserved with formaldehyde and gave off an unappealing chemical funk. Crack their chewy little shells and icky guts came out. This was not a task suited to a delicate flower such as young Miss Jennifer, even if she was Italian, and thus slightly less evolved than your average Tarpon student.

I guess I should point out that Tarpon Springs, Florida is home to a large Greek population, and kids boasting this heritage comprised more than half the student body. A large portion of the faculty was Greek. They even offered Greek classes for the language requirements. If there's anything I learned during my studies at Tarpon High, besides "ask what the pill does before you eat it," it's that everyone on the planet is less evolved than the Greeks.

In fact, I once had a teacher just come out and tell me, "Patrick, we had advanced mathematics and philosophy while your people were painting themselves blue, living in caves and poking each other in the ass with spears."

I pretended to be impressed but, honestly, the whole blue thing with the spears didn't sound too bad. Especially compared to advanced math. Shit, come to think of it, I'd probably still go with the cave today, given the choice. I mean, I can barely stand to put on pants. Plus, it's heritage.

Anyway, when I saw Jennifer balk at the dissection, I seized the moment. I walked over, pulled out my giant butterfly knife, whirled it around a few times like you do and stuck the blade right through the crayfish's head.

Jennifer looked me in the eyes and smiled. I stood there, held her gaze and smiled back. Our science teacher, Mr. Lelakis, smiled. He knew some heavy-duty ninth-grade butterfly-knife courtship when he saw it. Plus, the Greek kids were always stabbing the shit out of each other and setting off nail bombs on Halloween, so he was probably used to that kind of stuff.

Sadly, I think Mr. Lelakis died relatively young a few years ago. He was a great guy, even to students belonging to subhuman mud races, such as myself. For example, he didn't care that I was waving around a giant butterfly knife in his class like some sort of maniac. Like Jennifer, he thought it was cute.

These days they wouldn't see such a thing as innocent flirtation. They'd fucking call in a SWAT team to hang me from a gibbet in the town square.

Man, I just remembered . . . I got that knife from a Filipino kid named Gabe Sanchez. Once Gabe was hiding in the trunk of my buddy Scott Millard's car, shooting fireworks at traffic as Scott drove around. A cop came up behind them, and Gabe, not able to see it was ol' 99 with the trunk pulled down low, fired off a volley from a Roman candle right at it. A fireball stuck to the hood of the cop car, igniting the paint and instigating a chase. Gabe, assuming it was just some angry dudes behind them, continued his assault while Scott careened through the streets, trying to lose The Man.

Eventually Scott wrecked the car into a telephone pole. After it was all said and done, they ended up with a million hours of community service mopping floors at some Elks Lodge or something, where they somehow managed to boost several hundred dollars worth of booze from a closet, a caper that kept us all happily puking through weekends for almost two years.

Great guys, Gabe and Scott. And you know what? There's a lesson here. Parents and schools and shit overreact to everything kids do these days. Despite our hijinx, nobody brought out the gibbet for us, and we all turned out to be responsible members of society.

. . . Well, I guess. I don't really have any idea what happened to those two. They could be out there driving around right now, looking to fuck up a cop car or two with some big-ass bottle rockets. I suppose the jury's still out on me, too, even if I spend hours and hours each day sitting quietly in an office, staring at a computer screen and feeling my brain turn to mush, and very little time stabbing crayfish in the head with butterfly knives.

Which is a shame, because carving up that crayfish was certainly my in as far as Jennifer Testa went. We started spending a lot of time together, and it was great. She was smart and funny and just the damn prettiest thing I ever saw. Plus, she lived in the same subdivision as me, had cable with MTV and her mom didn't care if we smoked cigarettes.

I spent a few perfect weeks sitting next to Jennifer on the couch, bumming smokes from her mom, cracking jokes to make her smile, maybe dancing together when a Prince video came on—Jennifer had a ballet background and loved to dance. I loved watching her. After it was time to head home we'd call each other, talking about nothing for hours.

This short period was honestly the last time in my life I can remember feeling anything, anything at all, that could be described with a word like *contentment*. Pretty much everything—everything, not just relationships or whatever—before and since has basically been an endless string of disappointments and annoyances or, at best, a way to mark time until something better came along.

But I could have sat on the couch next to Jennifer forever.

I worked up the nerve to kiss Jennifer the night before I left to visit my mom, two hours away in Gainesville. It was just getting dark, and we were out in the street in front of Jennifer's house, saying goodbye. As I kissed her, she cradled the back of my head, pulling me into her, then started stroking the back of my neck.

I had kissed plenty of girls by this point (surprisingly), but never like this. It was deep and slow, with none of the awkwardness or frantic tongue spinning I usually associate with frenching ninth-graders I remember from my teenage years. She kissed the side of my neck, and a warmth I had never felt before in my life spread through my entire body, totally giving me a boner.

Running up the phone bill in Gainesville was a no-no, but I managed to call her a few times. The last time, she seemed a little sad, a little distant. When I got back to my dad's a few weeks later, I found out why.

Somehow while I was gone, Jennifer had started dating a dude named Philip. He went to another school and was a rich kid with a Trans Am and a fondness for showing off his skills with the nunchucks.

I couldn't figure out this situation at all. I was still spending a lot of time with Jennifer—hell, I spent more time with her than that creep Philip did. And Jennifer seemed more sad about the whole situation than anything, like she'd rather be dating me. When I'd ask her why she was with him and not me, something I did frequently, she'd just look upset and say, "He asked me first."

The irrational nature of this response drives me nuts to this day. I swear, I don't think it was a line. I think she really did like me more than him, and it made me insane. Teenage girls, pay close attention to this—"he asked me first" is a totally stupid reason to date someone.

Hey, maybe nunchucks just rate higher than butterfly knives? Nah, that can't be the case. I took those stupid things away from him once. I stopped by Jennifer's house and he was out in the yard, flipping them around like a retarded ninja. He knew how I felt about his girlfriend and kind of waved them around at me.

"Go ahead, you dildo," I said. "I dare you. Come at me."

He raised his eyebrows and did, while Jennifer yelled for him to stop. I grabbed a chuck mid-swing, yanked 'em out of his hands and casually tossed them through the open passenger window of his Trans Am. So fucking smooth.

There's no way I could pull that off today. I'd get conked in the brain and spend my waning years shitting my pants in a home. Teenage butterfly-knife romance gives you magical powers.

I could hear Jennifer giggling as I walked away. But still she stayed with that guy. It was breaking my heart.

Out of my mind with jealousy and confusion, I wrote her a letter, telling her how I felt about her and how much she was hurting me with this he-asked-me-first crap. I appealed to her sense of reason, her clear affection for me. That kiss we shared. For no good reason at all, I also described, in detail, how I shaved for the first time that day. Even though I totally didn't need it.

She called me and told me she loved the letter. She told me she'd keep it forever. But she wouldn't break it off with Philip. He asked her first.

I stopped talking to her. But I still loved her.

A week or two of ignoring Jennifer, and I was in bed, pining away while contemplating a photograph of her. It was taken when she was a bridesmaid or something at a wedding. She was all done up and smiling and looked so beautiful. I decided to jack off.

Now, in a lifetime of frequent and varied masturbation habits, this was the first time I ever whacked it to a picture of someone I knew instead of dirty porno pictures or even dirtier imagination pictures. It took a long time and was kind of weird. When I was done, I wiped myself off on the photo.

That sounds terrible, I know, but this honestly wasn't done out of any kind of psychosexual hostility. I had decided to beat off on the spur of the moment and, without time to prepare and get a tissue or something, it was just the only thing handy. Plus, at the time I thought I would never want to look at that photo ever again.

I was wrong. I regretted it instantly, and felt wholly disgusted. Despite the pain she caused me, I loved her with all my heart, and treasured that photo. Wiping myself off on it seemed like a cheap shot, at least after the fact. So crudely demeaning, even if it wasn't intended that way. Also, glossy photographs aren't really absorbent enough for efficient post-ejaculation cleanup, so it just kind of smeared all the goo around. Ugh.

As far as I was concerned, this unpleasant little coda meant it was all over. Somehow, I managed to soldier on with life and all that shit. My duties as magistrate of the Tarpon Springs Advanced Dungeons and Dragons Club helped distract me. Gamma World, an exciting new prospect that set D&D-style action in the post-apocalyptic milieu of *The Road Warrior,* beckoned for further investigation. Life was full.

At the beginning of tenth grade, Jennifer was dating David Burke. He was older, a senior, and enjoyed a rep as the school's second or third most promising artist. David rocked a cool new-wave style, with vintage clothes and long, swoopy bangs. He smoked clove cigarettes, drove a '67 Mustang convertible and liked some of the same bands I did, Black Flag and Dead Kennedys and Echo & the Bunnymen. I approved of his relationship with Jennifer. It wasn't me, but it was an improvement over that douche Philip.

I started chatting with the two of them in the halls between class, asking David to swap cassettes of hard-to-find bands and shit like that. I never once let on that anything had ever happened between me and Jennifer, that we had ever kissed or that I had spooged all over a classy photograph of her or anything. I could feel her watching me intently during these exchanges, but I played it real, real cool.

Now, at the time I was sporting a variation of the much-maligned haircut that's today known as the mullet. Near the beginning of the '80s, however, a version of this style, developed by David Bowie during the Ziggy Stardust years and locally known as "the spike," was really considered very controversial and avant garde. Forward-thinking soccer players and confident men in boundary-pushing bands such as Kajagoogoo and Dokken wore their hair in a spike, and so did I.

David Burke, however, had over the summer converted his spike into bangs. Clearly, this was the direction to go. So when he suggested I skip school with him and Jennifer one day so we could all get high and he could give me a new haircut, I was into it. I looked over at Jennifer to see if she minded and got a little smile that told me there would be no awkwardness, that it would all be okay.

The next morning I headed to her house instead of the bus stop. Jennifer and David were under the covers of her parents' bed, fully clothed. She invited me to join them, and I jumped in. Jennifer passed me a joint, and we spent hours nestled in there, watching MTV and cracking jokes. Laughing and snuggled up next to her, I felt something that wasn't entirely dissimilar from the contentment I experienced at her house pre-Philip. Later, David cut my hair, giving me bangs and a long rat tail. He totally fucked up the sides, though, taking it out in dozens of uneven chunks and acting like it was supposed to be like that. I suspected something was amiss, but knew the haircut would bum out Dad and get people to pay attention to me regardless, and so went along without a fuss.

The next few months were alright. I wasn't playing so much D&D, instead running with what my grandparents would call a "fast crowd." David drove me and Jennifer to school each morning in that bad-ass baby-blue Mustang, and he always had decent weed. Jennifer started calling herself Jenne. I'd crash at David's house and we'd drive into Ybor City for hardcore punk shows at the Star Club, or we'd go to gay bars like El Goya and dance to New Order. He knew an older crowd, high-school grads and artists and homos. It was very exciting. Once, someone shot at us in a parking lot.

I got a little disillusioned with this scene after discovering how much David's art ripped off a friend who had graduated a few years before. Plus, David had some weird thing going with his ex-best friend where I was pretty sure the two of them were, like, gay. It was no big deal, but

I could tell he wasn't being honest about it. And when Jennifer wasn't around he always wanted to discuss masturbation technique with me, in detail. It got to be a little much. Eventually, I declined the offer of a live demonstration.

Even so, I still hung out with the two of them a lot. We smoked a lot of pot.

Around this time I was driving along Alternate 19 with Jennifer (or Jenne, whatever) and her mom, sitting in the back seat as we made our way to some school function. Out of nowhere, Jennifer's mom blurted out that she knew who Jennifer was going to marry, and that it was me. I sat there, stunned. It was a weird thing to just come out and say, considering Jennifer was with David. But Jennifer turned around from the front seat, looked me in the eye and smiled.

I smiled right back, not saying a word. I was still in love with her, of course.

Not long after, I was out partying with a small group: David, Jennifer, the artist whose style David ripped off and my girlfriend at the time. We were all really, really high. Somehow we ended up drinking in a random patch of woods, I think because we didn't want to share our booze or drugs with the common folk at any of the weekend parties.

Staring at Jennifer, I dared everybody to start making out with each other. They went for it—with a crowd as self-consciously unconventional as us, I knew they would. So when my turn came I kissed Jennifer for the second time, and it was pretty good, just like I remembered. I could feel real love in that kiss, true love. The world spun and my whole body turned liquid.

Of course, ten minutes later I started vomiting forth long streams of clear, pure grain alcohol, so the spinny feelings and stuff might have been from that. It steamed in the cold air and burned my throat on the way out, but I could see the headlights from our car refracted through it, making rainbow patterns. I laughed, both from the elation of once again kissing the girl I loved as well as at what seemed like just a shitload of grandly absurd cosmic juxtapositions.

Oh—no, I didn't kiss either of the dudes. As far as I know.

When I was done barfing and laughing, we piled back into the car and hit a party. Our little make-out session gave us a secret, something that bonded us, and we stuck to ourselves, separated from the crowd. Someone mentioned how they just didn't feel like talking to anyone else, how they only felt connected to our little group. I said, "It's like we're the Breakfast Club."

Self-loathing instantly poured over me. I couldn't believe I said something so trite, so stupid. But everyone thought it was great, nodding and agreeing. "Yeah, yeah, that's it, it's like we're the Breakfast Club!" I should point out that at this time I hadn't actually even seen the movie.

Monday came, and after school I was at Jennifer's, getting high with her and David. This was the routine.

As David rolled a joint, I watched Jennifer go into a ballet routine, kicking her legs and twirling. And she started singing, "We're going to get high, we're going to get high."

I realized I hadn't seen her dance like that in almost a year. She used to dance like that all the time, just out of happiness. Horror and sadness began to expand in the pit of my stomach, and I couldn't bear to watch her. I went into the bathroom and stared at myself in the mirror, trying to recognize my reflection for what seemed like a very long time.

When I opened the door, Jennifer was standing there. She kissed me. She told me that kissing her in the woods that night reawakened her feelings. She wanted me. She loved me.

I kissed her back, briefly, but the horror just grew. I broke away and walked into the living room, where David was watching TV, and stood around awkwardly for a minute or two, then just left.

In the following weeks, I quit smoking pot. (Well, for a month or two, anyway.) I started riding the bus again and rang up my old D&D buddies. Jennifer would call me, but I never called her back. I was polite but distant to her at school. Eventually, I stopped talking to her. She would stare at me, and I would pretend not to notice.

I moved back to Gainesville just before the start of my junior year and never saw her again.

HERBS GO ON SPAGHETTI

2003

Last night I go to my dead aunt's house to help my mom and my live aunt move this futon. My mom, who is crazy, had told me on the phone that if she decides to take the futon—an event that was in question for reasons I'll get to in a minute—it would necessitate moving the three other futons she owns to make room for it.

"Why the hell do you need another futon if you've already got three?!" I asked her.

"There's nowhere to sit in my apartment," she replied. My mom lives by herself in a small, one-bedroom apartment and has no regular visitors, or friends of any kind for that matter. But whatever.

I go to the damn house, wait for my batshit insane family to show up and let me in, and then carry this futon and frame outside so my mom can smell them. Yes, smell them. Someone smoked cigarettes in the house back in like 1963, so Mom thinks everything in the house is tainted with deadly poisons. She cannot abide by anything that carries any sort of perceptible smell—perfume, cigarettes, paint, detergent, etc. You know, all the stuff every sane person in the world slathers over themselves on a daily basis with no notable ill effect. You could probably douse Mom in some kind of scentless military neurotoxin that's designed to boil human flesh right off the bones (for legal reasons, I should mention that I am not seriously considering doing this) and the loony old bat wouldn't blink an eye, but heaven forbid she has to be exposed to any kind of fume.

So I'm standing in the yard while my mom and my aunt start sniffing the wood frame—*the fucking wood frame!*—of the futon, debating over whether or not it smells like cigarettes, despite the fact that nobody has lit one up in that house for more than twenty years. I decide to take a sniff myself, just out of curiosity. I can't smell a damn thing, except crazy.

The futon is deemed unfit, which is fine by me since that means I don't have to go to Mom's lair and play the fucking futon shuffle. There's a lot of discussion about how at some point the stinky futon can be taken over from my dead aunt's house to my live aunt's house and exchanged for a theoretically acceptable futon there that can be brought over to my mom's, only we can't do it now because someone is sleeping on it and blah blah blah.

I had received a *Godzilla* DVD in the mail that day I wanted to watch, and finally bellow at my family to shut the hell up and get out of my way so I can put the damn futon back in the House of Many Awful Invisible Fumes and Poisons and get the hell out of there.

Before we all leave, my mom and aunt inquire about my visit to the doctor that day. I had gone to an ear-nose-throat specialist about two post-sinus-infection nosebleeds to make sure I didn't have a polyp or varicose vein or shiny quarter lurking around up in there, and the verdict came up negative. I mentioned that the doctor wanted me to get that allergy test where they inject you with stuff to see what makes you swell up. This set both my crazy relatives off and running:

"You don't want to do that! They'll inject you with *chemicals!* And then they'll just prescribe *more chemicals* to fix what they've done! What you need to do is get some herbs, or look into this alternative treatment where they inflate something inside your sinuses to reshape them, because these problems are often the result of deformities caused by sleeping on them wrong and . . . "

It was at this point that I completely lost my mind and started ranting, raving, waving my arms and dancing around.

"No! I do not need to get my fucking sinuses reshaped! Because you cannot deform them by sleeping on them! Because there is a bone in your head called the skull that keeps this from happening! And I do not need to eat any fuckin' herbs, because I am an American living in the twenty-first century, where we have a little thing I like to call science! Look! Look at that elbow! You see any psoriasis there? No! Hell no! It's all cleared up! That's because I'm a real American, not some cosmic fuckin' hippie, and I went to the nice doctor and I took the goddamn medicine they gave me! I don't eat any fuckin' herbs unless they're in my spaghetti, and I don't break out the crystals and the flute when I get sick! And I get better, unlike your crazy asses!"

They just laughed and drove off. And they'll probably outlive me, too, just out of spite.

HE WAS JUST HOLDING IT FOR A FRIEND

1993

People talk about food poisoning a lot, mostly in the context of lies they tell their boss.

It's a good excuse for taking the day off. You're too debilitated to work, but nobody expects you to go to the doctor. It doesn't last long, so you can show up hale and hearty Tuesday, with no need to fake any special symptoms on your return or anything. If someone starts quizzing you, just allude to bad stuff coming out of your pooper and they'll generally change the subject. Convenient—especially when one's only real affliction is a hangover or an intermittent inability to pretend like you like your boss.

I think lots of people, especially vegetarians, convince themselves that these occasional bouts with made-up food poisoning are real, despite mild or nonexistent symptoms. Even those without a full-blown Costanza can work up a little nausea after noticing the milk they just drank expired yesterday or whatever. And vegetarians . . . Man. Ever see a vegetarian find out their soup might have been made with chicken broth? It's quite a spectacle. Coughing, dry heaves, tears . . . They'll put on a nice little show, for sure. You'd think someone smacked 'em in the gut with a frozen ham. Not that I would know what it looks like if you just up and smacked some vegetarian in the gut with a frozen ham . . . I swear.

I was vegetarian for more than a decade. My crazy mom decreed us so when I was eleven or twelve, and I just sort of eventually went along with it. As my mom no doubt knew, being vegetarian was a good way to get attention and act all self-righteous and morally superior. When you're vegetarian, everyone has to fuss over you, make special plans. When they don't, it gives you an excuse to sulk, especially during Thanksgiving or Christmas, when the rest of the family has eleven different dishes they can eat and you only have two, corn and cranberry sauce, and you know this because you sat there and counted. And you can get even sulkier when nobody pays attention to you mewling out questions like, "Was this corn boiled in ham water?" Because they're all too busy eating delicious regular food to care.

Also, when you're vegetarian you always get to decide where to go eat, because the place all the normal people want to go, the place with "BBQ" in its name, "doesn't have anything you can eat." That's a funny word, *can.*

Vegans do all that shit as well, and usually ramp it up threefold in the self-righteous category, too. Vegans also spend sixty-two percent of their time imagining totally false but entertainingly nefarious origins for commonplace ingredients. "Don't drink that Mountain Dew, dude," they'll tell each other. "It's colored with Yellow #63, which is made from crushed bugs." Or, "The sorbitol in your toothpaste comes from rendered bear fat, dude. Better ditch it."

These sorts of lines are delivered with an air of disapproving gravity that suggests the recipient is ignorant, less of a vegan than the speaker. It implies they don't have the commitment or discipline required to be really pure. Mastering this tone is important, because veganism is more than a diet, or even a cult—it's a constant game of one-upmanship. You start out not eating meat and dairy then progress to throwing away all your leather belts and shoes. Soon, you'll be turning your nose up at honey, because it oppresses bees. Ever see two frantic, indignant vegans try to top each other by listing all of the fun, ordinary shit they won't do? It's a hell of a thing, less a war of attrition than a duel where the winner is the one who proves himself the biggest loser.

. . . Some people might think I kid with that whole bee thing. But some people are no doubt gritting their teeth right this second, thinking, "After we get done dismantling world capitalism, we're bringing our stupid giant puppets and firebombs over to your house, fucking bee-exploiter Hughes."

I have some insight into all this stuff, you see, because I was also a strict vegan for about a year and a half, at the tail end of my vegetarian period.

Mind you, during my time as a vegetarian before that I'd occasionally—very occasionally, like once every two or three years—get drunk and take a bite out of someone's hamburger, just to freak everybody out, since they were used to me being such a fucking drama queen about vegetables or whatever the rest of the time. And, every so often, as inevitably happens to every vegetarian, I'd find out something I ate included some insidious pork blood or something.

Unlike other vegetarians I knew whose "systems" had become too sensitive and pure to digest that poisonous interloper of succulence, meat, accidentally eating animal parts never made me feel sick. I'm not saying I didn't play it up a bit, because what's the fun of being a vegetarian if you don't do that? But, much as with all you lying fuckers and your fake-ass Monday morning food poisoning, I never experienced any real distress. In fact, I just assumed it happened all the time when I didn't know it, because it probably did. You ever wonder why vegetarians only get sick that way when they know they accidentally ate meat? Well, don't, at least not out loud in front of one, because you'll be in for a bracing lecture.

Shit, you know, I didn't even get sick the day I forswore veganism and vegetarianism forever, hitting a cheap Chinese food buffet to cram handfuls of every possible quasi-identifiable flesh nugget and MSG-laden gloop I could grab in my belly. Nope, on the contrary—that day I felt great! Not only was it psychologically liberating, it was probably the first time vitamin B12 hit my bloodstream in a decade.

Viruses and occasional stress aside, only once have I been really walloped by any kind of gastric rebellion. Absolutely 100% bona fide food poisoning—the real stuff. Borne on the wings of some funky sour cream, it was, and fearsome.

The evening it hit me, I had gone to a now-defunct local nightclub to watch some people make noise. And I mean "noise" in the direct sense of the word.

I understand that most people have no direct experience with out-and-out noise, at least presented in a context usually reserved for traditional musical performance. That's because most people, if not happy or well-adjusted, are too busy with rewarding careers and hobbies, perhaps spending time with friends and family, to notice this crap even exists. And even if they're unlucky enough to run across it, they don't pursue it or anything—no, the reasonable response to encountering noise is to shrug and go off and spend your free time doing things that are relaxing and pleasant.

But an audience for noise does exist, as well as what might be a surprising number of prolific performers and artists who make the stuff. People go to noise concerts, buy noise CDs and records. Nobody in their right mind ever need be able to make these distinctions, but noise actually varies pretty widely in texture, dynamics, volume and overall presentation. Much like with veganism, aficionados chiefly value it for the opportunity it gives to one-up fellow nerds with useless, arcane knowledge and the dedicated pursuit of unpleasantness. Frequently, though, noise enthusiasts pretend otherwise, making up a bunch of theoretical arty hoo-hah to smokescreen the fact that their devotion is more a symptom of emotional problems than reflective of a refined aesthetic sensibility or highly developed intellectual capacity.

I have to admit, though, that I personally love me some noise. When I was a kid, I'd hold up my heavy, black Panasonic cassette tape player to the tinny speaker of my small black-and-white TV during Godzilla movies and record the sounds of destruction and mayhem. I'd lie on my bed for hours, eyes glazed over in happiness, playing back the tapes and listening to the explosions and shrieks and roars. As an adult, the occasional noise concert serves as an amusing novelty, and, in private, some of that stuff can be useful to effect a kind of instant satori, deployed to override the mental circuits and scour the forebrain of thought-based clutter—a refreshing, controlled way to blast that pesky ego for a few minutes without the need for all that terrible Buddhism.

The night I experienced real food poisoning, I was hanging around this nightclub's warehouse space, waiting for the first noise act to begin. It was my friends Justin and Shannon—they had made their own feedback-loop machines and would get onstage and fiddle with them while playing a variety of warped easy-listening records on all these broken-down turntables. Another guy in the audience, on this night I think my friend Frog, would project old Super-8 home movies over them while they performed.

Please don't be fooled into thinking this is in any way novel. Since the late '60s, every metropolitan area and college town from here to China has had a couple of deep thinkers pop up every three or four years like clockwork and do exactly this. Sometimes they wear costumes.

This night Shannon came up to me and, smirking, asked me in a tongue-in-cheek way if I wanted to "jam" with them. (As you might have guessed, smirking and sarcasm are important components of participation in this scene.) I agreed and set about the warehouse looking for "instruments," silently congratulating myself at the spontaneity, conceptual audacity and overall cleverness of using "found" materials for my part of the performance.

I came up with some pretty good stuff, too. As they began fiddling with their machines and Frog cranked up the projector, I sprinkled a little sand inside a big metal bowl, then started rubbing a smaller metal bowl inside it. I held it up to a microphone and it made some neat noises, sort of like a cranky robot whale. The sound guy threw a little echo on that shit and we were on our way. The twelve people in the audience sat there, twitching in ways that communicated quiet appreciation, or maybe heroin withdrawal.

After a few minutes I started getting a little restless. It was too pastoral or something, too gentle. But earlier I had reckoned this particular bit of noise might end up needing a little action to spur it along, and had gathered up a couple of claw hammers along with this really awesome thick slab of metal. I arranged it on this podium thing and positioned the microphone while Justin and Shannon kept fiddling, looking over to see just what I was doing.

I got it all set and, grinning, took up a hammer in each hand. I had this mental picture of me hammering away like Hephaestus with those bad boys, slamming down on that slab with mighty force . . . I was going to give these passive noise pussies an ass-kicking night to remember, a performance filled with sweat and muscle and metal and sparks. I was going to evoke the propulsive rhythms of America's industrial age, conjure the mighty dynamo vigor inherent in the cars and machines and buildings and shit that filled our lives like a one-man Futurist Manifesto. I was going to blow their fucking minds.

I brought a hammer down, and it kind of went "clink." The other one, too. It didn't conjure up Hephaestus at all. It conjured up me, a dorky guy pathetically making a clink sound in front of a dozen or so pasty douche bags in a smelly, dark warehouse. So I started in a little harder. The clink got a little louder, but certainly nothing that would fucking blow a mind.

About nine seconds in, my arms got real tired, and I couldn't keep a steady beat. I looked out into the darkness and saw the skimpy audience, illuminated in the flicker of those stupid movies. They were wholly unimpressed, blankly staring at me. "Bring back those whale bowls, dude," they seemed to say. Frustrated, I picked up the slab and threw it on the cement floor in front of the stage.

The slab, solid metal, weighed about seventy-five pounds. When it hit the floor it made a sound like a bomb going off. People jumped and scattered.

"Ah," I thought. "This is more like it."

I did it again. It was so loud. The noise was almost unbearable, but I was too excited to stop. I'd heft that slab up, brace it on my chest, rear back and push it away from me as hard as I could in the direction of whatever little pool of audience members was closest. They'd run and that thing would hit the floor and BOOM. My arms ached and my ears were seriously ringing after two throws, but I managed to toss that thing maybe eight or nine times. By that point Justin and Shannon had given up and were unplugging all their little gizmos. My slab shtick was a little vulgar for them, perhaps. I collapsed on the cold floor, arms trembling. Maybe it wasn't subtle or artistic, but man, that big ol' slab kicked up some serious noise.

A short while later, Frog got up on stage. He had changed into a costume made from red patent leather, or maybe shiny rubber. It was like an S&M get-up for a cricket of indeterminate gender that was made out of candy. I grabbed a chair up front—this was going to be good.

Frog had a tape or machine sequestered away somewhere producing these great shimmering sheets of pure white crackle. These would kind of fade in and out, creating a simple rhythm. He had a guitar, too, that he used to overlay this with all kinds of roaring and squealing. Some kind of distortion effect had been applied to his vocals, rendering them a completely indecipherable electronic squawk. It was really loud, too, penetrating through even my damaged hearing.

I sat there, letting it wash over me, and wondered where Frog was going to take it. He stretched it out a bit, staying the course, and it was exciting, even a little nerve-wracking. He could do anything, but what would it be? I waited. Then I started getting a little antsy. And then full-blown anxiety kicked in. I stared at that creepy red costume, bathed in red light, and started getting really weirded out. The noise felt like it was smothering me.

I tried to tough it out, but could feel my guts churning. What the fuck? Had Frog figured out a way to generate one of those crazy secret military subsonic frequencies that made people shit their pants? Was Frog going to melt our brains in the name of art? If anyone was capable of it, it'd be him. Was I fixin' to die? I had to get the fuck out of there.

I ran outside, ears still ringing, and hopped on my bike, speeding home to safety. Man, I'd never reacted that way to noise before or, shit, anything else. "Frog must be some kind of mad scientist," I thought. "I wonder if he's even allowed to, you know, do that, like with the Geneva Convention and all?"

Once home, I nonchalantly hit the bathroom. I was standing in front of the toilet peeing when it hit me—I was going to barf. I slammed the seat up just in time, as before I could really prepare for it that evening's burrito dinner came spraying out of my mouth in liquid form, achieving a velocity that frankly shocked me.

The forward momentum, the force—deep inside me, I could feel it pushing something in the opposite direction. With great effort I clamped my mouth shut and spun around, aiming my butthole at the toilet just as a thin, swamp-green ichor pulsed out of my nether regions, hitting the ceramic bowl with enough force to make me worry about the potential for serious blowback.

As with the first eruption, it seemed like the force my body was using to banish these foul poisons triggered a reaction at the other end of my body. I squinched my ass shut as best as I could and spun again, once again barely making the switch in time to target the latest stream of watery horror-gruel into the toilet.

This pattern was repeated for what seemed like hours. I danced and spun in front of the crapper, alternately clenching and relaxing various orifices in an attempt to direct the vile flow. It was mostly successful, but exhausting. Finally, though, after who knows how long, I was finished. And dehydrated. Pretty much every drop of moisture, at least all the gross moisture, had been expelled from my body.

The next morning wasn't too bad. I drank some Gatorade but was a little hesitant about eating anything solid. By the end of the day I was still tired, but the gurgle in my intestines had ceased. Later, I found out that several people who had eaten burritos from the same joint that day had also gotten sick. The culprit, of course, was the dodgy sour cream, which I reckon on that day was just a shade or two too sour.

It was maybe a week later that I ran into someone who had been at the noise show the night I got sick, a girl with the nonplussed, laid-back attitude of the dedicated stoner.

"Hey man," she said. "It's too bad you split that night. Where did you go?"

"I had food poisoning—the real food poisoning, not that shit you make up to tell your boss—and had to get out of there. It was grisly."

"Right on."

"Did I miss anything? How was Frog's thing?"

"It was cool," she said. "But Dan Aykroyd liked that thing you did with the piece of metal better."

I stood there for a second, trying to process that.

"Did you say Dan Aykroyd? Like, Blues Brothers Dan Aykroyd?"

"Yeah. I smoked a joint with him up against the back wall," she said. "He was in town for River Phoenix's funeral and was just checking out the scene. He thought you throwing that metal around was great."

I just stared, trying to make sense of what she was saying.

"I thought it was kind of obnoxious myself," she said, and walked away.

MY LATEST COSTANZA

2004

"I wonder what kind of dying guy I'll make?" I thought. "Will I mope around making everybody feel bad? Or go nuts and start shooting up heroin and robbing banks? And what's the best way to parlay this into getting blowjobs?"

You see, I have this thing I do, where every so often I'm convinced I have some sort of fatal disease. I mope around for a few days, hyperventilate a little. Try to figure out who, if anyone, deserves my CD collection. Wonder if God is going to be mad that I don't believe in him, that sort of thing.

I usually do this during those rare periods when things are going well for me, or even looking a bit promising or hopeful. With nothing else to focus my gigantic neuroses on, I cobble together a handful of half-imagined symptoms and perform some complicated algebra in which the answer always equals imminent and painful death. The Internet is a big help, though I started up this little hobby without its assistance a long time ago.

From what I can remember, the first time I convinced myself I was about to die was when I was about eight. I was visiting my dad for the summer, playing a game in his bedroom where I had to hop from his bed to a square patch of sunlight on the rug. As the day progressed, the patch would move farther and farther away from the bed. To raise the stakes, I would bet God that if I couldn't make it, he could kill me within three days.

I pushed the game just a little too far that day. Couldn't make the patch. I tried again and again, becoming more hysterical with every jump. Fuck! I couldn't do it! I was going to die! I started to hyperventilate, pacing back and forth. God was going to kill me! And there was nothing I could do! I mean, a bet was a bet.

I ran into the living room, where my dad was lying on the couch watching TV. Tears running down my face, I shook my hands and frantically hopped around.

"What's the matter with you?" Dad asked.

Somehow, divorced from reality though I was, I knew telling him that I lost a bet with God about how far I could jump and was going to die would just make me sound like a dipshit.

"I . . . don't . . . know!" I choked out.

Dad sat up and stared at me for a few minutes while I gyrated and paced around and generally acted all hysterical. Eventually I tired myself out and kind of collapsed, resigned to my fate. No blood was visible, so my dad could safely chalk up this display to just more typically incomprehensible, borderline-autistic behavior on my part and go back to watching TV.

I spent the next three days hunched over and fearful, glooming the place up and wondering how it was going to happen. But God spared me that day. Obviously, he had a few more tortures in mind before my clock was going to get punched.

Like in ninth grade, when I was hanging around this guy named Lee Larko. Lee looked like Donny Osmond and was an awesome guy. He knew all kinds of slutty girls to fingerbang and had a hook-up with this dude at the Majik Market who would let us buy smokes and cheap wine.

He also had this great idea where we would get poker games going in half-built houses—at this time Palm Harbor, Florida was little more than a few thousand acres of scrub brush and half-abandoned orange grove in the process of being converted to cheap subdivisions, so there were plenty of construction sites we could use. We'd squat down on the cement floors, pour out handfuls of change and go to town, smoking and pokering it up like big shots.

One time a uniformed realtor, showing the house to a couple of potential customers, walked in on us while we were doing this. There was an awkward moment or two where we all stared at each other in surprise. Then, as if following some unspoken agreement, everybody ignored each other. We went back to our game, and the Realtor continued showing the house. Nobody said a word.

Awkward, yes, but not as awkward as the time Lee shot me. I was peeing in his bathroom, and he started shooting a BB gun through the door. Fucking thing hit me in the arm. I started yelling, zipped up and threw open the door.

"Motherfucker! You shot me! That fucking hurts!" I was pretty pissed.

Lee looked a little green, like he knew he was in trouble. "Is the BB actually in there?" he said.

"Shit, I don't know." We looked down at the hole in my arm. I poked it a few times. "I don't feel it. Maybe it hit the bone and bounced out?" Using this remarkable jump of logic, I convinced myself it wasn't actually embedded in my arm, mostly because I just didn't want to have to explain the whole thing to my dad. Lee went along with it, fearful the incident would wind up with him in prison, or at least detention.

Of course, the BB was in there. The lump became all too apparent as the hole healed. And I was obsessed with it. For years I would run my finger over it, convinced it was slowly dissolving into my bloodstream, poisoning me. It would keep me up at night. "Would they amputate my arm before I died?" I'd wonder. "Will I rot? Will the BB float to my brain, turning me into a gibbering baboon man who soils his drawers in public?" God forbid I just, you know, died. I'd need to be mutilated and embarrassed in some fashion first.

And so it's gone throughout the years. At various times I've been convinced that I had AIDS, schizophrenia, pleurisy (though to this day, not exactly sure what that one is), lupus, multiple sclerosis and a variety of cancers. I've come to call the phenomenon "my Costanza," from the episode of *Seinfeld* where George freaks out, thinking he has cancer. "I knew it!" he wails. "I knew God wouldn't let me be a success!" Not that I've ever been on the verge of being a success.

So my latest Costanza took place last week. I was fresh out of the tub and rubbing some Tinactin on my foot fungus (one of the many minor indignities I have no time to document here) when I noticed a dark spot about the size of a quarter on the bottom of my foot.

"Holy shit, that looks bad," I thought. "I better look this up on the computer." After all, nothing will supercharge a medical freakout like the terrible stuff all over the Internet, which after porn delivery seems to be running a secondary service as a repository of worst-case scenarios.

I fired it up, knowing full well that this was a bad idea. And it was. Turns out skin cancer on the bottom of your foot pretty much means you're fucked. A few choice words and a search engine provided all the impetus I needed to quickly become hysterical. Illustrations varied from huge bubbling lesions eating away the foot to small, fairly innocuous blotches that nonetheless no doubt spelled doom for the unlucky bearers. Of which I was now one.

Now remember that the power of my Costanza is so strong that it can override any contrary evidence. Instant-doom foot cancer, for example, primarily affects Asians and people of African heritage in overwhelming numbers, said the Internet, and even then generally hits the elderly. In my mind, though, this is no consolation.

In addition, I spend anywhere from ten to twenty hours a week training in full-contact kickboxing, performing repetitive motions where I pivot on the exact spot of my blotch over and over, grinding all 6' 2", two-hundred-plus pounds of me into the ball of my foot hundreds of times a day. Not exactly light on my feet, I've had blister after blister right in the Costanza spot, literally torn circular hunks of flesh out of it so many times that I don't even think about it anymore and just track blood all over the on the dojo carpet when I do my thing.

Note that bleeding all over the place—in most civilized countries, an actual, tangible medical symptom—doesn't bother me. Oh no, *bleeding is fun,* because you can chase children and girls around with a bloody foot. Providing you can keep your balance while hopping.

Anyway, you'd think I'd find some reassurance from that when poking around at my foot spot, but no. This time I was sure. Even more sure than the last dozen times I had cancer, but didn't.

You see, I, like many crazy people, have little voices in my head. But my voices are a little different. You know the old-school crazy stereotype, the normal guy who hears the voices telling him to kill and go awry and stuff? And he fights those voices off for as long as possible before just snapping? I'm the opposite. I walk around pretty much just nuts, listening to the voices in the back of my head that go, "Look, relax. You're being an a-hole."

This go-round, though, my little voice of reason was no help. "Dude, that thing on your foot looks bad," it said. "You're fixin' to die."

I called my dermatologist and made an appointment. I didn't know what good it would do, other than to put an official stamp on my fate.

On the drive there I mulled things over, wondering which dying-guy tack would be the best to take. I was really hoping that chemo wasn't going to keep me from getting hard-ons, because I planned to milk the sympathy thing and get as many blowies as possible before croaking. People always talk respectfully of the stoic guys after they croak, but I knew there was no way I was going to get laid if I kept quiet about it and acted all strong.

The dermatologist took a look at my blotch. "It's probably just hemor-rhage, but I'll need to define it," he said. I climbed on to his dermatology table while he daintily poked at my foot. I relaxed a little. Shit, maybe I wasn't going to die! Maybe it was just my Costanza kicking in again!

"Hmm, your epidermal layer is very thick. I'm having trouble defining it," he said, picking away. "I think we should do a biopsy."

Biopsy?! Fuck, that's exactly what you do for cancer. I started panick-ing again. "Now, Mr. Hughes, a biopsy will require one or two stitches in your foot. You'll have limited use and blah blah blah . . . " he said.

"Whah? Can't you just carve that sucker out?" I asked, swiveling around for a look.

"No," he said, looking bewildered. "I'm trying to not cause you any discomfort." Yeah, like a fucking biopsy, stitches in my foot and waiting for lab results wouldn't cause me any discomfort.

"Just go for it," I said. He seemed frustrated. "Look, doc, I grind that spot into a carpet until it bleeds on a regular basis. I can take it."

He still seemed reluctant, but started picking away anew. "Oh dear, you're bleeding," he said. I could barely feel a tickle. "Yes . . . Yes . . . okay. Well, this is dried blood. It flakes, and the skin is pink underneath. And I see the source of the hemorrhage. I'm reasonably sure this is just hemorrhage as a result of your training."

"I haven't heard anybody say 'hemorrhage' this much since Christmas," I thought. But *reasonably* sure? That's not good enough.

"I'm going to prescribe a salicylic acid pad. I want you to wear this pad for two weeks, then come back and see me," he said. "It'll macerate that thick epidermic layer so I can take a better look. But I don't think you have anything to worry about."

I left, not really feeling better. Sure, he said I didn't have anything to worry about, but he seemed rather grave when he said it. He's just being nice, isn't he? He knows I'm a goner and is just trying to use maceration to give me two weeks of false hope as an act of kindness. Fuck!

Knowing that education and the cold light of reason have the power to banish these sorts of childish Dark Ages phantoms to the realm of, um, banished phantoms, I got home and read up some more on this foot-cancer business. I would use good, solid information to drive the Costanza from my mind. Once again, the Internet did not fail me, and in short order I was completely hysterical.

"Fuck this," I thought. "I'm not waiting no two damn weeks." I pulled out my pocketknife, inserted the tip in the incision he made and in a few short strokes sawed off the thick yellow skin.

I held it up to the light and looked closely. "Gross," I thought. Then I swabbed at the skin with a fingertip and some spit. The brownish shit came right off. I got in the bathtub and scrubbed my foot. The whole area was soon pink.

Even this wasn't good enough. I spent the rest of the weekend looking at the spot in different lights, scrubbing at it and poking it. Showing it to people. "Does this look cancerous to you?" I showed it to my friend Kalpesh, who's ridden out a Costanza or two, having known me since I was twelve. He smiled. "Don't die," he said. Does that mean he thinks I'm going to die, I wondered?

After a few more days I started to relax a little. Looking back on the hysteria of the past few days, I thought, "Man, I've had blood blisters in that spot a bazillion times. What the fuck is wrong with me? Why get so worked up over a blotch there now?"

But that's just it. That's the way the Costanza works. It lurks, waiting for a blotch or a rash or a cough to take root and feeds off the Internet and . . . Shit, I just realized, now I have to make up some lie for my dermatologist. I can't tell him I sawed the skin of my foot with a pocket knife. Well, actually, you know what? I think my dermatologist might be kind of a douche bag. Fuck what he thinks.

Ugh, the stress is making my BB start to throb a little, I think, and . . . Oh, the BB? Yeah, still in there. I forget about it, most of the time. A few years ago it set off a handheld metal detector at the airport, and I had to roll up my sleeve and explain to the guy that Lee Larko shot me there with a BB twenty-two years ago while I was taking a pee. The airport guy just smiled and looked confused. He didn't speak English.

C'mere. Wanna touch it? You can touch the BB if you want. Go ahead! Rub it for good luck! Touch it!

A FEW WORDS ABOUT SALTWATER CATFISH

2002

Whenever someone asks me what kind of fish I caught on a particular day and I grumble, "Just a bunch of catfish," the response is inevitably positive: "Oh, great! I love catfish! Gonna fry 'em up? Mmmm-mmm!" Etc.

NO. *NO NO NO NO NO NO NO!*

Saltwater catfish (or "Osama fish") are different from their freshwater cousins, and I want to set the record straight: there's nothing positive about the existence of these animals. At all. Many strange and terrible creatures, no matter how superficially despicable, play important roles in the vast, delicate balance of the natural world: experts tell us that mosquitoes, rattlesnakes, mean wasps, poodles, stupid people, Chihuahuas, ghosts and pterodactyls all have their place in the grand scheme of things, like nasty pieces of some huge, scary puzzle.

But the saltwater catfish is less a fish or other necessary food-chain element than a plague . . . Some sort of cosmic retribution dreamt up by God to punish humanity for its worst sins. Every time scientists mock the natural order by grafting an afro onto a chicken or inventing a remote-control banana, or some idiot South American peasant cuts down a tree in a rain forest somewhere to pay for those acid-washed jeans, that terrycloth shirt and that carton of Dorals, Mother Nature's fetid womb opens up and spews forth onto my fishhooks a thousand or two of these hateful, finned child molesters of the sea.

Yeah, that's right—they molest children. They also:

• Complain about being hooked in a loud, persistent and distinctly flatulent bark.

• Shit all over the place the instant they leave the water. Or maybe they're just constantly shitting—I wouldn't be surprised. Regardless.

• Are covered in a thick, translucent, boogery slime that permanently adheres to your line.

• Have needle-sharp, venom-coated spines sheathed in their dorsal and pectoral fins.

• Are inedible. Some lunatics swear that a certain variety is alright for the table, but how they even made it through all that *bukkake* dripping off of 'em to skin 'em and give 'em a try is beyond my understanding.

• Are plentiful. I have had days where I caught one on every single damn cast, one after the other for hours at a time.

• Are indestructible. I release most of my catches and make it a point to be as delicate as possible with fish in general—the poor things didn't ask to be caught, after all, and I want to do everything I can to ensure their survival after I get through harassing and yanking on 'em. Some people delight in killing every saltwater catfish they haul up, but I'm a conservationist at heart and figure I may as well apply my standards across the board. This isn't to say that I haven't occasionally gotten frustrated with the little fuckers and poked 'em in the eye, beat 'em up a bit or launched 'em a few dozen feet into the air during the release process. But no matter how roughly I handle these fish, they just bark, shit, ooze, stab me with one of their spines, flip me a bird and swim off laughing and getting ready to jump back on my hook at the earliest opportunity.

I'd rather catch the dread stingray than a saltwater catfish (and believe me, I catch plenty of those fuckers too), even though stingrays have a brittle, poisonous barb on their whiplike tails, not to mention a really, really gross mouth that looks like that movie of a pulsating ventricle or aorta or whatever it was that I had to watch in sixth grade health class. As bothersome and potentially crippling as a stingray encounter may be, these weird alien fish do have a few positive qualities. They're occasionally eaten by the very bored or hungry, and they're usually pretty docile (I even had one bond with me after I unhooked it—damn thing followed me around for half an hour, gazing up at me like a lonely puppy and freaking me out until I dropped a brick on it).

Saltwater catfish, on the other hand, go into some kind of supersonic death twist when they get hooked, rolling and twisting up your line while barking, trying to stab you with their deadly fins and getting as much fish poop and slime everywhere as they can muster.

A few years ago I got some crazy idea into my head (fancy that) where I was convinced the sharp spines of the saltwater catfish weren't truly venomous. I figured it was just a misconception based on infections resulting from the occasional puncture, or some old hillbilly canard drummed up to frighten yankees. Then I got stuck. Right in the meaty part of my hand. I didn't die or anything, but it hurt like nothing else I've experienced in an action-packed lifetime filled with injuries, indignities and a significant lack of self-regard.

I seem to have recovered pretty nicely, thankfully—some people have experienced permanent paralysis in a finger or hand after a good catfish jab. Though I must admit that since it happened I have had Musical Youth's "Pass the Dutchie" going through my head on a loop, and sometimes get distracted trying to figure out what the hell is a "dutchie" and wondering if maybe those kids weren't a little young to be messing around with dutchies in the first place, if a dutchie is what I suspect it is. And I'm pretty sure that it is.

Anyway, I'm starting to get a little worked up here just thinking about this shit, so to summarize: saltwater catfish are real bad. Don't act all excited at the thought of getting a hold of a mess of 'em for a fish-fry, or people in the know will deride you as a hopeless landlubber. And for the good of America, heckle and demean them every chance you get. Thank you.

FRANCIS FORD COPPOLA IS A DICK

2001

Now, I'm just a simple old country boy without a lot of your fancy book-learnin', but I'm pretty sure that I once heard something about that Dante feller planning on making Gainesville, Florida's Friends of the Library Book Sale the eleventh or twelfth circle of Hell in his famous book *All Your Dead Friends and Relatives and Pets are Burning Eternally in God's Lake of Fire*.

For those not living in Gainesville, the Friends of the Library Book Sale is held twice a year at special times when the moon is full, the wolfbane blooms and the spirits of the restless dead return to exact their terrible vengeance on the living. Ostensibly, the event sells books and donates the money to various programs at the local public library, including such favorites as the Vegan Astrology for Self-Righteous Lesbians class; that cheery construction-paper Anne Frank diorama they put up at Christmas;

the ongoing Sleepy Bum Round-Up; the Parents: Leave Your Loud, Illiterate, Surly Children Here All Day While You Hit the Crack House initiative and the special weekend appearances by Batshit Crazy Guy Who Says Hello to Everyone in a Really Loud Voice.

Funding from the book sale has also gone toward buying up every available copy of *Pluto Nash* on Betamax for the library's extensive archives as well as underwriting subscriptions to favorite magazines such as *White Belt Karate, Crocheting without Hands* and *Southern Nostalgia for Segregation*.

In execution, though, the book sale doesn't really resemble a book sale so much as it does a steel-cage, no-disqualification wrasslin' battle royal held at the Senior Citizen Special Olympics. "Man," you're thinking, "Sign me up! I'd sure like me a piece of those goddamned short-bus senior citizens!" No, no, no. Simmer down, there, Remo Williams. While not necessarily physically tough, the book-sale patrons can overwhelm anyone with sheer numbers. People come from miles and miles around to mob this thing, and they're especially determined, often showing up several hours before the 4 A.M. opening time to mutter obscenities at imaginary antagonists and vibrate in anticipation.

Okay, to be fair, the sale patrons aren't all old. Plenty of miserable hippies attend to buy books on organic Volkswagen repair and ensure the place reeks of patchouli and armpits, and the record bins always have a nice glut of hipsters clotted around 'em searching for ironic two-dollar Dexy's Midnight Runners albums they can play at their "old wave" DJ gig, something everyone with a star tattoo and messy black hair apparently has.

I'd say a full ten or fifteen percent of the crowd actually consists of children. They're my favorite, both because it's heartening to see such young folks aglow with a sincere love of reading and also because they're a lot easier to shove out of the way when you need to dive in and grab some good shit before some other motherfucker gets it.

Ah yes, the shoving. Plenty of shoving at the book sale. In fact, pretty much any pretense toward being a polite, contributing member of society is dropped upon entry. The heritage of hundreds—if not thousands—of years of civilized development just sloughs off like so many flakes of dandruff the instant people walk in the door. And begin stabbing each other in the genitals with rusty hypodermic needles while desperately trying to snatch that last copy of *The Bible Code's Chicken Soup for Oprah* or *Cornholing for Dummies*.

One year—and I'm even not making *this* part up—I was standing in the middle of the rabid throng and trying to decide which section to peruse next, guns or porn, and how best to navigate through all the mess, when one little wretched gnome put his gnarled hand on my chest and, head down, tried to shove me out of his way. I stared down at the top of his mottled, crusty head in disbelief as he applied all the pressure he could muster, breaking out in an oily sweat from the effort and grunting, "Nnnnnng! Nnnnnnng!"

Now, I'm admittedly a lot more goofy than fearsome, but I'm slightly taller and thicker than average, not to mention covered in scars and prison-quality tattoos of shit like pirate flags and Misfits record covers. And I couldn't believe this little troll thought he could just shove me aside, like normal people do with cripples. Actually, I don't think the frenzied little monster even knew what he was doing. After a minute or two of pushing, he looked up, saw me glaring at him, gasped and scuttled off into the crowd while I pondered what book could possibly be worth entering into this kind of madhouse. (Turns out that year it was a pristine, first-edition copy of *Spalding's Field Guide to North American Homos*.)

Mentioning porn reminds me of something that happened at the sale a few years ago: they really do have a porn section, kind of . . . Off in one discreet, roped-off corner they always have a few tables stacked with shit like collections of bawdy limericks and copies of that infamously randy men's magazine, *Esquire*. Mostly I ignore this section, because frankly there just ain't anything in there that can out-dirty the dirty stuff in my head, but this particular year I had spent about two minutes casually sorting through its piles of *Sports Illustrated 1986 Swimsuit Special* and tattered, jism-stained biographies of Dr. Ruth while looking for cool old *Playboys* or whatever when I heard someone call out my name.

I look up, and standing there is, of all people, my mother. I'm holding the section's one legitimately dirty item, a copy of *Penthouse Forum* from 1978 with the pages open to a story about a geisha giving a dog a blowjob or something, and Mom proceeds to introduce me to her six or seven elderly female friends. I put down the magazine and actually have to reach across the rope separating the dangerous, disgusting perverts like myself from the nice, well-adjusted patrons with the ability to form normal relationships to shake each of their hands, tainting each of them with my filth while they fix rigid, insincere smiles, pretend not to notice that I'm Caligula and make mental plans to go wash off the dried orgy juice as soon as humanly possible

To tell the truth, it kind of turned me on.

Anyway, this year the book sale was pretty much more of the same. I always tell myself I'm not going to go, and I always do. I get punched by

112-year-old lepers, poked in the eyes and gonads with the huge cardboard boxes everybody totes around and headbutted by hysterical, book-mad *Star Trek* fans who have all the grooming skills of comics-shop employees.

Regardless, at the sale I know I can count on flinching when some cheese-stuffed housewife next to me suddenly squeals with delight at scoring a copy of *Flowers in the Attic* for a buck. I know at some point I'll mistakenly make eye contact with one of the drooling spastics left to fidget in the corner or wander through the crowd unattended, and feel my IQ drop fifteen points. I'll rub shoulders with four-hundred-pound adult D&D players and other men who think it's okay to wear their hair in a ponytail. I'll wince as various rocket scientists loudly recommend *Angela's Ashes* or drone on about John Grisham and Mary Higgins Clark. If, while browsing, I leave two inches between me and a shelf or table, some circus contortionist will slip into the space and grab all the books I want while I'm left staring at the back of his head.

Inevitably, I'll get rammed with a wheelchair or something, stumble and accidentally knock over a stack of books being sorted in the middle of a busy thoroughfare by some bespectacled, hostile and beige forty-five-year-old James Taylor fan of indeterminate sexuality. I'll eventually grab eight or ten books and wait in line an hour to pay for 'em. And I'll get home and at least one of 'em will be something I already have.

This year they had initiated a challenging little puzzle for everyone and asked people queuing up to pay to separate into two lines, one for people with checks and one for people with cash. It gets a little confusing, seeing as the lines snake around the huge warehouse for at least six miles, crossing each other and looping back on themselves multiple times. Occasionally one of the volunteers, friendly folks who happily devote their time in return for the judge not sending them to prison for raping the comatose (or whatever), would walk up and down the lines, making sure people were being herded into the proper group.

One guy, a squat little runt in a loud Hawaiian shirt who kind of looked like if Francis Ford Coppola had a sort of midget-y thing going on, had apparently missed the constant, megaphone-delivered announcements about the necessity of getting in the right line. Not long after I began the internal debate over whether the handful of books I had were worth another thirty minutes or so of waiting in this stuffy, loud hellhole (a debate I engage in halfway through the line every single time I go), Coppola is informed that he's in the wrong group.

It's actually kind of understandable how this idiot managed to not hear the line announcements, despite the fact they're being regularly delivered at brain-splitting volume. See, Coppola has the most remarkably thick patch of coarse, black hair covering his entire ear. The fucking thing looks like a piece of bread with mold growing all over it. You could probably put Motörhead in his fucking ear and he wouldn't hear it.

So anyway, instead of getting in the correct line, or just trying to work something out, Coppola starts loudly berating the volunteer: "What?! What are you gonna do?! What goddamn difference does it make what line I'm in?!" The volunteer keeps his cool, but this man-wart keeps it up. People are trying to ignore him, but he keeps getting louder and more insulting. He's at least nine or ten people away from me, so I can't actually reach out and grab him, but I start glaring at him with all of my might and trying to will him to shut up with the power of my mind.

Meanwhile, he's ignoring me and continuing: "What?! What?! Are you gonna not take my goddamned money?! My money's no good?! What?!" The volunteer throws his hands up and starts walking away. I'm fantasizing about what I'd tell him if he was in line next to me: "Look here, pubic ear, if you want to keep all of your blood inside of your body you're going to shut your loud fucking Francis Ford Coppola-ass mouth and wait in line without complaint like a proper sheep, just like everyone else is doing. Because, so help me God, if I have to listen to one more stupid, diseased word out of you, I'm going smash your balls between two volumes of that there *Encyclopedia Britannica* so hard that your grandchildren will turn blue and die."

Eventually this human skidmark, sensing the murderous mood of the crowd, settles down and goes back to grooming his homemade earmuffs. I return to my patient wait, struggling to tamp down a barrage of panic attacks and trying not to stare at the awesome boobies of the three sixteen-year-old emo girls standing in front of me. Or at least trying not to look too obvious while I'm doing it. Hmm, I wonder if those little darlings would like an escort to the "adult" section . . . Ahem. Well.

Anyway, after another seven hours of pain, humiliation and oxygen deprivation I pay for my books. Emerging into the sunlight, I gasp at the beauty of the sky and the trees and burst into tears. My clothes have turned to rags and my hair is gray. (Well, that happened before I went, but still.) I kneel and kiss the ground, sobbing. I can't remember my name, but I know that I'll regain that, and the ability to feed myself, as the horror eventually recedes.

After I get home, I notice one of the books I bought, *Redbirds,* by the talented, disgraced journalist and author Rick Bragg, is a retitled British edition of something I already have. *Fuck.*

MAYBE I'LL SPROUT WINGS AND FLY AWAY

1993

Sometimes in life it's necessary to let a motherfucker stick a razorblade in your eye. Really.

Ah, I sense your skepticism. Please allow me to explain.

I have an uncle-in-law who's a builder. Back in the early '90s he would occasionally employ me for odd jobs at his various construction sites. Because I didn't have a car, he'd pick up me and my hangover, drive me to a worksite while talking about Jesus, drop me off and leave me to do stuff like smash up pesky chunks of cement or sweep up the beer cans, burger wrappers and crack pipes left by his crews.

I like this uncle. He's kind of like a cross between Ned Flanders and G. Gordon Liddy. The house where he, my aunt and their two kids live is chock-full of flavorless religious health food, wall hangings stitched with inspirational homilies and the kind of Christian analogues to secular pop-culture items that make me feel like I'm standing on the edge of a deep, dark hole. They also have lots of awesome guns.

My aunt and uncle also used to always be involved in some kinda pseudo-religious Amway-styled scam or another. Before they got it out of their system, my uncle would always have some entertaining, cockamamie endorsement of some damn thing or another to share, like when he was on this preposterous blue-green algae kick.

"You know, I was puttin' up a fence the other day, and a piece of the post snapped," he once started telling me. "The tension from the wire swung that post around, and it ended up smacking me in the arm real hard."

"Really?"

"Yup. And you know what I did?"

"Nope. What?"

"I made me a poultice out of some of that blue-green algae and put it right on the spot where the post hit. It didn't even bruise. Now, this thing hit me hard enough to almost break the bone, but I didn't get a mark on me. Blue-green algae. That is some wild stuff."

"Wow," I'd say, while thinking, "Shut the fuck up."

This is the same uncle-in-law who was responsible for one of my favorite Christmas memories. A few years back, we had convened at his place to open presents. He was telling me about the radical construction materials he had used to build the place, including plumbing made entirely of blue-green algae, and invited me upstairs to take a look at some exciting new insulation. Well, I'm hardly one to turn down a chance to check out some insulation, so I followed him up to the attic.

He grabbed a handful of this stuff that looked like the weird powdery cardboard material in padded envelopes that gets everywhere if you open 'em wrong and spread it out on his palm. Then he put a penny on top of the material, grabbed a blowtorch and melted the goddamn penny. I mean he *melted* that fucker. Right in his hand.

Then he asked me if I liked brandy, and we went down to the garage to drink some he had stashed out there, away from the womenfolk. I noticed a big, wooden board in the corner that had a bunch of knives sticking out of it.

"Oh, those are my throwing knives. It's a great stress reliever," he said, then started giving me a demo. Thwok! Thwok!

"Hey," he said, "Do you like guns?"

"Sure!"

He unlocked a trunk that contained dozens of pistols and started pulling out a few of his favorites.

"Here, hold this Beretta nine millimeter. It's not loaded—go ahead and dry-fire it, you won't hurt it."

So I'm standing there next to a board full of throwing knives, holding a gun and a glass of booze, and my mom calls out to the garage to ask me to take her home. Shit . . . Just when I was starting to feel all Christmas-y.

The whole eyeball thing started when this uncle hired me to lay some sod at one of his job sites. While wearing contacts, I had got a chunk of the stuff in my eye. I just wiped it out and kept working. I slept in those contacts, and the next day woke up startled to see my eyes shot through with an intricate network of bright red, tiny veins. At first I was hoping that this was the fulfillment of a lifelong wish, that I had finally been granted the ability to make things burst into flame just by staring at them. But this was not the case.

I peeled the contacts off of my eyeballs and tried to get on with my life, but I could tell something had gone horribly awry. My eyes were itchy, turning redder by the minute (I estimate at least .7 on the Tommy Chong scale) and extremely sensitive to light. I always hate it when a formerly compliant body part turns rogue on me, and the fact that I use my eyes fairly often made this whole thing pretty disconcerting.

So the next day I visit that paragon of advanced medical technique, the University of Florida infirmary. Now, I had visited the infirmary plenty of times before, but never as a patient (the infirmary's where college girls go to get their chlamydia cleared up, so it's a good place to meet chicks that are willing to, you know, "do it").

After a bit of the usual stuff anyone has to go through when visiting a doctor (you know—sitting in the waiting room for three hours, filling out questionnaires, signing release forms absolving the clinic of responsibility after they accidentally graft a hamster head onto the side of your neck, having a gallon or two of blood needlessly drained, having a few different people stick their fingers in your butt, becoming increasingly restless as various screams, gasps and desperate pleas for mercy echo down the hallway), I was sent to see a nurse. She put down her cigarette, took one look at me and pronounced that I had pink eye.

I was skeptical. "I've had pink eye before, and this sure doesn't feel like pink eye. Are you sure?"

"Yes . . . Well, no. We'll perform a few more tests, just in case."

I was ushered into a room filled with the latest medical technology, circa whenever Dr. Frankenstein stitched that Herman Munster dude with the square head together. They strapped me onto one of those Frankenstein boards, spun me around a few times, punched me in the face, cackled, threw a few of those big wall switches, fired up the antenna thingy with the little lightning bolts and shined some really bright lights in my eyes. As the winds outside howled and the roar of the thunder built to a hellish crescendo I passed out, and when I woke up there were pictures of me on the Internet naked and getting a blowjob from what appeared to be Ernest Borgnine. They also said my eye condition was beyond their understanding, and I should hoof it like pronto over to the nearest hospital, the world-famous Shands, to see just what the fuck was wrong with me.

Shands is a fun place. You can walk around in there and see all kinds of weird shit you'll wish you never saw, like two-headed babies in jars. I had just finished a summer job there, Xeroxing gigantic, wasteful stacks of paper designed to ensure the daily dumpster-capacity quota was met. While I spent a lot of time at that gig freaking out secretaries by sticking paper clips through my recently abandoned nose-ring hole, I had overheard a thing or two about sick people getting better there, so I figured Shands would fix me up right.

Well, Shands is the kind of place you want to go if a tornado drives a coat hanger through your skull or some weird bug crawls into your ear and lays its eggs in your brain. But it's a teaching hospital, so unless you've contracted something really interesting from a meteor or you're holding your brain in with duct tape, the real doctors can't be bothered with you and will send out some medical students or residents to practice on you some.

During the check-in, I had a conversation with a resident that went like this:

"Mr. Hughes, are you allergic to any medicines?"

"Yeah, penicillin."

"What happens when you take it?"

"Huh?"

"I said, 'What happens when you take it?'"

"Uhhh, I dunno. I'm allergic . . . So I don't take it."

"You don't know what happens when you take it?"

"No, I don't know, motherfucker! Maybe I sprout wings and fly away!"

Someone snuck up behind me at this point and whacked me across the back of the head with one of those big reflex-testing mallets, knocking me unconscious. When I woke up, there were pictures on the Internet of me wearing a Speedo and getting dangled over a balcony by Michael Jackson, and the resident said I had some kind of grisly, sod-induced infection on the surface of my cornea. They were going to have to scrape my eye to clean out the infection.

Scrape my eye.

So they put a few drops of an anesthetic in my eye. I had to sit in this chair and stick my chin on one of those things that eye doctors use when they're torturing you with that air-puff glaucoma thing. They turn the lights out, shine a beam into my left eye, and a guy pulls out this disposable scalpel with a blade pretty much exactly like one of those X-acto knives.

And starts scraping. Scraping my fucking eye.

I had always thought of my eyeballs as being kind of squishy, like a pair of jelly donuts or silicone implants or something that'd just pop and spew eye-juice everywhere if you poked 'em too hard. But the surface of my eye provided a surprising amount of resistance. I could feel the keen edge of the scalpel pressing into my eyeball, as well as see its shadow moving across my field of vision.

Go ahead—imagine someone doing it to you, cutting through the tiny, moist layer of surface gelatin to grind at the brittle goods underneath . . . Scrape, scrape, scrape . . . Scrape, scrape, scrape . . .

They did it to me for what were twenty of the longest minutes of my life.

And that wasn't even the last indignity they were going to visit upon me. They loaded me up with a bunch of eye-salves and drops and shit and informed me that I'd have to apply 'em around the clock for a few days. The catch was I had to wait two full minutes between applications, which meant that I'd get up at four in the morning or whenever, put some drops in, try to focus on the clock for two minutes while hallucinating rows of soft, comfy beds dancing around me and listening to fluffy, imaginary pillows seductively whispering my name. I honestly spent more than a few minutes wondering if having eyesight was even worth this bullshit.

After a few days of this exquisite torture, I went back to the hospital. My eye sockets had swelled up, the actual eyeballs were still as red as a baboon's ass and some kind of foul jism was seeping from my tear ducts. The resident gave me a pill that made me dizzy, and I passed out. When I woke up, there were pictures of me on the Internet wearing a Catholic school girl's uniform and a saddle while getting ridden around the room by a very excited-looking Al Roker. I also overheard this conversation:

"Doctor, we called you in because this guy's eye is all evil and puffy, and it's seeping some kind of wretched goo. We can't figure out why."

"It says here you gave him penicillin-derived eyedrops. But his records say he's allergic to penicillin. Why in the hell did you prescribe him that stuff after he told you he was allergic to penicillin?!"

"Uh, we didn't believe him."

"Didn't believe him?!"

"He said he'd sprout wings and fly away."

Well, the fuckers eventually got it all straightened out, and I retained the use of my eyes. And I have to admit, the experience did have a few positive aspects. I skipped a few weeks of college classes (that, frankly, I probably would've skipped anyway, but still). I got to wear a cool, pirate-y eyepatch for a couple of weeks, even though I never really needed it. I got to pretend maybe I was gonna sue those quacks for billions of sweet malpractice dollars, even though in my heart I knew I was way too lazy to actually go through with a scheme like that no matter how justified. Oh, and I got a blowjob from Ernest Borgnine. Apparently.

MORE INDIGNITIES THROUGH THE AGES

Age three: I become enraged upon meeting another kid named Patrick. Soon after I become completely inconsolable when it's pointed out to me that he's older than me and therefore has an original claim to the name, which I cannot legally challenge. Bitter feelings of resentment toward my parents that stem from this unfortunate situation linger on well into the twenty-first century.

Age seven: Oh, that nickel I swallowed? I did it to impress a girl who told me I was "almost as funny as Paul Lynde."

Age nine: Desperate for attention, I pretentiously decide to start using my full name on class assignments. It's only after taking a few papers home months later that I learn I don't actually know how to spell my own middle name.

Age eleven: While wrestling with my seven-year-old sister, I slip, fall on her and bust her nose, causing no small amount of blood to start pouring out of her face. It doesn't hurt her at all—in fact, she doesn't even suspect anything's wrong until she sees my horrified expression. The crying starts after she runs into the bathroom and gets a look at the gory mess, but she's not upset for long—oh, no. Her panic is displaced as a plan forms in her devious little mind.

As she quiets down, I plead with her through the locked bathroom door to not tell our mom about the incident. She doesn't answer, but I can hear her doing . . . something. This makes me nervous. After a few minutes, she comes out of the bathroom. She's no longer bleeding, but she's smeared thick, dark red nose-blood all over her face and neck. It's already beginning to dry, setting into a kind of grisly, cracked death mask.

"I'm going to get you into trouble," she says.

Age twelve: I make a friend, Matt Krogh, whose interests happily run parallel to mine. We spend a lot of time making homemade explosives out of model rocket engines and black powder, playing Dungeons and Dragons, getting ignored by snooty chicks at the skating rink and beating the crap out of each other.

We invent this game where one guy puts on swimming goggles and wraps himself in blankets, pillows and puffy jackets while the other guy blindfolds himself and then spins around in circles flinging ninja stars, darts and throwing knives full-force around the room at random.

Amazingly, this little pastime inflicts no serious injury on either of us, unlike the time in the backyard when I become momentarily distracted by a bee or something and take my attention off of Matt for a split second. Feeling an unexpected impact on my chest, I look down to see about seven feet of sharpened bamboo spear sticking straight out of me at a right angle. Matt, at the other end of the yard, stands pale and frozen.

"Shit," I say, because it hurts. And also because I'm admiring his aim a little.

Age fourteen: Tisza Langford comes over to talk to me while I'm mowing the lawn. She's wearing a bikini, and I get a hard-on. I have to turn my back to her because I'm wearing these stupid little soccer shorts. She continues trying to chat with me, and moves to face me while I keep turning away from her. After a few minutes of staring at my back, she gives up and pretty much quits talking to me altogether.

Age fifteen: If you have heartburn and decide to take some Alka-Seltzer, it's important to wait for the tablets to completely dissolve before drinking 'em down. You should not swallow them like huge aspirin. Extreme discomfort and forceful projectile vomiting may ensue. Let me stress this: Wait for the tablets to completely dissolve.

Age sixteen: My foofy new-wave bangs catch fire when, stoned, I lean just a little too far into the stove while lighting a joint.

Age eighteen: I meet Mike Watt, a famous rock 'n' roll musician who has played with some of the world's greats, including the Minutemen, fIREHOSE and the Stooges. Well, by "meet," I mean, "scream because I look over in the parking lot before the fIREHOSE show and see a man's naked hairy ass and he jumps up and screams too and it's Mike Watt."

Age nineteen: Chuck From Hell and I get a couple of cases of beer and crawl through a muddy creek to get into this weird cave under University Avenue to drink. When that gets boring, we go visit Eileen and Tracy. We destroy their apartment and empty the fridge and pee on stuff we shouldn't pee on and somehow I get to make out with Eileen a little, but we don't stay long because the sun is coming up and adventure calls.

See, Chuck had been in a terrible car accident several months prior, where a guy in another car fell asleep at the wheel, strayed into Chuck's lane and killed his girlfriend. He wanted to go to Tallahassee and have a look at where she had just been buried. We start driving and I fall asleep. I wake up at a rest stop barely half an hour north of Gainesville, where Chuck had wisely stopped to nap after getting tired.

It's very bright out, and I am half-buried in a pile of empty beer cans, wearing a leather jacket with skulls and spikes all over it and covered in mud and condiments. Families are staring at us. Despite the presence of perfectly serviceable bathrooms at the rest stop, we decide to hit a gas station to clean up. By "clean up" I mean we use an entire bottle of gooey pomade to sculpt our hair-dos into giant, greasy rockabilly pompadours. Fueled by warm beer, we eventually make it to Tallahassee, where we spend thirty seconds looking at Chuck From Hell's girlfriend's grave. He pronounces this depressing, so we go to the mall, where he buys a Zodiac Mindwarp cassette and some clove cigarettes, and two huge bikers wrinkle their noses at us in disgust.

After cruising around for a little while, Chuck remembers he knows a girl in Tallahassee who "likes to get fucked up the ass." I stand next to him at a pay phone while he tries to track her down. A bum sitting on a park bench and swigging from a brown paper bag looks over at us disapprovingly. A car with two girls in it pulls up next to us. They look over, and I look back and smile. They lock the car's doors and run the red light.

Age twenty-three: I'm using the bathroom during a Radon show at the Hardback. Clay Smith, musician and reprobate, is at the stall next to me. As I finish and give my penis a few hygienic, manly shakes, Clay looks down and says, "Wow, you have a big dick!"

Startled, I look up, and Clay uses the opportunity to smack me right on the head of my dick. Hard. I stand there in shock for a few moments as Clay, giggling, runs out of the bathroom and onto the dance floor. After taking a few moments to gather my composure, I run out and tackle Clay from behind, knocking him completely unconscious.

Instantly, six or seven pretty girls run to Clay's aid, cradling his head, whispering comforts, stroking his brow with their soft, ripe bosoms and feeding him sweet, cold beer. I am not a victim but a bully, and nobody is impressed with my sore little pee-pee.

Age twenty-five: New Year's Eve festivities start early for me and, after drinking just a bit too much, include firing bottle rockets into large, open buckets of house paint, spattering and angering innocent bystanders. Not long after using this same paint to execute a huge pentagram and an anarchy symbol on the host's garage, I experience a brief moment of clarity and decide that I should head home before I get into real trouble. While stumbling home in a blurry haze, I fall flat on my face at least once.

At home, I disrobe, head to the bathroom and begin vomiting. At midnight I shiver, naked, and rest my head on the toilet seat while listening to people celebrating outside my window. "Happy New Year," they cheer, over and over again. "Happy New Year!"

The next day my girlfriend calls me from Tallahassee to tell me she's in love with some dude. A week later she sends me an invitation to their housewarming party. It has a cartoon of them carrying boxes into their new house together while giant hearts float above their heads.

Ages twenty-six to thirty-seven: *Good times.*

ANSWERS TO READER QUESTIONS

Dear Sir,
Will those skinheads really beat my ass?
Sincerely,
Dick Hertz

Well, Dick, if it's 1988 and the skinheads in question happen to be those thirty or so Nazi behemoths from Tampa and Orlando, then I can assure you the answer is yes. In fact, if your ass-beating experience is anything like mine, they'll probably do a thorough, professional-grade job of it too.

Sometimes people ask me, "Why did they beat your ass?" Well, Dick, they're Nazi skinheads. They didn't really need a reason. First of all, they were skinheads. And second of all, they were Nazis. The skinhead chapter of the Hello Kitty fan club doesn't need a reason to whoop someone's ass, you know? Ass beating just falls under general duties in the job description.

But in a roundabout way I brought it on myself. Back then, pathetically enough, I had aspirations toward thuggishness, and (while eschewing any racist or fascist sympathies, please note) attracted the gang's attention by trying to be like them: bald, menacing and angry. I did this in a wholly goofy and pussy-fied way, of course. It was pretty easy to bum out local hippies and knock down the occasional drunken fratboy while scowling around town in my boots 'n' braces, but you're dealing with a whole 'nother standard of whoop-ass when it comes to a cross-eyed mob of crank-fueled, big-city muscle-heads with tattoos of swastikas.

My beating started out pretty mild. I was waiting to go inside a hardcore show at the local VFW hall when my head started jerking forward uncontrollably. I spent a few confused minutes trying to figure out why this was happening before someone pointed out to me that three or four skinheads were taking turns running at me and hitting me in the back of my head. (Little did they know that they couldn't get my attention that way, as my head doesn't house any vital spots.)

Disturbed by this development, I retired to the parking lot, where the beating began in earnest. My first combat strategy involved talking—frankly, I was terrified that if I fought back I'd incur a higher level of butt-kick than might originally be in store for me. It wasn't until I was curled up on the ground with them in a circle around me, kicking me, that it occurred to me that my designated stomping was going to be turned up to eleven no matter what I did.

So I hauled myself up and started swinging wildly. The mob backed off a step or two, and I heard a few voices call out for the attack to resume under "one on one" rules. Although I certainly appreciated this chivalry, I thought to myself that it would have been much nicer if the one-on-one thing had been instigated a little earlier, alas.

Regardless, a gigantic representative was selected from their ranks to carry on with my thrashing. I adopted the Marquis of Queensbury pose, and he hit me four or five times in the face. I then landed one feather-light blow to his kneecap, which of course was the signal for the other twenty-nine gentlemen to resume punching me from all sides.

Somehow I fought to my best friend's car and sat on the trunk, wiping blood out of my eyes while kicking at the mob, who really seemed to be having a good time. Strangely enough, considering his dark-brown skin and long, curly hair, my friend was allowed to pass through the crowd unmolested. In fact, one of the Nazis politely handed him his hat, which had fallen off while he vainly tried to pull me from the fray. He started the car, I fought my way into the passenger seat and after a short discussion we agreed that it was probably a good time to leave.

I was so glad that I didn't die that as we pulled away I started laughing. My friend was looking at me in horror, and I figured out why when I glanced down and had the unique experience of seeing blood pour out of several holes in my face and splash across my lap. My nose was broken in two places, my clothes were torn and the entire left side of my body was turning into one solid bruise. My ghastly appearance didn't prevent us from stopping by the video store on the way home, which gave us the chance to warn a punk-rock buddy working there that he might want to avoid the show. "There are a lot of mean skinheads there," I said, perhaps unnecessarily.

You'll be happy to know, Dick, that I learned some important lessons from this experience. One is that no matter how tough you are, there is always someone tougher. In fact, there are thirty of those tougher someones, and they like Hitler and will punch you in the face while wearing spiky metal knuckle-rings.

Another thing I learned is that everyone will treat you like you're some sort of bad-ass fighting machine if you have two black eyes, a broken nose and cuts all over your face, despite the fact that these accoutrements would seem to suggest your skill at fisticuffs is somewhat lacking. Weird.

Oh, I mustn't forget this one: pushing pieces of your nose back into place makes disturbing crackly noises and kind of sucks.

Thanks for your question, Dick!

Hello,
Can Jim Marburger really pee and ride a bicycle at the same time?
Skeptical,
Hugh Jass

He sure can, Hugh. And despite being drunk and bleeding because he jumped off of that really high porch into those bushes to make amends for busting your hand open when he hit you with that chair, he's as graceful as a greased-up Nadia Comeneci frolicking naked in an inflatable moonwalk with Mary Lou Retton while he's doing it.

Hola,
Powdered cocoa won't put out the fire?
Ciao,
Amusingo Genitalio

No, paisan, it won't. And that shit doesn't exactly give the kitchen a nice chocolatey aroma when it explodes all over the place, either.

YOU DONE KILLED HIM

1988

There's this kid named Fessie, okay, and he's a total punk-rock drama queen. The type of 1980s suburban shithead who's always derailing a good party by swallowing fourteen aspirin or lightly mincing his wrists with a steak knife and siphoning off all the hot goth babes, whose sympathetic nature and love of posed histrionics irrationally draw them in just as surely as Super Extra Hold Aquanet, clove cigarettes, fishnet stockings and gooshy, pale boobies never fail to hypnotize me.

Anyway, Fessie chalks up more than a few black marks in his column throughout the course of a year or so, trying to hit me with his car and trying to bait my friends into fights, no doubt in an attempt to further his wretched martyr act.

I find it easy to ignore the little attention whore, for the most part, until an incident where, adopting a particular sort of obnoxious bravado

I've observed in many lower life forms, he tries to shake my hand at a keg party. Not only am I disinclined on principle, I'm also using both hands to pour myself a beer during his attempt. I point this out to the little creep (and, all things considered, rather politely, I might add), finish serving myself and walk off.

A few minutes later, I'm in the kitchen staring down the cleavage of some foxy little Morticia and making small talk about Bauhaus or something when Fessie starts fussin'. Supposedly outraged at my snub, he has two or three guys "holding him back" in the other room while he rants and raves about "what a dick" I am. Having seen similar tableaus played out many times, I shrug and return my attention to little miss spooky. After a few more minutes of . . . of . . . shit, I don't remember, probably enthusiastic discussion about the Sisters of Mercy's *Temple of Love* twelve-inch, brave young Fessie taps me on the shoulder. When I turn around, he hits my jaw with a sucker punch that boasts all the destructive force of a kitten parachuting into a bowl of flowers.

Fessie is pulled away while, enraged, I make my way to the back yard. Muttering my murderous intent, I empty my pockets and strip off my jacket, watch and shoes. Barking out challenges and threats, I begin a short regimen of stretching, followed by a warm-up routine that includes what I hope is an impressive-looking collection of kicks and shadow boxing. After a minute or two of this, I am out of breath and starting to get cold. I am also wondering why I'm the only one in the back yard. I gather up all my stuff and go inside—the place is deserted. Confused, I go out front—ah. Fessie's there, bellowing his plan to kick my ass to the entire party, who mostly look bored.

I walk over, hit him with a straight jab and follow it up with a sloppy roundhouse kick to his ribs. He collapses. I look around. People stare at me, disgusted. The goth girls get on their brooms and fly over to the other side of the yard, putting as much space as possible between themselves and me, the big Fessie-beating bully. People start to file back into the house, keeping their distance from me. Angry and frustrated, I steal a Skinny Puppy tape from the host. Then, feeling bad, I put it back.

A short while later, I'm sulking in the corner when some guy comes up to me with blood all over his hand. "I thought you were a dick for beating that one guy up," he says, "But look—he just bit me in the hand!"

I walk into the front yard, where Fessie is going apeshit. He starts screaming at me again. He rushes me. Trapped in some *Twilight Zone* nightmare where, despite recognizing my fate, I am doomed to repeat the same actions for all of eternity, I grab him by the hair with my left hand

and deliver a stiff right square to the center of his forehead. His eyes roll back in his head as he slumps to the ground and starts twitching.

"You done killed him," says the laconic guy next to me. I start panicking and hopping from foot to foot.

"No . . . No! There's no way!" I kneel down to check on Fessie, who, thankfully, is still breathing.

"If'n you didn't kill him, you at least gave him brain damage," the guy mumbles before wandering off uninterested, along with pretty much everybody else.

With visions of prison running through my mind, I sit on the front lawn for the next twenty minutes with Fessie's head cradled in my lap, desperately trying to revive him and make sure I didn't give him brain damage. After a while he comes to, looks around and blinks. He's strangely quiet, but he doesn't seem . . . well, any more brain-damaged than before, and I am relieved.

"Why, Fessie?" I ask. "Why do you do all this stuff? Honestly, man, what's the deal?"

Head still calmly resting in my lap, he looks up at me for a moment before answering.

"You don't respect women," he says.

STRAIGHTS VERSUS THE GAYS

1999

I've never been one for nostalgia. But sometimes—when reclining on my deathbed, for example—I like to look back and reflect on life, this strange journey we all share . . . Perhaps even try to make sense of it all, or compact three and a half decades of hard-won experience into some golden nugget of wisdom I can pass on to loved ones . . . Invariably, when these philosophical moments strike, I return to this one thought more than any other:

For a supposedly straight guy, I sure have spent a lot of time in gay bars.

And that's it! That's the diary entry this week. "For a supposedly straight guy, I sure have spent a lot of time in gay bars." Hope you enjoyed it, and thanks for stopping by.

. . . Okay, I reckon leaving this where it is will only trigger more of the already all too-common aspersions as to my sexuality (it was just one buttplug, for fuck's sake, and I couldn't even feel the vibration), so I guess I'll elaborate.

First of all, I should point out that a gay person raised me. Well, a supposedly gay person. My mom came out of the closet as a lesbian when I was nine or ten, you see, but in a way that didn't really say, "I'm finally comfortable enough to be who I really am," as much as, "I'm fucking nuts, and please pay attention to me." This is a subject for another entry (as well as an estimated $750,000 worth of therapy sessions and Paxil), but I bring it up to illustrate that I was brought up around lots of openly gay people and was lucky enough to view this sort of thing as perfectly normal from a fairly young age.

Yes, despite lingering negative stereotypes, I'd like to go ahead and take this chance to inform any bigots, 'phobes or doubters reading this that the gay race (or whatever they are) are entirely normal—just as boring, petty, stupid, small-minded, reactionary, dull, fucked-up and square as everyone else, for the most part. However, as a teenager I did notice one important difference between the worlds of gay and straight: the former would let me into their bars.

I liked gay bars. They often featured cheap drinks and good music for dancing. Nobody ever called me a fag there. There were always a handful of open-minded straight chicks, and less competition for their attention. And the sights . . . Oh, the magical sights I did see . . . Like the midget female impersonator singing "Over the Rainbow." Or the time (this still brings tears of joy to my eyes) some stray fratboy shoved a girl and Jimbo the burly, chivalrous bartender went after him with a baseball bat while hollering, "I may be a faggot, but I'm a 250-pound redneck faggot with a baseball bat, and you will not put your hands on a woman in my presence!" Or the time I saw Mike Watt's hairy ass in the parking lot. Cherished memories all.

I've also hooked up with what I'm reasonably sure were attractive girls at gay bars pretty often, for me anyway. One time, while still in high school, I was drunk and leaning against the dumpster in the parking lot of an infamous bar on the outskirts of town called My Friend's Place and making out with a totally hot punk-rock college chick. She was super nice, had bought me a bunch of drinks and even kept making out with me after I turned and ralphed into the dumpster a couple of times, causing one patron walking by to clap his hands and gleefully dub us "Gainesville's version of Sid and Nancy."

Of course, it wasn't all dumpsters and ralph and baseball bats. There were a couple of rough patches, too, which is to be expected even when friendly cultures mix. For example, one time some gay friends told a pimp-flavored male stripper named Sweet Dick Willy that it was my birthday.

Or there was the incident involving an amorous Rosie Greer look-alike cornering me in the bathroom. Me: "Sorry dude, I'm straight." Him: "Hey, that's cool—I'm straight too. I just like to suck a little white dick every now and then." Me: "AAAAAAAGGGHHH!!! . . . Hey, wait a minute. My dick's not little."

And then there was the time just a few years ago when I turned my back on my stylish, witty (but still stereotype-refuting, mind you) queer friends and became a gay basher.

It all started with a friend I'll call Kristy Moss (because that's her name) somehow convincing me (I think she appealed to my love of booze after unfairly clouding my mind with her abnormally large bosoms) to go drinking and dancing with her at a local gay bar. We arrived early and sat at the bar for a few hours, drinking many crisp, refreshing gin 'n' tonics.

At some point her then-boyfriend, Hank, showed up, and we made our way downstairs for dancing. Hank wasn't as confident in his abilities as I was (and by that I mean "not as drunk") and sat off to the side while Kristy and I tested the goodwill of the assembled gays by taking up valuable space on the dance floor. At one point a girl Hank was friends with stopped by to chat and flirt with him, sending the jealous Kristy and her propensity for heightened emotional states storming out of the club in a huff. I volunteered to go after her.

We spent a few minutes arguing near the club's entrance, a deck at the top of a single flight of stairs, while assorted patrons snickered at us, assuming since we had been there together all night that we were the feuding couple. "Ha ha, straight people," they said, "So foolish with your silly old-fashioned mores and relationship stuff. After Point Six of the Gay Agenda is implemented, you all will be rounded up and exposed to the rays of the Homotron, which will . . . " Er, did I just say something about the Gay Agenda? Shit, I promised to keep that a secret. Alright, just pretend you never heard that.

Anyway, Hank eventually walked up. Almost immediately, a middle-aged guy sitting on the deck with his arm around some dude who looked twenty-five years younger than him pipes up with some sass like, "You *need* to tell your *friends* that they should . . . "

Hank cuts him off: "Hey, mind your own business, alright?"

"Don't tell *me* to mind *my* business when *you* need to . . . "

"Why don't you shut the fuck up and make out with your little boyfriend, there?" Hank says.

That last line came out sounding a lot more homophobic than it was meant. All conversation had stopped, and Kristy and I quit arguing. Everybody was staring at Hank, and nobody looked real happy.

Sensing this, Hank tried to defuse the situation. "Aw, c'mon, I didn't mean it like *that*," he said. "Here, I'll show you—let me give you a little kiss." Everyone stiffened up as Hank leaned toward the guy with his lips puckered. Springing up, the guy swung a quick roundhouse that caught Hank off-balance, sending him sprawling. And without even thinking about it, I threw a right cross that smashed right into the poor sap's nose, breaking it with an audible crack and a generous splatter of blood.

After the punch, there was a brief pause before the place went apeshit . . . Everyone started screaming and jumping up and down all at once. Total hysteria. Kristy burst into tears: "They're fighting over MEEEEEEEEE!!!" The guy with the broken face picked himself up and ran down the stairs. A black drag queen who had a good two inches (of height) and about fifty pounds of muscle on me started jumping up and down and screaming, "STRAIGHTS VERSUS THE GAYS! STRAIGHTS VERSUS THE GAYS!"

I stood there for a few seconds, an oasis of calm in a splendidly colorful storm, looking at my bloody fist and thinking, "Goddamn. I'm bad-ass." Then I heard someone scream something about calling the cops. Though I didn't feel like I had done anything wrong, I really didn't want to tempt fate and chance getting my ass beat by that big drag queen, so I split and hot-footed it down to the parking lot.

I stood alone in the darkness of the lot for a few minutes, watching the mayhem. Kristy, still crying, tried to explain things to a group of patrons while Hank apologized to everyone. People raced around, running in and out of the club. The drag queen leaned over the railing of the deck, pointing at me and screaming, "THERE HE IS! THERE HE IS!" I was wondering if I should wait for my friends or just get the hell out of there when someone walked up behind me. It was the guy I hit. I raised my fists.

"No, no," he said. "I've learned my lesson. I deserved it." Blood was pouring out of his face.

"Okay," I said, a little puzzled. "Say, uhhh, sorry about your face, there."

"I'm glad you did it," he said. "I shouldn't have hit your friend. And I should've minded my own business."

"Well, frankly, I agree with you," I said. "But you're bleeding pretty bad. Are you gonna be alright? Can I give you a hand or anything?"

He made a few noncommittal protests while I looked around on the ground, finally scrounging up a dirty napkin. I handed it to him, and he held it to his nose. We stood there quietly for a minute or two, staring up at the chaos at the entrance to the bar. I looked over at him, and he looked down at the blood all over his shirt and shrugged.

"I wonder how I'm going to explain this to my wife," he said.

DOES A BEAR SHIT IN THE WOODS?

2003

I don't know about the bear, but I shit in the woods. Once, anyway. And let me tell you, if you're looking for a good indignity to thoroughly scrub away those last few pesky shreds of self-esteem, squatting down pants-less in the brush to let one rip will do the trick. My sense of self-worth was shot off in the war many years ago, of course, but I feel that I can speak authoritatively on this matter nonetheless.

I was camping one Saturday, you see. Enjoying the natural splendor and blah blah while drinking myself cross-eyed at Blue Springs State Park. By the time I hit the sack that night I was exhausted. That morning I'd had an invigorating kickboxing sparring session (an experience you can recreate at home by wrapping a moist dog around your face and letting a laughing guy punch and kick you while you wave your arms around at random, and girls laugh, and also you must stuff a large hunk of plastic in your mouth and be very tired); it was a fairly long drive to the campsite, and the afternoon had involved lots of strenuous bottle lifting and beer swallowing and standing around holding a fishing pole. So when I went sleepies I crashed hard.

This didn't prevent me from waking up at four in the morning, guts all a-churn. Was it the cookies? The supper of nearly raw steak? The estimated fourteen beers? Who knows, but it was itching to find its way to the outside world, and like pronto.

In vain, I tried ignoring the low-end rumble coming from my nether regions. It was to no avail. After several torturous minutes of trying to go back to sleep while feeling the pressure build, I knew I had no choice but to get up and relieve myself if I was to reclaim comfort. I crawled out of my tent, grabbed my flashlight and, half-delirious from sleep and booze, stumbled out into the night in search of succor.

The campground featured a large bathroom and concession stand, located about a ten-minute walk from my site. All I had to do was follow the path through what the map called the Midnight Death Forest of Spooky-Ass Horror and sweet relief would be mine. I squinched my ass cheeks together as tightly as I could while still retaining mobility and toddled down the very dark path. At some point during the day, thoughtful children had chalked inspirational messages along the way: "My mom is STILL a bitch," "Hell Road," "Haunted," and, my favorite, "TURN BACK!"

Woodland goblins and vampires, disturbed by my frenetic waddle, rustled in the brush alongside me. I paid them no heed, remaining intent on my mission and trusting the yellowing light of my flashlight to keep anything nefarious at bay. Plus, I am a big boy now, and do not need daddy to hold my hand in such situations, no matter how comforting it would be.

Fifteen terrifying minutes later I found the bathrooms. Like every other damn thing at the campground, they were totally dark and scary. "I hope there's a damn light switch inside," I thought as I pulled on the door. But the darkness soon became the least of my worries: the door was locked. "Fuck it," I thought, "It's 4 A.M. I'll go on the ladies' side." But no, I wouldn't go there either. The entire thing was locked down.

Tired, boozy, sick and experiencing severe gastric discomfort, I stood there, reeling, and briefly wondered if this wasn't some kind of stupid nightmare. No, it all pretty much fell right into line with the rest of my stupid life, so I re-squinched my butt and hobbled back toward what the signs said was the Soul-Chilling Forbidden Path of Inescapable Bloodcurdling Pants-Shitting Doom.

I hit the path and had a little conversation with myself: "What if you're walking along, and all of a sudden there's a guy, just standing there?" Fuck, that's scary. Better cut that shit out. "What if he's standing there, just staring at you, like he's been waiting for you? And his skin has the chalky pallor of the grave?" Holy shit, where are these thoughts coming from? "And what if he's holding a knife?" Oh my fucking God, brain, I have to take a dump so bad I can taste it, so I'd really appreciate it if you'd stop with that Stephen King shit right now.

Suddenly there was some kind of spastic commotion in the bushes right next to me. I jumped about six feet, somehow managed to keep my poo in my ass and swung the flashlight around so I could get a good look at the chalky-white evil ghost dude that was fixin' to knife me. The light uncovered a small alligator that I had apparently startled. He wouldn't make eye contact—in fact, he seemed embarrassed and was acting like he didn't see me. So I split before he called up his friend the Pale Stabbing Ghoul of Creepy Woods to do me in.

Back at the campsite I tried to stop hyperventilating and climbed back into my tent. My intestines continued their protest, and relief was nowhere to be found. I knew I had no choice but to go natural if I was to make it through the night. "Maybe it'll be like communing with your robust monkey ancestors," I thought. "More likely you'll poo on your ankle," my stupid brain replied.

I crept back out of the tent and, quietly as possible, rummaged around looking for paper towels. I grabbed a handful, removed my shorts, removed my underwear, removed my fishnet stockings and stood for a few moments, bare-assed, and contemplated the step I was about to take. After a deep breath, I squatted down, did my business while praying that nobody would wake up and take pictures, wiped and got the hell out of there. My physical relief overcame the deep sense of shame and revulsion, and I was soon asleep.

The next morning, I asked my buddy Brian if he had brought a shovel. "I woke up in the middle of the night and had to take a shit," I explained, pointing to the mess just a few short feet from our tents. "I need to bury it."

Understandably, Brian looked disgusted. He stared at me for a minute and asked, "Why didn't you go to the bathrooms?"

"Believe me, I tried. I had many adventures and the bathrooms were locked. That path is scary as shit at night, too."

"Path?"

"Yeah, I took that dark-ass path and saw a fucking alligator."

Brian pointed to a break in the brush across from the campsite, maybe twenty feet from where my tent was set up.

"The all-night bathrooms are right through there, dude."

STILL MORE VARIOUS HISTORICAL INDIGNITIES

Age two: Learning to pee like a big boy takes a nasty turn as the toilet seat slams down on my pecker like a giant clam snapping shut on a helpless diver's leg. I am trapped, screaming, for hours.

Age seven: Swallowed a nickel.

Age eight: I spent many years obsessed with catching crayfish. After a birthday party that features a daunting blue cake made strangely lumpy by small marshmallows in the frosting (which nobody would eat and which I had designed and specifically asked for) as well as a dozen or so kids somewhat aghast at encountering my shoddy house and annoying family, I singlemindedly drag the bored and reluctant revelers to a local creek to engage in my favorite pastime. I splash around with a determination and focus I've not since been able to recapture, while the other kids stand on the bank and stare at me. I don't catch any crayfish, and as a result of everything I am relegated to the bottom of the social stratum for the remainder of my school years.

Age nine: I lose my only friend, a kid named Bay, because I beat him up during a dispute over who would get to go out with actress Kristy MacNichol.

Age ten: I do catch a crayfish, a big one that promptly clamps down on my thumb. I ride my bike home several blocks, crying and with one hand outstretched. From it dangles the crayfish.

Age eleven: After I wear a cape and a helmet to school, some kids begin calling me "Captain Weirdo." I embrace the nickname and for a short period become known as "C.W. Hughes." It all comes to a stop when I move up a grade and this name appears on my report card, and my mom calls the school to make sure they don't have me mixed up with another kid. My teachers don't really seem too surprised to find out what those initials actually represent.

Age twelve: The day after I convince my mom to let me get this swell new haircut, I am confronted by older thugs while playing air hockey after school at the local rec center. They call me "Devo" and prepare to beat me, as to them my haircut implies I am a "new wave faggot." Though proud of my haircut and a big fan of Devo, I lie my way out of the beating by telling them that the haircut is because I'm planning to be a punk rocker for Halloween. Oh, and the avant-garde hairdo in question? Today it's known as the "mullet." This was also the year I went to school dressed up as Dr. Who.

Age thirteen: After losing my virginity on a beach, I wander around in a daze for an hour or two. Sand in my swim trunks rubs the skin off of my crotch and inner thighs, and I become convinced that I am now the carrier of some sort of heinous strain of fast-acting super herpes. I do not have sex again for many, many years, starting an unfortunate trend that continues to this day.

Age fourteen: Trying to fit in with the current fashion, I convince my mom to buy me an Ocean Pacific-brand shirt from a thrift store. The first day I wear it to school I am confronted by the delighted younger brother of its previous owner, who had written his initials on the tag. It is also remarked that my retro-styled low-top Converse sneakers "make me look like I play basketball." I'm not really sure how that's supposed to be bad, and don't get a chance to ask before the beatings begin.

Age fifteen to thirty-seven: Basically two decades of bliss. I am cool and well-liked.

BEN WAS THE VAMPIRE

1991

One time I narrowly missed becoming another man's woman. Apparently.

It all started with my old high-school buddy Chris Robertson. Chris was a great guy, and one day after a couple of beers, he took my hand, unexpectedly kissed me full on the mouth and, eyes full of tears, said, "I want you to be my woman. I've wanted it for a long time, and there's nothing in the world I want more. Be mine."

Ha ha! Not really! . . . As far as you know.

Anyway, Chris was kind of moody. He was significantly younger than his two older brothers and diabetic, and had been coddled by his parents to some degree, making him a bit spoiled. And when he'd drink, his blood sugar would go awry and he'd just become a total mess, alternating between sloppy rage, crying jags and an incomprehensible, yet vaguely menacing, sort of mumbling and giggling.

This stuff was all in good fun, really. He attacked me with machetes and butcher knives a few times, and I had to knock him unconscious once or twice. And there was the time he drank half a bottle of cough syrup at a party and decided to strangle himself by using a necktie tied to his bedroom doorknob. That was sort of funny and pathetic at the same time, something a slightly more sober Chris readily admitted a few hours later, laughing at himself with a self-deprecating cackle. In fact, even when these little dramatic episodes occasionally got out of hand, the fact that Chris himself would be the first to mock and belittle his shenanigans was a huge mitigating factor. And it always made for a good story.

But it's one thing to have a buddy who has a fat sullen streak and the propensity to freak out every once in a while, and it's another thing entirely to *live* with a buddy who has a fat sullen streak and the propensity to freak out every once in a while.

Yes, Chris eventually moved in with me. And living together was a challenge. When he moved in, it was his first time leaving the nest. He had never developed certain life skills most people take for granted.

Once I saw him use a metal fork to fetch something out of a plugged-in toaster. I hollered at him, telling him that he could kill himself doing that. He told me to fuck off and went to sulk in his bedroom. Later, he called his mom to complain about me, but she confirmed the potential dangers of the deceptively placid toaster and even sent him a special non-conductive wooden tong he could use should he ever again need to pry a goodie from the machine's infernal maw.

Another time, while eating hamburgers on the back deck of a local punk club, I warned him to slow down on the booze . . . Predictably, he told me to fuck off, and not long after I saw him vomit on himself. Not feeling particularly compassionate that night, I lost track of him, but when I staggered home at 4 A.M. he was passed out on the bathroom floor, curled around the cool, comforting porcelain of our toilet. This wouldn't really be notable except that months later while we were doing laundry he discovered a chunk of semi-digested burger from that night in the rolled-up cuff of his jeans. It was remarkably well preserved.

You know, I just remembered . . . Not long after the toaster incident, Chris started dating a girl who was his match in the life-skills department. He had met her when I brought her home and had sex with her, but decided not to pursue a relationship after she smacked me in the face full-force when I told her I thought a sucky punk band called the Dead Milkmen sucked. A day or two later she turned up in his room. I snickered a little, but tried to conduct myself around them with as much politeness as I could muster. I couldn't muster too much, of course, and as a result the tension around our place increased.

A week or two into this and, unbelievably, I caught her doing the very same metal-fork-into-the-toaster thing. Once again, I screamed, and she ran crying to Chris. He very gently explained that she could hurt herself that way and demonstrated the use of the wooden toaster-tong. It was kind of heartbreaking and sweet, really, like watching someone with Down Syndrome teach a monkey to wear pants.

They seemed perfect for each other and eventually got a place together. However, she was an English major at the college, and soon after entered her society-mandated humorless lesbo-commie phase, parading around with a vaguely militaristic cap, overalls, a stern expression and armpit hair. I didn't see Chris too often around this time, but when I did he looked even more miserable than usual. Chris had always hated commies.

Anyway, before he moved in with her and had his balls removed, we were living together and it was a little tense, but it's not like we didn't still hang out. One night we were drinking on the porch and decided to hit the town. At one point during the revelry, Chris says he's going home. I find another ride, but remind him that I had lost my keys, so he'll need to leave the door unlocked. A pretty straightforward exchange.

Complications arise when I make it home, a little after the bars close at two. The front door, you see, is locked. I commence to pounding and yelling, hoping to rouse Chris, but it's to no avail. Perhaps because of an alcohol-induced coma, or possibly just out of meanness, he's refusing to let me in.

I'm drunk, pissed-off and panicked. My ride, a vague acquaintance, tells me that she wants to get home soon, lest her husband become enraged at the late hour and beat her, but she's willing to give me a ride to a friend's place. Pondering that creepy fucking statement through the drunken haze in my brain, I ask her to take me to Ben's house.

Ben is quiet and reliable, the kind of person you can count on in this sort of crisis. He's also deeply, deeply weird. Before I met Ben, I used to work with a jolly fratboy who referred to his mysterious, nocturnal roommate as "the vampire." The first time I went to Ben's place, I thought it looked familiar . . . I looked around for a minute, then remembered I had been there for one of the fratboy's parties. Two and two came together in a flash and, delighted, I exclaimed, "Ben! You're the vampire!"

"Yes," he replied. Ben never said much.

But he was as demonstrative during sleep as he was reserved in the waking hours. He'd sleepwalk like a motherfucker, creeping around performing arcane, inexplicable tasks and having detailed, peculiar conversations with people while totally unconscious. A girlfriend once woke him during one of these esoteric somnambulant rituals and asked him just what he was up to . . . "I was holding down the blue rays," he said, sighing.

So I had this strange woman drive me to Ben's, thinking he'd be awake, or at least involved in some ghastly mockery of wakefulness, and I could use his phone to call Chris and wake his stupid ass up.

But Ben isn't home. The abused wife leaves. I stagger around Ben's neighborhood for what seems like hours, drunk and tired and wondering what I'm going to do. I decide the best course of action is to go back to Ben's and sleep on his lawn.

I get there, and Ben's home. He was out running errands, buying groceries and, possibly, draining blood from his victims. As best as I could in my state, I mumble my way through an explanation, and he lets me in to use the phone.

I call home, and after a few rings get our answering machine. Fuck, Chris still won't wake up. I call back again—still nothing. On the third call, I try yelling into the machine. "Wake up! Chris, wake up! I need to come home and sleep! I have to work tomorrow!" No response.

Desperate, I call back a few more times. Ben sits on the edge of his bed, quietly watching. "You know," he says, "It's possible that Chris never made it home."

Never . . . made it . . . home. The idea fills me with anger. He knows I don't have my key! He promised to leave the door unlocked! And he never even bothered to go home!

"Give me the damn phone," I say, finding a sudden focus in my rage. I dial our number again. "Chris, I know you're out there, partying, even though you said you were going home and would leave the door unlocked for me. Well, this is it—I'm really pissed this time! Really pissed!" I slam down the phone.

After about thirty seconds, I decide that my message didn't sufficiently convey the extent of my feelings, so I ask for the phone again. "Chris, I don't think you know how pissed I am, man. I'm going to get you," I growl. "I'm going to get you, and there's nothing you can do about it. You can't hide." I slam the receiver down again.

I sit there for a minute or two, thinking about the situation and becoming even more enraged. I grab the phone and dial. "Chris, I'm going to beat the holy living shit out of you. You're going to wish you had never been born. I'm not even going to give you the chance to make an excuse. I'm just going to open up and start hurting you the second I see you." Slam!

And, predictably, a minute later I dial again. "You're going to feel pain like you've never felt before, you miserable piece of shit. I'm going to break every bone in your worthless body. You've done a lot of crummy shit to me, but this takes the cake. I'm going to beat you, and beat you, and beat you, and there's nothing you can do."

This pattern repeats itself for about fifteen more minutes, with my invective getting increasingly violent and detailed. "I'm going to peel your skin off, Chris. I'm going to light your fucking head on fire and piss it out, and then do it again. I'm going to rip out your right eye, but leave it attached, so I can point it at your other eye, and you can watch that eye being ripped out up close and personal." Etc. Ben sits there, amused and a little alarmed. I finally tire and crash on the floor.

The next morning, after a few shitty hours of drunken, uncomfortable sleep, Ben takes me to work. We stop by my apartment, hoping Chris will be there so I can grab a quick shower and change of clothes. Sure enough, he's there. I throw open the door and burst into the room, snarling. Chris, who's standing at the answering machine, jumps a few feet into the air and starts trembling. I push past him into my room and get ready for work. When I come back out, Chris is sitting on the couch with some kind of a homemade bandage wrapped around his head. I glare at him and leave, thinking, "If he thinks pretending to have some sort of head injury is going to spare him a beating, he's got another thing coming."

On the way to work, Ben tells me how obviously terrified Chris was. He was just shaking and pacing, Ben says, and wouldn't say a word. "Good," I say, but inwardly I start to soften. The guy was a fuck-up, but he was still my pal. The scare ought to be punishment enough. I'd let him stew until I got home, and then make up with him.

I'm at work a few hours when Chris calls. He's crying, and I feel terrible. "Dude, I'm not really going to beat your ass," I say, trying to console him while wondering why he's being such a blubbering pussy. He's sobbing, making weird mewling noises and incoherently mumbling. The first articulate thing I can make out is him saying, "Last night I took some acid . . . "

Oh boy.

It turns out Chris had given this girl a ride home when he left. She invites him in for a drink, and he accepts. After some drinks and foolin' around, they decide to go to a party, and she offers him a hit of LSD. He accepts that, too.

So they get to this party, and he starts tripping, but gets freaked out by "these weird paintings of monsters" all over the place. Before long, he's in the midst of a full-blown, drug-induced panic attack. He wants to go home but is in an unfamiliar part of town and is afraid to drive. So he decides to wait it out a bit.

A few terrifying hours later, he makes it home. He's still feeling kind of wobbly and nervous, but decides to listen to the messages on the answering machine. Not surprisingly, he finds the tape of insults, screaming and violent threats somewhat less than soothing. He starts freaking out again, pacing around and wondering if he's going crazy. Maybe those messages were just some kind of sick hallucination . . . He listens to them again to be sure. And a minute or two in, I burst through the door in a homicidal rage.

So Chris isn't doing so hot.

I do my best to talk him down. I also make a few calls to friends and his girlfriend, who agrees to go keep an eye on him. Apparently, by the time she gets there the crisis is pretty much over. He's giddy, and dancing around in some kind of homemade tinfoil hat. And he's back to "normal" by the next day.

A few weeks later, Ben and I are laughing about the whole thing. "There's something else to the story; something I didn't tell you before," Ben says.

"Oh yeah? What?"

"Well, that night, while you were crashed on my floor, I did some sleep-walking."

"Uh oh. What'd you do?"

"Well, I woke up at one point, and I had ahold of your boot," Ben says. "I was dragging you across the floor by your boot. You slept through the whole thing."

"What were you doing? Holding down the blue rays again?" I laugh.

Ben suddenly turns very serious.

"I suspect you were fixin' to be my woman," he says.

CHATTING WITH CAROLA

2004

"Hey Pat, do you remember what happened when we made out that time?"

"Uhhh . . . Kinda."

"I had a big crush on you, and I was too young to drink, but I was nervous that we were hanging out, so I drank a lot, and we were kissing in the front yard . . . "

"Oh yeah, yeah . . . "

"And right in the middle of us making out, I had to stop."

"Uh oh."

"We were kissing, and I said, 'Stop, stop.' And I got sick, and I turned my head and threw up."

"Oh, God . . . I totally remember that now."

"I was so embarrassed. And then the next day I go into your record shop, and all your friends are there, and they see me walk in and they start laughing."

"Oh . . . Shit. I'm sorry."

"And I felt terrible, and they're laughing at me, and you just shrugged and said, 'This is what I do. I kiss girls, and they get sick and throw up.'"

SECONDHAND CRACK FUMES

1987

I used to want a good nickname. In my teens and twenties, it seemed like every third guy I knew had a good nickname: Chuck From Hell, Bob Chicken, Frank Boy Cool, The Saucy Pirate, etc. (Okay, I admit I totally made that last one up. But I think it'd be hard to argue its potential.)

Anyway, one day I realized I had a nickname: Pat Hughes, spoken real fast like it's one word. "Hey, it's Pathughes! Get him!" "Put your damn pants back on, Pathughes!" "Do me a favor? Don't tell Pathughes about the really fun party I'm having." It doesn't confer any special attributes, reflect superhuman abilities, incorporate the word *atomic* or have any kind of a ring to it, but it'll do. At least it doesn't serve as a blatant warning, like say Stabby Jim or Dirty Mike.

Not that warnings are always heeded. When I was seventeen, I got kicked out of the house and overlooked the obvious, signing a lease on an apartment with Dirty Mike. At the time, I thought a shared love of punk bands such as the Misfits and Naked Raygun was a perfectly solid foundation for becoming roommates. As it turned out, though, there were compatibility issues of a much higher degree of complexity than anything I anticipated lurking just behind our happy domestic facade. Like, for one example, Dirty Mike liked to snort a lot of bathtub crank and smoke a little crack cocaine once in a while. And I didn't.

Well, I didn't like to smoke the crack, anyway. I must admit I gave the speed a try once or twice and discovered it pretty much made me feel like I always felt—anxious, nauseous and borderline violent—only crappier, and so I ditched that shit pronto.

Before I had moved in with Dirty Mike, he told me the story of how he had earned his nickname. As a teen, he went to school on Halloween dressed like a hobo. To create his costume, he took a shit and wiped his ass with his shirt. Which he then wore.

His creativity resulted in expulsion, something that needled him even years later. "I mean, that's what bums *really* do," he would mutter while relating the story and grinding his teeth down to brown little nubs. "I was just trying to make a *realistic costume.*"

Somehow this anecdote didn't dissuade me from moving in with him. In fact, at the time, the story seemed to land him somewhere between "genius comedian" and "brave martyr." "Subhuman asshole" didn't get added to the mix until after I had lived with him for a few weeks and my precious Samhain tapes ended up stolen and sold to support his drug habit. And I watched him smoke crack.

At first, he would be fairly discreet about it and retire to a back bedroom to enjoy a rock or two. Occasionally, he'd invite a few redneck biker friends over for a little crack party. Eventually, he'd just fire it up while we sat there with our friends, enjoying the special garbage-dump ambience we'd created.

I didn't even give a shit. I was pretty beaten down by the time Dirty Mike started openly huffing down that sweet crack rock. In fact, I was as sick as I'd ever been in my life. Stress, poverty, booze and poor nutrition—er, make that no nutrition—had put the atomic whammy (say, that's not a bad nickname) on my immune system something fierce.

The first physical manifestation of my malaise occurred the day after a show by a punk band called the Descendents. I woke up around noon, briefly considered going to school (I had fallen out of the habit, mostly because I was lazy and hung over all the time but also because it was when I was at school that my tapes tended to disappear) and finally decided to shower, shave and go hit up the goddamn Hare Krishnas for a free meal.

Rubbing my hand over my strangely lumpy face, I thought, "Man, the pimples sure came out in force last night," and started to squeeze a big one. Then I noticed the "pimples" were all over my chest, neck, arms, legs and ding-dong. What the fuck could this be?

Hmmm . . . I had recently been over to a friend's house, where his little brother was sick with chicken pox. Could this be chicken pox? Shit, everyone has that when they're little, right? Turns out the answer was no. A quick call to my mother revealed that, indeed, while I had contracted my share of entertaining rashes and ailments as a child, somehow I managed to dodge the pox. Well, no longer.

Chicken pox wasn't so bad, actually. I had transmitted it to at least three or four people at the Descendents show, which for some reason seemed really funny at the time. And it gave me a solid reason to stay home from school and get high on Benadryl for a few weeks.

And the thick, pink layer of dried calamine lotion that covered my face and neck came in handy when the cops dropped by. They didn't seem to like standing too close to a lumpy, crusty, candy-colored leper, so I'd get trotted out in my ratty blue bathrobe to tell them we didn't know anything about the case of beer just boosted from the 7-11 (actually sitting in our refrigerator) or the runaway kid whose parents were desperately looking for him (actually hiding in my closet). A few cursory questions from them and a (very real) wheeze or two out of me and they'd be on their way, off to something safer and more fun, like getting shot at by bank robbers.

Toward the end of my pox convalescence, my mother broke into my apartment around 7 A.M. and started throwing things around and screaming like a lunatic. Seems the school had called her about my absences, and this was her way of checking up on me. I wasn't a big fan of my mom at the time, seeing as I wanted her to give me money out of the child support she received from my father so I could buy food (and, um, smokes), but she refused. Instead, she'd bag up totally random old stuff I recognized from around the kitchen before I got kicked out, like canned pumpkin from 1963, and bring it to me, calling it "groceries."

Anyway, Mom was rampaging around and hollering, rousing me and the three or four dudes who had crashed on the floor the night before. We sat there, bleary, for a few minutes, trying to decipher her incomprehensible ranting, when I decided I'd had enough and took action.

And spit on her.

Yup, I spit on my mom. Does it get any lower than that? Just hocked a big, green loogie (no shortage of material for that, either) right out of my mouth and onto her.

Look, I know this is indefensible (well, unless you've seen my mom on one of her loony rampages), and I'm not proud of it, but I have to be honest. It felt pretty damn good at the time. And it shut her right up, too.

I glanced over at Dirty Mike and the other guys, their faces lit up like Christmas. Clearly, my act of defiance was the greatest thing they had ever seen. They couldn't have looked more surprised and delighted if I had spray-painted the Black Flag logo on President Reagan (R.I.P.) while jumping a skateboard over a tank of piranha and Nazi skinheads. After a few seconds the shock wore off, and they actually started cheering. Mom cleared out.

Soon after this wonderful exchange, my dad came to Gainesville to pick me up and take me to the doctor. Ostensibly, this was to give me a check-up after all that chicken-pox nonsense, but really he wanted to get me tested for drugs, after hearing about the mom-spitting incident. And who could blame him? Though I suspect he probably knew exactly what I was feeling at the time and was maybe even a little jealous.

No secondhand crack fumes had flown up my nose or anything, and the visit to the doctor turned up no evidence of drug use. It did uncover that, in addition to chicken pox, I was also suffering from pneumonia and viral bronchitis. No explanation for why I occasionally threw up blood, but whatever.

Satisfied that I wasn't on drugs and not really giving a shit about the other stuff, Dad returned me to Gainesville. Soon after, the carpet caught fire and we were evicted. Dirty Mike took to the streets, and I moved back in with Mom. Things went downhill from there.

Dirty Mike? Why, he got his act together, passed the GED and through hard work and perseverance eventually became a successful investment banker and philanthropist, of course, and . . . Shit, you know, I don't know what really happened to Dirty Mike. And I don't fucking care.

WHEN I QUIT TRYING

1980

I've never been one for regrets—all too often I'm generating indignities so fast that I don't really have much time to stop and reflect on all the dumb shit I've done, except of course when I'm writing them down like I am now. But if I did pause to really savor the various layers, shades and nuances of historical heartbreak in my life, I'd be giving short shrift to the hot flush of shame that hit me this morning, for example, when I cut my ear. Trying to shave it. Fucking ear hair. What the fuck kind of cruel biological joke is fucking ear hair?! Anyway, while I'm not one for regrets, if I could go back and give a wee Patty-poo some advice from the future, it'd be something along these lines: "Don't try. Just don't do it."

Because some people just aren't equipped for cool. Maybe it's the result of an inherently comical physical appearance—cool people sure as shit don't have to try and shave their ears, you know?

Or it's because of a geeky enthusiasm for minutiae and detail: "Excuse me, that's incorrect. Devo released 'Girl U Want' as the first single off their 1980 breakthrough album, *Freedom of Choice*. The surprise success of 'Whip It,' which is often attributed to their novel use of the video medium, paved the way for an upsurge of interest in 'Girl U Want,' as well as future singles, which, while not performing as well on the charts, still blah de blah de blah . . . "

Or maybe it's because someone doesn't drive a Trans Am while waving nunchucks around like a fucking idiot and has to get around on their dad's old ten-speed and pay for lunch with those big, pink tickets that announce "I'm poor" to the world, Jennifer Testa, so fucking sorry I wasn't a rich karate dickhead with a Members Only jacket, just a sincere, decent guy with a pretty good record collection for a ninth grader; a guy who made you laugh and who walked you home from the bus every day and who your mom liked and, uh . . . Ummm . . . Was I just saying something? Well, whatever. Sometimes it's a combination of these factors.

Style plays a big part in this stuff, probably never as much so as in middle school. In sixth grade I was aware that style existed, mostly because many other kids didn't miss a chance to remind me that I didn't have it. Occasionally I'd even try to give it a go, in hopes that other kids would think I was cool. Not surprisingly, this never worked out to my benefit.

Partly, this was because I just didn't relate to the popular style at the time, which in Gainesville was kind of a mellow California surfer look based around the brands Ocean Pacific, Lightning Bolt and, for borderline losers, Hobie Cat. If I would've been loyal to my personal aesthetic, I would've dressed like Sid Vicious or maybe Dracula from the neck down, topping off the ensemble with a full-head Godzilla mask, Dr. Who scarf and samurai sword. But I got my ass whooped often enough without drawing excess attention to myself, and swords weren't allowed at school, so I never really gave that look a proper try.

I loved rock 'n' roll music back then, mostly punk and new wave stuff but also classic groups like Led Zeppelin, The Who and The Kinks. There were a handful of older proto-stoner kids at my school who dug similar stuff and dressed in a classic dirtbag style—lots of denim and black band T-shirts. They weren't exactly popular, but they were tough and the jocks and popular kids gave them a wary kind of respect that was pretty appealing from my somewhat battered vantage point. There was no way I could afford all that Lightning Bolt shit, but the dirty rocker look was certainly within my budget, so I grew my hair long and decided to give it a whirl.

I used to tag along to garage sales with my mom on weekends, mostly to buy old records. I started looking through piles of T-shirts too, trying to score some tough-looking rock gear. I scored a Who concert shirt, which was good enough, but unfortunately yellow. I also picked up a T-shirt with a Mr. Bill logo. Now, "Mr. Bill" was an unfunny *Saturday Night Live* segment featuring a clay guy who got crushed a lot and, while I had never actually seen it, I was vaguely aware from reading *Rolling Stone* that *Saturday Night Live* had some counterculture/rock 'n' roll cachet, so I started wearing Mr. Bill about three times a week and even had it on when they took school pictures. It was dark blue, too. Still not black, but a good start.

Around this time, my mom would sometimes take my sister and I to Lake Wauberg on the weekends. Access to the lake is now limited to University of Florida students, who mostly use it to scream and thrash around and tip their canoes and generally become hysterical upon sighting three-foot alligators sunning themselves on the bank. And swimming is prohibited, I think because of some deadly water virus or poison moccasin infestation or something biological. But back in sixth grade, the south end of the lake was operated by the county as a kind of piss-warm, murky pool-alternative for poor, scumbag area kids who couldn't afford the seventy-five cents it cost to swim in the city pool, and it suited me just fine. We'd go, I'd submerge myself in the dark, gooey water and then go home and pick ticks off my legs while mom poured hydrogen peroxide in my ears to kill off mites and bacteria and such.

And one day, while splashing around in the dark green slime and pretending I was about to emerge from the depths and level Tokyo, I found it.

A rock 'n' roll T-shirt. A bit faded . . . But black. Just floating there, waiting for me. Holy shit.

Bob Seger, it was. A black Bob Seger shirt, with a design that featured some horses running majestically in front of a mountain or lightning or some shit like that.

Now, I fucking hated Bob Seger. The only thing I knew from Bob Seger was that shitty "Old Time Rock & Roll" song, which I recognized even at that young age as a wholly bogus chunk of small-minded bullshit. It didn't seem like there was room in Bob Seger's world for exciting new groups like my favorites, The Clash, so as far as I was concerned, he and the rest of the dinosaurs in the Silver Bullet Band could go fuck themselves. But remember, I was desperate to adopt an aesthetic that would help me more smoothly navigate through the treacherous shoals of Westwood Middle School social life, even if it was one I didn't truly feel. All I saw in the shirt was a possible entry into the mysterious world of cool, or at least potential camouflage.

So I snagged the shirt, wiped off some of the algae, and got my mom to wash it. And then I proudly wore it to school the following Monday.

It was exciting. I just knew I had entered into a different world. One, I anticipated, with fewer beatings and insults. I sat in my first-period class, thrilled and feeling truly alive.

A few cool kids were sort of neutrally checking me out, glancing at each other with raised eyebrows. Probably figuring out the best way to induct me into their ranks, I thought. After a few minutes, Julie, a popular blonde girl with very white teeth and an impressive collection of expensive Jordache jeans, looked over at me, sneering, and in a quiet, flat voice said, "Nice shirt, dude."

"I know!" I replied, too excited at the attention to hold in my enthusiasm. "I found it in a lake!"

AT ONE WITH NATURE

1997

I confess—something I share with many hippies is a desire to connect with nature. The modern world focuses so much on the superficial, you know? The blinking and beeping and chirping of computers and cellular phones, the numbing comfort of sitcom laugh-tracks, the overwhelming spectacle of big-budget action movies, the compelling lure of naked boobies all over the Internet . . . Think of the knowledge and peace we as a people could gain by turning away from these distractions from time to time and instead savoring the pastoral.

It's perhaps no surprise, but while the hippies and I have this yearning in common, our paths significantly diverge. For example, hippies seek out the tutelage of shamans, spirit guides, healers and visionaries to learn about the natural world. They frequently sit around being all natural and filthy. Some smoke or ingest a selection of natural, psychedelic flora in order to melt the shackles of mundane reality separating us from our animal brothers and sisters, fostering an embrace of the Cosmic All. And I can certainly respect all that, if by *respect* you mean *deride*. But me . . . Well, I prefer to instead put nature in my mouth and stomach, if at all possible after it's been killed, or at least reasonably subdued.

One time I sat on a bar stool and listened to a very attractive young woman tell me about some rough times she had experienced (I think she had said her ex-boyfriend was too focused on his band, boo hoo hoo). Her life had been turned around during a morning jog, when she saw a deer. The deer looked at her, and in that instant she felt a jolt of spiritual connection. It was quickly over—the wise, noble deer went back to nibbling at the spoiled cottage cheese mixed with dogshit stuck to the side of the dumpster, and she made her way back to civilization, where she became a vegan and devoted herself to . . . to . . .

Shit, I can't remember. Reminding humanity of that which has been lost by the artificial lifestyle of Western culture, or something. At the time I was completely dazed by her total stupidity, which had made my penis go irreparably soft. I abandoned my hope of using it to feel a jolt of spiritual connection with her vagina and excused myself to seek adventure elsewhere.

After waking up the next afternoon and waiting for the tremors to stop and the feeling to come back to my legs, I enjoyed a few moments of quiet reflection. Piecing together the previous night's activities, I had to admit to feeling a bit jealous of the pretty cretin and her supernatural deer. If only all my encounters with the natural world could be so enlightening, so free from spines, fangs or toxins.

But you know, as Gandhi once said, "Dude, there's enlightenment, and then there's enlightenment." Why does enlightenment always have to result in inner peace and be topped with a fruity, mystical foam? Shit, there have been a few instances when I've felt my consciousness expand faster than Michael Jackson's pantaloons at a Chuck E. Cheese, and it wasn't because some flea-bitten varmint beamed me with a ray of woodland wisdom. It was because some rogue piece of nature, apparently forgetting the way the food chain is supposed to work, was trying to eat or kill me.

Like the time I was in the yard jacking off with a beer bottle in my ass and fell into this nest of angry scorpions. As they began to sting me in the eyes and genitals, I yelled out to the priest to put down the video camera and . . .

Okay, that never happened. But you know the only damn reason you're reading this is because most of these stories end up with something terrible getting stuck in my pee-hole. So don't judge me.

I may never have managed to get any scorpions stuck in my pee-hole, but one time a giant spider attacked me. It wasn't at all action-packed and exciting, like the scene in that movie where the two intrepid, gay midgets with the ring have all the magical adventures. I did, however, feel my consciousness expand. It expanded to include the thought, "Holy shit, big hairy spiders are totally fucking scary."

It happened on the lovely, pristine waters of the Itchetucknee river. Despite the fact that you can't bring booze in there, unlike Ginnie Springs, the crystal-clear, spring-fed Itchetucknee is a popular summertime destination in this area. People of all ages rent big, black inner tubes from nearby merchants and pay a nominal fee to spend a few lazy hours floating down the river, enjoying the cool water and gorgeous scenery. No additional fee is necessary to enjoy the thrill of having a multi-legged piece of that scenery break off and attempt to stab you in the face with poison.

I had only been on the river for a few minutes—my inner tube was still partially dry—when my buddy Jim looks over and says, "Hey. You've got a really big spider on your tube."

Now, I grew up in a town built on a swamp, and I've spent a lot of time harassing the local wildlife. We've got these things around here called banana spiders, which can spin a giant web, say across your front door, in about two seconds. I've been walking face-first into these webs and emerging sticky but unharmed about nine times a week since I was a kid, so big spiders don't freak me out.

Calmly leaning over the front of my tube, I see the spider. It's hard to miss—the damn thing is as big as my hand. Not to mention ugly, brown and covered in hair, just like pop singer Ashanti without her makeup.

"Man. That is a big spider," I say, and give a little chuckle. Jim gives a little chuckle, too. He doesn't know what's going to happen, but he suspects that whatever it is will be plenty entertaining. "Alright, Ashanti. I've got nothing against you. But this is my tube, so you're going to have to hitch a ride somewhere else."

I purse my lips and blow a little air toward my arachnid hitchhiker. Nothing. I try again, blowing a little harder. It ripples the spider's fur, but engenders no response. Jim smiles. I blow again, this time with more force. The spider turns to face me, as if noticing me for the first time. "Look, dude, you're going to have to go in the water," I say, furrowing my brow and blowing once more, this time really trying to push some air.

The spider races up the side of the tube, heading right for me, exactly like those fucking things in the *Alien* movies. Wisely, I let out a piercing, high-pitched scream and flop backwards. Of course, I'm in the middle of an inner tube, so heaving in that direction lifts the front of the tube, launching the giant spider toward my face at a velocity that surprises both of us. My scream ratchets up in both pitch and volume, and at the last second before the horrid beast's fangs pierce my skull and fill my brain with fiery venom, I slip through the tube and duck under the water.

I thrash around under the water for a few seconds then pop up, out of breath and wild-eyed, and start batting around my tube, flipping, shaking and submerging it until I'm satisfied it hosts no giant spiders.

I climb back aboard and look over at Jim. He's incapacitated with happiness, quivering with glee at how the events played out. I get my bearings, the adrenaline stops flowing and after a minute or two my breathing starts to return to normal. Jim is still obviously delighted. Thinking about what it must have looked like, I start laughing a little as well.

"Heh heh! Whew," I say. "Close one. Biiiiig spider! I didn't even know I could scream that high, heh heh heh."

A few minutes later, and I'm totally relaxed. The river is beautiful, the water is cool and the sun is shining. It's like paradise. This type of thing is one of the reasons I put up with living in this ass-backward state in the first place. All the trees and plants and shit are pretty and green. It's nice. I float over some fish and think, "What's up, fish?" I see a turtle on a log. He's just hanging out, soaking up the sun and enjoying life. We're not so different, me and that turtle. You know? I float past a banana spider suspended on his web between a few branches of a nearby tree. "What's up, banana spider?" I think. "Sorry about that scene with your spider cousin a little ways back there. I may have overreacted. But I have nothing against you spiders." The banana spider nods. Me and the spiders are cool. In my own drowsy, mellow way, I'm beginning to feel at one with nature.

About twenty minutes later, a group of teenage girls comes floating up behind us. We can hear them swimming, gossiping and splashing for five or six minutes before they come up on us. Just a bunch of all-American girls having wholesome summertime fun. They come around a bend and see me and Jim drifting along.

All of a sudden the girls become very quiet. Before I can turn around to get a look at them, one girl's voice shrieks out:

"OH MY GOD! YOU HAVE THE BIGGEST SPIDER I'VE EVER SEEN ON YOUR BACK!"

CHRISTMAS FUN

God help the fucker who tries to get between the Hughes family and a good time. *God help them.*

Brother Craig communing with a member of the mullet family. A fickle breed, though not immune to Craig's charm. I think fish in general are attracted to his yellow rain slicker and generally beardy, nautical appearance. Yes, he's one god-damn corncob pipe away from adorning a box of Mrs. Paul's, and the fish seem to dig it.

This is what Craig got Flo (she's his mom and my stepmother). A kit for making Jell-O shots. How awesome is that? Answer: really, really awesome.

ALLISON AND THE THREE STAGES OF HUGHES FAMILY CHRISTMAS JELL-O SHOTS:

Stage 1: Deployment.

Stage 2: Euphoria.

Stage 3: THE BURNING.

Santa, what happened to your red coat?

I am fascinated, yet mildly terrified, by this squat, Santa-based homunculus.

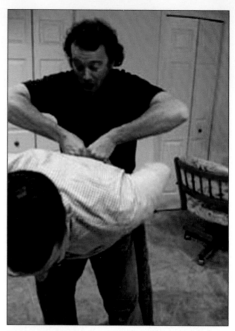

Brother-in-law Kyle accidentally smashes a glass, makes the crucial mistake of bending over to clean it up in front of Craig.

Neil dug up a Batman costume Flo made him when he was like six or something. After a few drinks, Dad agreed to try it on.

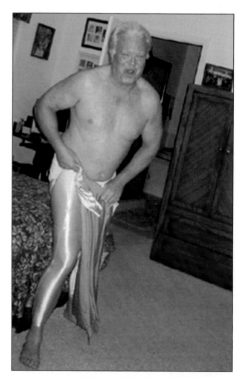

I check on Dad after a few minutes of grunting noises. "Get the hell out of here, I'm not ready," he yells.

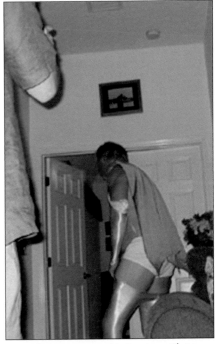

AAAAAARRRGH!! WHY?!

It is done.

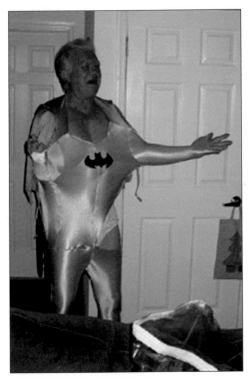

I can still see it when I close my eyes.

Around these parts, it's just not Christmas until someone gets stripped down to their tighty-whities.

My brother Craig got a chainsaw. Anyone else think this is a bad idea?

Later, some of Neil's friends show up with a radar gun we use to measure the force of our various punches. Frasier there is actually wearing the bat-panty around his neck as a jaunty ascot.

My jab registered a whopping 14 MPH, and for a while Frasier was in the lead with 25. Dad's turn, of course, rendered competition moot after he topped everyone with a terrifying 174 MPH blow.

Neil, preparing himself for a Jell-O shot.

Stage 1: Excitement.

Stage 2: The Burning.

Stage 3: Quiet contemplation.

I love Flo. Don't you? Dad said when he first met her she was swinging from the chandelier at this bar.

We also heard the story about the time some burly construction worker tried to heist $60 worth of booze from her in a parking lot. Instead of calling the cops, she grabbed his collar and jacked him up against the side of his car. He turned over the goods. Dude obviously had no idea who he was fucking with.

When I was fifteen I was living with Dad and Flo and they forced me to get this job at a McDonald's. It sucked. After a week or so, this manager fired me because, as she put it, "You do everything we tell you fine, but if we don't tell you to do something, you just stand there." Dad and Flo gave me a huge ration of shit over it: "What kind of reason is that? Nobody gets fired for that! What did you really do?!"

After I got fired they sent me down there on Dad's old-ass rickety ten-speed to turn in my uniform and pick up my check. That bitchy manager wouldn't give it to me, saying it wasn't ready or something. After another week or two, Flo was running errands and drove me by the place to get it. She had picked up Craig and some other kids from school, and they were all screaming and jumping around the car like maniacs while I ran inside. Keep in mind I was still in the doghouse for getting fired.

So I go inside, and that cunt manager still won't give me the check. I can see the damn thing, not ten feet away from the front counter, sitting on a desk in the office, so close I can read my name. The manager says she can't leave the front, because she's the only manager on duty. Even though the restaurant is almost deserted. I go back out to the car, where Flo is sitting impatiently while all those kids flail around and yell. I tell her what happened, and she grabs the uniform from me, barks "Wait here!" and runs inside. Through the window we watch as Flo grabs the manager around the neck, pulling her off the floor and half over the counter.

She gets the check. The kids are suddenly quiet.

Later, Dad and Flo went to war with McDonald's over my dismissal, which was suddenly viewed as some sort of epic injustice. The manager got transferred to Siberia and they offered me the job back, which—thank God—Dad and Flo refused to let me take. They still refuse to eat at that particular McDonald's, twenty-one years later.

Here I Poke Easy Fun at People Who Are Much Happier Than I Am.

My original plan was to go with a girl and get a bunch of pics of me and her doing terrible medieval stuff so the comedy would doth ensue. No dice, though. Seems as if the combined prospects of spending the day with me and mingling with faire nerds didn't turn out to be much of a draw. Imagine my surprise.

If the first goddamn thing you see when you walk in isn't some robey Friar Tuck-ass motherfucker gnawing away on a turkey leg, run and get your money back, 'cause you're at the wrong place.

So did the Medieval Faire invent big fat bellowy ponytail dudes, or do big fat bellowy ponytail dudes just naturally gravitate there, like spawning salmon?

Ha ha, ye olde rabbit ears. No doubt Crab-ass Da Vinci's enormous right shoulder quivered with rage when he saw the tricketh his impish gay brother hath wrought.

I stood in front of this for like nine minutes, reading the sign over and over again to make sure it wasn't just a beautiful dream.

"You see, Billy? Keep yourself parked in front of the Xbox instead of going outside once in a while for a football game and you'll eventually end up on the other side of this rope with Baron von Clownypants and his band of half-assed d'Artagnans, instead of out here where the pussy is."

His stylish Oakley Blades hath caused Aerobics Gypsy to yearn for the touch of his robust build, but, alas, his stripey wand longs to caress only ToriAmosKitty771326 at hotmail dot com.

"Sorry, kingly decree sayeth thou must don puffy sleeves before thou canst breach the rope and challenge yon band of scrappy beekeepers."

Prithee, good shopkeep, but mightst thou stock ye modern wizards and dragons or . . . Ah, nevermind.

If that thing comes up Maid Marian your dad's going to leave you here.

Hmmm, methinks the fence sprite hath caused mine loins to sprouteth a boner.

Yeah, there's nothing that'll whirl your imagination back through time like a bored soccer mom dishing you up a greasy slice of pepperoni.

Doth grass stains mar thy breeches? Try a little lemon juice.

The Blueberry Witch emerges from haunted Ersatz Castle to cast a spell on the audience. Now they all like anime.

Sir Rudy Hat realizing he locked his keys in his Acura.

I'd joust it.

If thou don't getteth thy stupid velour robe out of the way of my camera, I'm telling the Cartoon Network to cancel *Naruto*.

When did all these little plays and shit they do get so creepy and misogynistic? Everything that happened involved some knightly dude choking or sworded or spanking a hapless maiden. I saw as many dastardly rogues swat indignant maidens on the ass as I did robey dudes eating giant turkey legs, and you know I saw a lot of those motherfuckers. Anyway, the nerds need to learn a damn social skill or two or get some better clothes or something, because the lack of poontang is twisting their minds and as a result their skits bum me out.

Although, to be fair, all that working-out-our-fear-of-women stuff doesn't stop the nerd girls from going along with it. Hell, these ones had their own little cheering section, complete with all kinds of preplanned rhymes to heckle their favorite squire or whatever. Listening to them made me feel very cold inside.

Squire Julio spins to engage his nemesis, an actual female, while in the background the Tardy Cossack scrambles to keep his bowl of gruel from getting kicked over.

If you look to the left, you can see how the excitement of furious intergender melee causes Sir Rudy Hat to levitate, slightly.

Squire Blooming Onion's generous rump doth present a most inviting target indeed!

Something about the desperation in their eyes suggests they think that if they just juggle fast enough they can maybe outrun their fate, maybe trade in their split ends and billowy garb for good grooming and man-pants, and maybe—just maybe—as a result someday feel the naked titty of a normal, fully conscious woman in their hand.

But they can't.

You know what else I noticed about the fuckin' Faire? You can't just joust or swordfight or have a human chess match in a normal, direct way. All the nerds have to fancy everything up in these elaborate storylines where Robin Hood is rivaling King Arthur for Snow White's hand in marriage and the Princess Bride is secretly in love with Jethro Tull and how am I supposed to keep track of all this shit? You think you're going to see a couple of knights have a good old-timey duel and the next thing you know two pirates, three clerics, a squire, a dungeon master and the queen disguised as a handmaiden have all run in to labor over some point of exposition and drastically reduce the amount of time the dudes in the armor spend whacking each other with fake swords. Hey, nerds—I'm sorry your community theater production of *Our Town* isn't as fulfilling as you want it to be, but I'm totally calling bullshit.

Dude totally jumped off that horse onto that other dude.

Elf boy, what is it that scores you the fair maidens? Is it thy pimp suede vest? Thy magical cloak? Thy very recent trip to Super Cuts?

Yeah, that's what you want to do with a crowd of teenage Insane Clown Posse fans—sell 'em swords. Is anybody regulating this? Can't the government swoop in and round up these little Trenchcoat Mafia protegés before they go ballistic and start carving up the normal kids?

Wait, a black man? At the Medieval Faire? Poor guy must have lost a bet or something.

Oh dear, looks like chinstrap here has been converted from regularity to medieval ways and will have to trade in his chinos for... Hey, what the fuck is Mae West doing hanging around with a fucking conquistador? Just what time period is this supposed to be, anyway?

Katie loves the Medieval Faire because it's the one weekend of the year anybody talks to her. Anybody at all.

It could be worse. At least he's wearing *something*.

Holy shit, I'm totally freaking out.

Hey! Grampa! The Dr. Livingston I Presume Faire is next week.

At what hour doth thy minstrels Slipknot commence?

That asshole district supervisor for Geico will rue the day he halved the per diem allowance of Count Spectacles.

Jesus Christ, it's a nice day to be doing something, anything, and . . . Ah . . . Ahhh . . . I, ahhhh . . . I think I'm having a panic attack.

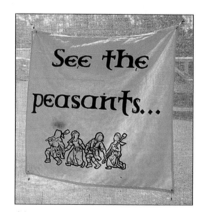

No.

No Hores.

My brother Craig married a wonderful woman named Allison at the lovely Spirit of the Suwannee park, located an hour or so north of Gainesville near metropolitan Jasper, Fla. Hey, you know what "country jamboree" really means, right? That's code for "there are no black people in here."

Allison and Craig, who's obviously pretty aware just how much he lucked out on this deal.

Me and Craig. He's a great guy. Well, okay—that's a lie. Like the rest of the Hughes clan, he's a sociopathic menace. But when Allison is around he's practically like a normal person, everyone says so. We're all pretty grateful.

Seriously, I wasn't there ten minutes before I drank three of those colorful little brainsmashers. And, I think, two beers.

So we drank a lot that night. In this photograph, I'm peeing.

Believe me, I'm well aware that I'm not winning any beauty contests over here, but the next morning I woke up looking like Abe Vigoda's butthole. Even though Dad and Flo had rented out these little cabins I totally could've crashed in, I decided to sack out in the bed of my truck. My head got all covered in weird bug bites, and I can't seem to focus my left eye so good anymore. And those Jell-O shots aged me like a decade, each.

Eventually I managed to get up and get mobile. Everybody had rented these boss little golf carts to tool around in. This is me and my cousin Crystal, and I think it also just might be the greatest photo ever taken, ever.

We thought this was pretty great.

This is the bank of the mighty Suwannee and the spot where the ceremony is going to be. Me and Dad spent four hours tracking down everything we needed to assemble that trellis. And by "trellis," of course, I mean, "three fucking sticks jammed into the sand."

Later, the ceremony begins. This is Barney. He's performing it. I think he might be a genie.

This was really something. Barney started wailing on that bongo drum, and Craig and Allison had to start a fire.

I thought we were going to be there all damn day while they sawed away at their twigs or whatever, but it actually went pretty fast. I think Craig might have primed it with a Jell-O shot.

Now it's time for the reception.

Here you can see Barney go apeshit.

Hey, if I had that physique, I'd show it off too.

Neil does the best-man thing, donning the ritual mask we use when we make toasts. Ethnic.

Dad is going to beat someone's ass.

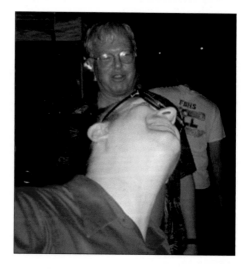

The end of the party. Taken just minutes before unconsciousness.

You'd never guess it, but I actually showed a lot of promise the first few years after I was hatched. For example, you can see from my pudgy Aryan glory here that up until the devil got into me, I was mysteriously blonde, healthy and happy. I got me a zippy Speed Racer sort of sweater on, and while I don't really recommend pairing long sleeves with short pants, my get-up at least seems free from grime, stains and tears. And that football? Man! Sports! Talk about your wholly misguided parental optimism.

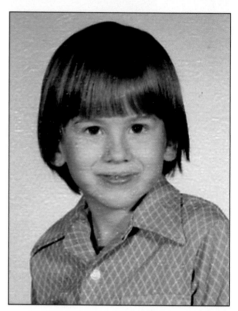

It wasn't long before the real me emerged, though, in all my creepy and possibly homosexual glory. It was right around this time I decided I would devote myself to emulating Paul Lynde. I'll let you know how it works out.

Best Cthlulu Award, 1984, goes to Patrick Hughes.

Look at that robe! I mean, it was for a school play and all, but, frankly, I would've happily just walked around in that thing year-round, oblivious to the heckles and catcalls of society, and casting little gay spells in my head all the live-long day.

I lied to Mom about the date for school pictures so I could get 'em taken with my favorite shirt, not hers. Look closely and you can see where the print is damaged, at the top of that first O. I was a little excited that morning and wanted to iron it, so I'd look my best.

Oh, I should point out that I hadn't actually seen Mister Bill at that point, despite wearing his shirt at least four times a week. I knew from reading *Rolling Stone* that he was a character on *Saturday Night Live*, a show the magazine assured me had a rebellious, counter-culture rock 'n' roll edge. Plus his clips always ended up with him all mashed and on fire and stuff. That was all pretty much good enough for me.

Oh! And also check out my pinkie. Weird!

"Why, hello there, sailor. Fancy a game of footsy?"

Because it's how I felt on the inside, damn it.

This isn't too bad. The whole vampire cowboy thing could have been pulled off a little better without the Down Syndrome haircut, but you gotta work with what you got.

"This is the kind of bed the astronauts sleep in," they'd say. I'd slip into dreamland seconds after hearing the click of the padlock.

A glimpse at the New Wave Years. You can see here how the family continued the tradition of torturing children with terrible outfits. They've got poor Neil tricked out like a fucking *Batman* villain.

I'm still not sure how I didn't end up a serial killer.

Here's Dad, contemplating the possibility someone switched out his blonde sporty football kid with an evil gay Paul Lynde homunculus somewhere along the way. I imagine he finds the thought comforting, probably to this day.

I was going through all these photos at my Mom's house a week or two ago, and at one point I was like, "Mom, holy shit, look at me. I'm gay. Totally gay, all these years, and I never knew it."

"What?! Are you really?! Are you gay?! Please don't tell me you're gay," she said.

"Ma, you can't get upset by that," I said. "You're a lesbian. It's not logical."

"Well, are you or aren't you?" she said. "Because my friends ask me all the time."

Ha ha, we got to pretend she has friends.

Fishing with Jim Marburger in January. Despite what this looks like, I am not about to cry here. I am about to break into a jaunty tune. That's what we rugged types do when the wind picks up, you see—we stave off the cold with a song: "Ohhhh, I'm so cold, so fucking goddamn cold, my balls are cold and we're not catching fish and I want to go back home and I'm cold cold cold . . ." I don't know if you knew this, but I can compose songs of manly adventure like that right off the top of my head. It's a gift.

Jim Marburger. He can pee and ride a bike at the same time, with a minimum of fuss.

Fishless after several minutes, Jim postulates that agitating the bait a bit might make them more lively and attractive to our prey.

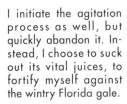

I initiate the agitation process as well, but quickly abandon it. Instead, I choose to suck out its vital juices, to fortify myself against the wintry Florida gale.

It was obviously way too cold for the fish to bite, so we decide to hunt supper on land. Seasoned outdoorsmen like ourselves know how to read the signs—the wind, the waves, the smell of the air. . . These things reveal their secrets to those such as us, red-blooded men with the spirit of the wild in their hearts.

Tonight, the secret of the wind went something like, "Dude, it's really fucking cold. This sucks."

Note: proper equipment is crucial to a successful and rewarding camping experience.

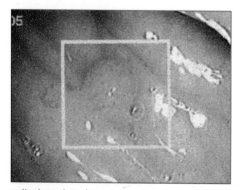

Polly the Polyp, the cutest intestinal nubbin you'll ever see. I guess it's maybe the only intestinal nubbin you'll ever see. If you're lucky.

A Black Cat fireworks logo with crossed bottle rockets—my own visual love poem to the joys of mayhem and extended adolescence.

First day on the job at Burger King.

This is Jon Resh, the guy who did all the swank design for this book. I've known the dude for a long time. In fact, back in like 1994 I apparently filled his car with Styrofoam packing peanuts. I don't remember doing it at all.

FUN WITH SCIENCE, PART 1

1993

In the modern world, where most folks are dumber than a fucking bag of rocks, science is little understood. Or, despite the innumerable benefits of science we experience throughout the day, even viewed with disdain and suspicion—how often have you heard the word used in a pejorative way? Yes, for many, *science* evokes misguided or even sinister goings-on off in some secret lab.

Compounding the problem are the hippies, mystics, graduate students in cultural studies, religious nuts and other such dipshits or charlatans who are fond of using the term to add a little authority to their chosen brand of made-up bullshit, referring to any vague discipline with its own jargon as a "science" and further degrading our understanding of its role and importance in almost every aspect of modern life.

In short, I find it useful to think of science as a process, a strategy that reduces the subjectivity inherent in the human experience. Of course, I also like to think of science as misguided or sinister goings-on in some secret lab, because that's where you get zombies and weird powers and experiments gone haywire and other shit that makes movies with giant, intelligent sharks fun to watch.

Although I'd like to champion the former perspective here, I have a really short attention span, so if something doesn't involve drinking, boobies or violence, I can't be bothered. So, not having actually any aptitude for serious, tedious scientific study, I'm only qualified to champion the haywire-type stuff. Hell, maybe if some kid is reading this, he'll start out interested in scientific mayhem and migrate over to the kind that involves bona fide book-learnin'. I think that'd be great. You paying attention, kids? Don't do drugs, stay in school.

So I'm a big proponent of looking around for the kinds of cool experiments one can integrate into everyday life, just to keep your personal awareness of science piqued. But this can be a challenge. For example, my youthful, innocent interest in homemade explosives can't be recommended—these days, igniting a toilet-paper tube filled with scraped-out model-rocket fuel and black powder and other such lighthearted foolin' around will get the goons from the government to shitcan your ass faster than a Reichstag burns, and you don't want to end up at the bottom of a dog pile in that damn Abu Ghraib. And I have an ethical problem with stuff like giving your dog bong hits, no matter how much he likes it or how hilarious it is.

For these reasons, I think it's good to start with experimenting with yourself. See what's it's like to drink a six-pack at 6 A.M. Look in the fridge—mint jelly, what's that for? What does it taste like on a peanut butter sandwich? What happens if you add coffee grounds? Horseradish? But this is entry-level stuff. It's all in good fun, but soon you'll want to graduate to some more in-depth style inquiry.

One time I realized I had gone a whole day without eating or drinking anything but Yoo Hoo. "Here's my chance for some top-notch science fun," I thought, and determined to go as long as possible surviving on nothing but Yoo Hoo.

I lasted four days, quitting after the little dancing Yoo Hoo gremlins in my peripheral vision started looking at me with pity. For the first two days, I was giddy and chock full of sugary vigor. But by the end of my experiment I was dizzy, eight pounds lighter and was experiencing some strange gas symptoms . . . Or more of a wind, really . . . A cool, chocolatey breeze that constantly blew out of my ass. Oh well, I regret nothing.

Though the gremlins left after I ate some spaghetti, and I kind of feel like there was a missed opportunity with Bobo, the shy gremlin with the nice rack. Definitely some sparks there. Ah, Bobo. Do you ever think of me, I wonder? Do you ever long to once again feel the caress of my chocolatey breeze?

MORE ADVICE FOR CHILDREN

Strictly speaking, ranch dressing is not an ingredient.

Yeah, I know Sid Vicious wore a lock on a chain around his neck just like that. But the first time you try and pogo with that thing on it's gonna chip a tooth, Road Warrior.

Sure, she's good-lookin'. She's also crazy. Crazy as a shithouse rat. Run for your life.

Just because one of those made you feel nice and two of 'em made you feel even better, taking the whole bottle will not exponentially increase your good time. In fact, you may get dizzy, or throw up, or end up spending half of the next day wondering where the hell your pants are. Or die.

The bouncer at Mons Venus always knows best. If he says you should stop, then you should stop.

Yes, you got grounded for having the very same porn stash that turned up in Dad's closet six months later. You still can't bring it up. The cosmic scales of justice will never tip in your favor on this one, trust me. Bide your time patiently, and one day you might get the chance for revenge. Like, by unplugging his dialysis machine. Or something.

Now that you've climbed up there, it's a lot higher than it looks, isn't it? Dumbass.

You can use Krazy Glue in lieu of surgical stitches. For when you're, you know, too poor to go to the emergency room. Or trying to avoid explaining things to the police.

The Renaissance Faire may not be the source of all your problems, but it sure as shit isn't helping any.

You're probably doing something that bugs the next guy twice as much. Clam up and get on with your life.

If you accidentally rear-end another car while driving, Florida law dictates that you must stop and confer with the affected party. Turns out just waving to let folks know you're alright while driving away is a little something the state troopers like to call "leaving the scene of an accident."

When it comes time to pick out that first tattoo, remember: It doesn't matter how much you like that one comic book. There's always a chance that eight years later someone will make a movie of it that stars Sylvester Stallone. And you'll be fucked.

Always look behind you before you make that first cast. That boat may be smaller than you think. And Jim Marburger's dad might be taking up more space than you think, too.

Dungeons and Dragons never goes away. Girls will still sense that shit twenty years later.

If you don't want Sweet Dick Willy to give you a lapdance, don't sit so damn close to the stage.

CHATTING WITH TODD CAMPISI, PART 1

I was going to ask you about your biggest indignity, figuring it was the time you shit your pants in the video store, but I seem to remember that didn't particularly embarrass you. Is this correct?

Oh, I was pretty fuckin' embarrassed, alright. But since it was just me and Scott Adams, and he was my roommate at the time, I knew I could trust him to help me through the shitstorm. I had to ride all the way back home sitting on a plastic Publix bag so I wouldn't leak my bowel chowder onto his car. It's all funny to think about it now, and I'm pretty sure that Scott thought it was damn funny then, too. I think the funniest part is that despite my hellacious bout that week with a bona fide, doctor-diagnosed intestinal virus, I just couldn't miss the big closeout sale for all those beat-up, old, used video tapes that I'm now fighting to get rid of on eBay. I hate them.

Did you turd it up and keep looking, or were you on your way out the door? Did you drip? Did anyone notice?

I was sizing up my haul, just about ready to go, actually. (Man, you can really take that sentence in two ways when you think about it.) I had a stack of about ten videotapes in my arms and I thought, "Well, one tiny little innocent fart couldn't hurt now, could it?" It could. And did. A burning hot deluge of butt soup shot out of my ass and went half-way down my right leg. Fuuuuuck. I went, "Pssst, pssst" to Scott and whispered to him, "Hey, remember what happened to Scot Huegel at the Spoke warehouse? Well, it just happened to me right now. Only worse."

Scott immediately recalled the Huegel incident, which as legend has it is as follows: Once, in mid-song during an intense, emo-filled practice by his band, Spoke, Huegel let out what he also thought was an innocent little bottom burp that resulted in a single round turd rolling out of his shorts and onto the warehouse floor. The whole band stopped to a silence, and Jon Resh (who's responsible for designing the book you now hold) exclaimed, "What's that, brother?" To which Huegel replied, "Dude! It's my shit." And walked off in humiliation. Now, whether or not it all happened exactly like that, I'm not sure. But I like to believe that it did.

Anyways, Scott agreed that we had to get the fuck outta there ASAP, so I cautiously walked up to the line to pay, trying to keep the mess all up in my ass region as best I could. When I got to the front of the line after what seemed like a year, I quickly paid for my stupid videotapes. I distinctly remember the clerk making a funny face, as he must've gotten a whiff of the thunder from down under.

I managed to scoot out to Scott's car and that's when he wisely offered me the Publix bag to sit on. God bless him. When we got home, I shut myself in the bathroom for a half hour and cleaned myself up. I threw my jeans away. Anyone wanna buy some videotapes?

How does one "keep the mess all up" in one's "ass region" anyway? And it didn't drip at all?

I just kinda got all clenched up and waddled when I walked. Thank-fully, my jeans were very absorbent.

What videos did you get? Was it worth it?

Let's see: *The Killer, Slam Dance, Gigantor, 8th Man, Re-Animator, Three O'Clock High* and *Inframan*. I can't remember the other two. But yeah, at the time it was definitely worth it. Videotapes were cool, man.

Oh, I'd totally shit my pants for Three O'Clock High. *So how does this stack against all the other indignities you've suffered in life? Any-where near the top?*

It's definitely up there, just because of the comedy factor. I've done a lot of other stupid things in my life that weren't really funny and don't make for a good story. Only a good ass beating.

What's the dumbest thing you've ever seen me do?

Damn, aside from you deliberately smashing flower pots on your forehead, that's a hard one. Anything really stupid would've most likely occurred while we were extremely loaded, so I don't remember.

There were a couple times when you stupidly listened to me when you shouldn't have, like that one late winter night when I left that note for you on my front door in a drunken stupor, insisting that you stay in my roommate's bed instead of going home. You thought something bad happened to me, so you stayed and didn't plug in the electric blanket before you passed out. I came home the next morning and found you all wrapped like a cocoon in Scott's bed, shivering to death, eyes all bloodshot and hung over as hell, and ready to wring my fuckin' neck. You were like, "Well, what the fuck happened to you last night?" And I said something like, "Dude, I slept with that retarded Angela girl." The look on your face was terrifying. You shouted, "That's it?! That's why you made me stay here?! I thought something bad happened to you. Come here. I'm gonna fuckin' choke you. Come here." Or something like that. Anyways, you were pissed.

Angela? Are you talking about that teenage runaway girl who talked all fucked up after her tongue got infected when she let the piercer use a stud he had dropped on the floor?

Yeah, that was her. Bleh.

She was a catch, a delightful flower. But I don't understand the connection between sleeping with her and it being so important that I crash at your place.

I walked home from the club with her and her flask of whiskey, and by the time I made it home I was out of my head. But I vaguely remembered telling you that you could crash at our place if you couldn't find a ride home. I was sitting there makin' out with her, and then she suggested we go to her place to drink more, which sounded like a brilliant idea at the time. So we went, and I left you that note on the door saying to go inside and sleep in Scott's bed. For some reason, I made it sound really serious and important.

Well, it turns out that you ended up getting a ride to my house, and whoever was giving you the ride said that if I wasn't home then they would just take you to your house. When you got to my place and saw the note, you told them to go 'cause you thought you'd better stay and find out what was going on. That's why you were all pissed the next morning.

Man, you were scary looking, and ready to kill me.

I was so, so cold. It was twenty fuckin' degrees, and I had an electric blanket that I was too drunk to figure out how to turn on. I'm surprised I survived.

THE DIARY OF TRIUMPHS

Age seven: My mom schedules a doctor's appointment. I learn I'm to receive an immunization booster shot at this visit. Although I've never been particularly afraid of injections, I become terrified. During the two or three weeks prior to the appointment, I obsess over it, sweating and feeling nauseous at the thought of that needle entering my skin. I start having trouble sleeping at night, because I lie awake thinking of ways to escape. The day of the appointment arrives, and I become hysterical. My mother has to call my grandmother over, and somehow the two of them manage to force me into the car, crying and screaming. We get to the doctor's office, and I'm sticky with tears and racked with deep, troubling sobs. The doctor looks at me, smirks like I'm the biggest pussy he's ever seen and pulls out the needle. I turn away, feeling dizzy. He jams the needle into my shoulder without a word. It doesn't hurt—in fact, it doesn't feel like much of anything. I stop crying and turn to look at it as he injects the medicine, thinking, "That's it?"

Age nine: Mom decides she can't live with "poisons" in the house anymore, so traditional methods of controlling fleas and roaches are out. For the roaches, we're now to use boric acid, a thick, white powder. Soon rows of this stuff line every windowsill and doorway in the house, clumping up with the humidity and collecting dirt and dead bugs. For the fleas, we place some sort of pungent leaves, many of which are still attached to their branches, all over our rugs and carpets. They soon turn brittle and brown. We leave them there. The few kids that were inclined to ever come over . . . stop.

Age eleven: It's time to get a new bike. I decide I want one with a long front fork, like a motorcycle chopper. The model I get is cherry red, with a big plastic hump in front of the seat that resembles a gas tank. I am stoked. Upon seeing my kick-ass new ride, pretty much every other kid in the world decides I am the biggest loser who ever lived. I regret my decision less than a week after getting the new bike, realizing I'm looking at least a year of bike-related abuse from my peers. Plus, the thing weighs, like, a thousand pounds and is a huge pain in the ass to ride. One day, I'm cruising along my street, and the glue holding the rubber handlebar grip gives out. The grip, along with my left hand, slides off, and I crash my face and right shoulder into the curb in front of a neighbor's house. I get up, dazed, and take stock of my injuries. My shirt is torn, my shoulder is scraped and blood is pouring out of my face. The neighbor, a churchy type who's raking his front lawn as this happens, stops, looks me dead in the eye and says, "That's what you get for riding that bike."

Age nineteen: I'm making out with a punk chick in a dark back corner of a bar. Even though I've generally held nothing but open disdain for the contrived, self-destructive side of old-school punk, doing something tough and sleazy seems appropriate, so I give myself a lighter burn. This involves heating up a disposable Bic for a minute or so and pressing the hot metal into skin. I jam the top of the lighter into my left bicep, instantly raising a blister in the shape of a happy face. Not wanting to be outmatched, my makeout partner hikes up her skirt and requests one as well. I burn a smiley face right on her tender inner thigh. She winces. We now have matching smiley-face burn blisters. My arm hurts.

Ages twenty through thirty-seven: That was it, that was all of them. No more indignities. Ever.

MEET ANTHONY

2003

Last weekend marked my mother's sixtieth birthday. This was celebrated in her typical fashion, crazy.

I know, I know . . . Everyone thinks their parents are crazy. Whenever I say I was raised by a crazy woman and would've been better off with a pack of wolves, the response is an indulgent chuckle and a few patronizing words about how the details may change from family to family, but there's a cosmic sort of balance at work that ensures everyone's family gets an equivalent dose of the crazy and blah blah blah.

Well, bullshit. My mom is crazy. I love her and everything, I suppose, but we're talking really, really fucking crazy. Years ago, at a previous place of employment, she stopped by my office unannounced, despite the fact I had specifically forbidden her from doing so. I wasn't there, and a co-worker admitted to me the next day that it took a while before they figured out she was my mom. Everyone thought she was some sort of lunatic bag lady or mental patient who had wandered in at random and started babbling nonsense at everyone. Unfortunately, they only misjudged the "random" part of that scenario.

Nothing I can write comes anywhere near to accurately depicting the full experience of mom's robust, distinctive brand of crazy. Every so often at a dinner party or something I'll loosen up after a few drinks and start relating some childhood anecdote, invariably blacking out before I can finish. The last time this happened I woke up several days later, naked and shivering in front of my computer. On the screen I could see where someone had typed I LOVE YOU, BLOCK OF CHEESE, ONLY YOU COOL THE BURNING in big, scary letters. I guess it was me.

My friend Mr. Stabs, a ventriloquist dummy who sleeps under my bed, says I should put off attempts at writing too much about Mom until I can afford that shiny bucket of Xanax I've had my eye on . . . Mr. Stabs gives pretty good advice (well, generally, but I don't want to go into it), and he's got a big knife, so I try to do what he says. Hence, this particular entry isn't meant to offer anything but the tiniest glimpse into the whirling tornado of horror that is my relationship with the woman who thirty-seven or so years ago pooped me forth from her 'giner.

But we're celebrating the day Mom was pooped forth, not me. She's rented out the meeting room and kitchen at the local Unitarian church for a party, and called me fourteen times during the week leading up to it to ensure I'll be there three hours before it starts "in case they need to move tables." I show up reasonably early and find the other twenty or so assorted family members and friends she's badgered into service, making up useless little jobs for themselves. Mom is nowhere to be found.

I'm enlisted to hang streamers, which gives me the chance to check out the many bulletin boards and dioramas and shit around the room. Of course, this being a Unitarian church, these things contain no discernable religious content. No, instead of addressing spiritual concerns, the place is positively wallpapered with posters, flyers, poems, brochures and macramé devoted to the modern liberal political agenda. I've always wondered where they indoctrinate people into the local NPR-and-a-Volvo-station-wagon brigade, and I guess it's here . . . Oh, look. Canvas grocery bags with a picture of a tree on them. What a surprise.

All this doesn't really have any effect on me, other than causing the same mildly deflated feeling I get when faced with any other brand of reflexive, partisan political or religious stuff. I manage to stop myself from correcting some bad science in a display designed to frighten children into caring about global warming, and continue hanging my streamers, making sure the loops are all uneven and shitty-looking in an obligatory display of juvenile passive-aggressiveness.

A few guests start to arrive, people who look like they know my mother from her medical support groups. For many years my mom has defined herself through various support groups, and they provide her with the bulk of her social activity. If it has an acronym, vague symptoms that can't be detected by doctors who don't use crystals or wands and gives you the opportunity to act all victimized and oppressed, my mom's got it.

Her main deal is that made-up Chronic Fatigue Syndrome thing that went out of style like ten years ago. Ironically enough, she's absolutely tireless in her involvement with various Chronic Fatigue Syndrome support groups and in a normal week expends enough energy to power a crazy-powered rocketship trying to rally support for her fellow not-really-sick Chronic Fatigue comrades.

Mom eventually shows up, a little late to her own party, but whatever. I walk outside to greet her and see if she needs help with the oxygen tank she wheels everywhere she goes. It, like her, is covered in balloons, ribbons, sashes, glitter and stickers. One might think this is to reflect the celebratory nature of her birthday party, but—Oh ho!—one would be wrong. She dresses like a cross between a rodeo clown and Steven Tyler's microphone stand no matter the occasion.

"Look! You can see my wings!" she says. She raises her arms and starts flapping her grotesque, flabby upper arms back and forth.

"Haaargh," I say. My jaw clenches, exploding a back molar into a fine powder.

"I'm old! I have wings!" she chirps, and flaps herself inside while I try to fight off a panic attack. I wonder if any of those goddamn Unitarians have some beer or something stashed in the back of the fridge . . . Some organic microbrews or something . . . Fucking hell.

After a few deep breaths, I walk back in. My sister is chastising my conservative brother-in-law for writing "George W. Bush" on his name tag, which considering the setting is actually pretty damn funny. Especially for a Republican.

My sister's new kid, just a few months old, is a beautiful little girl. But she has a little red patch of baby eczema or something on her forehead, and I'm compelled to devote the next hour or so to referring to my niece as "baby jam head" and pretending to scrape strawberry jam off of her with a cracker. This mortifies a few guests, but shit—if I can't get a drink during this ordeal I need something cheerful to get me through it.

But things get cranking and the party turns out to be okay. I enjoy insulting the infant, and the food's good. I like watching my shell-shocked Southern Baptist in-laws stagger around, confused by all the Democrats and lesbians. When I concentrate real hard and pretend I'm not actually related to any of these people, I have little flashes of something resembling . . . fun. This little soiree is actually one generous application of booze away from being a legitimate good time. Who would've thunk it?

My reverie is soon broken, of course. A crazy guy walks in and stands in the middle of the room, mumbling and staring around bug-eyed. This dude is obviously nuts, but a different kind of crazy than my mom, who manages to maintain just enough of a tenacious, self-absorbed grip on consensus reality that we can't really lock her up or anything. No, the new arrival is closer to what I think of as a classic street crazy, all google-eyed and twitchy and clearly just fixin' to snap and start ranting or killing people.

This is disconcerting—downtown Gainesville is filled with wandering psychotics, and dealing with them when you leave the house is just another fact of life. I used to own a little record shop on what passes for our main drag and garnered plenty of experience calming or pummeling agitated nutjobs and drug addicts as the situation warranted. But we're in a fairly affluent, outlying section of town without a lot of foot traffic, so this guy's appearance is extra disturbing. I mean, we're set back from the road a ways, so it's not like he was just walking by, saw people and decided to crash the party. He had to make an effort.

My instincts are to deploy my bum-hustling skills and toss him out, but I hesitate. He's recently bathed and is wearing pants, so there's the chance that he actually might know my mom from some schizo support group. Maybe the Unitarians keep him around for comic relief; what do I know? Or more likely they keep him around so they can, like, help him and stuff, and therefore feel all liberal.

A minute or two of this guy swaying back and forth and listening to his own synapses misfire and my sister goes over to talk to him, asking him how he knows our mom. A few vague, mumbled answers and it quickly becomes clear that he doesn't know my mother or anyone else there. I start walking across the room, assuming the next step is to ask the guy to leave. My sister just shrugs and fixes the guy a plate of food.

Shit. Feed 'em and they'll never leave.

The next half hour is kind of stressful. He's quiet and seems content to just mumble to himself and stare at things. Mom and Sis say they don't care if the guy sticks around and tell me not to confront him. Everyone else is pretty much just ignoring him, even though he has a crazy person's idea of what constitutes appropriate personal-space boundaries. I can't relax, though—I've seen way too many guys like this just unexpectedly freak out, and I keep having visions of what would happen if he lashed out and hit one of the kids or fragile, old commies mincing around the place. The guy isn't tall, but he's thick and has big arms, and I keep seeing disaster. Potentially hilarious disaster, sure, but disaster.

So I shadow him, waiting to pounce in the event he goes ballistic. Every once in a while he whips around to see what I'm doing, and I quickly look away and act interested in the ceiling. We circulate through the party like this for some time.

Eventually, I get fed up. I tell my sister I'm going to ask him to leave.

"Wait, I have an idea," she says. "I'll fix him a plate of food to go, with the emphasis on 'to go.' He'll get the hint." Yeah, because crazy people are so good at getting hints. This guy is getting the hint that the Pope controls all monkeys through the use of magical foot rubs, and that's about the extent of it. But a few minutes later she shoves a plate of goodies into his hands, points him toward the door and thanks him for coming.

He immediately turns around and tries to come back inside. I stand in his way. "Sorry man. Party's winding down. You take care." We stare at each other for a few seconds, then he turns around and walks off.

"Whew, that went alright," I think. "I wonder if God would've been mad about me beating up a crazy dude in a church? Fuck it—God obviously hates me anyway, and I don't believe in Him. Plus this isn't so much like a real church as it is an issue of *Utne Reader* come to life."

I relax a little and have a glass of punch. I make fun of Little Baby Jam Head and start to enjoy myself again. Then I glance out the side door and see the damn crazy guy again. He didn't leave, but walked around to the side of the building. Fuck. And now he's becoming more agitated by the second, whipping his head back and forth and yelping out random crazy stuff. I'm sick of this shit, and go to tell Mom I'm calling the cops.

Mom is having a conversation with her friend Susan, who's some kind of Unitarian high priestess or whatever. I mention the police, and Susan looks at me with open disdain. "I really don't think such steps will be necessary, Patrick," Susan says. I notice other guests staring at me, shaking their heads. What the fuck?

Oh yeah—these people are rank-and-file NPR/Volvo liberals. They think I want to call the cops on the crazy guy because he's black, not because he's crazy. Being capital "L" upper-middle-class liberals, they don't actually know any black people, of course, and might even think *all* black people act the way this guy acts. Regardless, they sure won't miss a chance to act all patronizing to someone, so Susan tells me to stay put while she goes to talk to him and learn all about his needs and feelings.

Susan lets the guy back in a few minutes later. "His name is Anthony, and he doesn't have anywhere to go," she says. This seems to satisfy everybody. Somebody slips Anthony twenty bucks, and you can be sure he really doesn't have anywhere to go now. He might be crazy, but he's not so crazy that twenty clams don't brighten up his day. So Anthony's part of the family now, and we resume our weird dance, where he walks around staring at things and startling people, and I follow him around and think about different ways I might kill him, should the need arise.

The party eventually winds down, and guests start drifting out. Occasionally, invisible forces compel Anthony to follow folks out to the parking lot. He's not menacing, but he's damn weird, and a few people ask me to walk them out to their cars. As I'm still not allowed to directly confront the guy, our little dance becomes even more absurd.

When there's just a few of us left, we start cleaning up. Anthony grabs a mop and starts attacking the floor with a zeal that's quite impressive, if not actually very effective or thorough. My attitude softens a little. He seems honestly grateful we let him hang around and wants to help out in any way he can. He seems less sinister to me now and more like . . . I don't know, just a lonely crazy guy who's happy to stumble on some nice folks willing to give him money and cake. Shit, I reckon I'd be happy, too.

We close up. Anthony helps me carry some leftovers and shit out to Mom's car. As she bends over to put a box in the back seat, Anthony takes a step back and starts openly checking out her butt. His google-eyes get even googlier, and a big smile spreads over his face.

I stare at this scene, barely able to comprehend the twisted wrongness of it all. Anthony glances over at me and gives me a big grin and a thumbs-up. It's too much for me—I can't speak or move. Anthony spends a few more moments gazing with open appreciation at my mother's sixty-year-old, lesbian ass. Then, without a word, he walks over to what I assume is his car, gets in and drives off.

CHATTING WITH A CO-WORKER WHO KEEPS FINISHING MY SENTENCES

2004

" . . . Well, *Mad* magazine served a very important function in my life, and I'll tell you why. As you know, I obviously grew up kind of deprived and—"

"And your family didn't even have forks?"

"Actually . . . Heh heh, I had kind of forgotten about this, but we didn't have forks for a few years. My mom decided she didn't want to 'have the taste of metal in her mouth,' and I think she was trying to make some point about Western cultural dominance in the, er, West, so for a while we ate with chopsticks, which was—"

"You didn't have forks?"

"Nope, we—"

"You really had to eat with chopsticks?"

"For a few years, yeah. Oh, man . . . I had totally repressed that. It all comes flooding back and—"

"Well, you're starting to make a lot more sense. Okay, maybe *you're* not making sense, but I'm beginning to understand why you're the way you are."

"God, the fork thing . . . I just wanted to . . . be . . . a normal kid, but—"

"Did you sit around eating cereal with—heh heh heh—chopsticks?"

"No . . . We had . . . spoons . . . Harrrgh, the memories burn! They burn!"

"So if she didn't want metal, why were spoons okay? Was it a thing with . . . the . . . tines?"

"Look, you're trying to find logic in this, and there was none. But as far as I can remember, it was more of a political issue, like she—"

"Didn't you care? You just went along with it?"

"By the time the Great Fork Blackout of 1976 happened, my resistance had been totally worn away. I mean, it's not like that was the weirdest thing I ever had to deal with. For example—"

"I still don't get it. Was it a safety issue? Did you have knives?"

"Sure, we had knives. In fact, we had big kitchen knives. Right around this time is when I started playing this game with my sister where I'd turn off all the lights in the house, grab a big-ass butcher knife and a flashlight, and hide . . . When I'd hear her get close, I'd pop up, grinning, and flick the flashlight on, and she'd scream and—"

"And you plan to use the fork thing as some sort of defense of this?"

"No, no . . . Look, this is all beside the point. What I was originally trying to say is that because we were poor, I couldn't go to movies, so I'd get *Mad* magazine and—"

"And sit there reading it, eating popcorn with chopsticks."

"Heh heh, no, no . . . I ate popcorn with my hands. Of course, it was covered in yeast . . . "

"Yeast?"

"Yeah, we ate yeast on our popcorn . . . This dusty, yellow yeast . . . Oh God, it's all coming back to me now. Nutritional yeast . . . and seaweed . . . "

"*Seaweed?!*"

"YES, SEAWEED. AAAAAAGH!!! ALL I EVER WANTED WAS TO BE A NORMAL KID!!! *AND I HAD TO EAT YEAST AND SEAWEED ON MY FUCKING POPCORN AND WE DIDN'T HAVE FORKS!!!*"

"Um . . . Did other kids ever come over to your house or anything?"

"No. Not more than once, anyway. Don't forget, we also had those special tree branches and leaves all over the floor to get rid of fleas."

" . . . "

"ANYWAY, since all I ever wanted was to be like other kids, kids who were being raised by members of their own species, so when they would talk about movies, I'd pretend that I saw the movies too, only I hadn't. I just got really good at guessing what happened in movies by using the *Mad* magazine movie spoofs as a rough guide."

"You know, I'm pretty screwed up in some areas myself, but you—"

"Yeah yeah yeah. I'm gonna go in my office now and lie down. And, possibly, never get back up"

MAYBE EVEN A LITTLE SCARIER THAN A DR. WHO MONSTER

1988

Okay, so when I was nineteen years old I was homeless and went to go live on my friend Lou's couch in Palm Harbor. Lou and a couple of friends I had known since high school were all employed at this really busy Burger King at the corner of U.S. 19 and 584, and they got me a job there.

I spent six or eight months living on Lou's couch, eating his mom's food, bumming rides to places, working at Burger King and spending my paycheck on Kool Moe Dee cassettes before splitting in the middle of the night to move back to Gainesville and freeload off people there.

Basically, I was a selfish dirtbag with bad tattoos and limited social skills, barely employable and chiefly interested in getting loaded and beating people up. (The first chucklehead to pipe up with something like, "What's so different about you now?" gets one of these here empty beer cans upside the head.)

Anyway, we're talking a real high point in my life. In fact, if the me of today met the me of then today, me of today would punch me of then in the balls to teach me of then a much-deserved lesson. And then me of today would run, because me of then was a big, angry, drunken thug who welcomed those bright flashes of pain for the all-too-brief respite they provided from a life spent gazing at the cinders of its own dead soul. And me of today is a puss who watches Truffaut movies and wears glasses and khaki pants and stares at computers all day long and knows about wine.

But working at Burger King wasn't nearly as bad as I thought it was going to be. First of all, all my shithead buddies worked there, and we could do shit like coordinate dance routines to Misfits songs while assembling the delicious materials we sold as food. It was also the first steady paycheck I ever earned in my life, and dealing with the gig's meager demands gave me a glimpse at that mystical, fabled land others called "responsibility."

In addition, on my first day I got to dress up in this bulbous Rodney the Reindeer costume and scream obscenities at passing cars. That was alright. Plus we got free soda, and there were some rock 'n' roll chicks working at our shop who were usually up for dirty break-room shenanigans. And there was also the occasional adventure, like when someone would shit on the floor of the customer bathroom or the time Lou figured out a way to operate the microwave without having to close its door and was happily irradiating everyone who walked by.

One of the mightiest struggles of the Burger King era involved a "Be Capable" named Kim. Be Capables (get it? "Be Capable?" "BK?") were people with various mental and physical problems who were placed in the less demanding, more menial (believe it or not, there was a slight gradation) Burger King jobs in an effort to teach them skills that would benefit society. I had nothing against most of our Be Capables, probably because at that shitty point in my life I was barely one or two Y-chromosomes from being designated Aspiring Be Capable For Life.

But Lou hated this one particular Be Capable named Kim. She was in her early thirties and prone to these weird fits where she would turn into the Mummy and start lumbering around all glassy-eyed and stiff-legged, wrecking things and choking people. Though tiny and suffering from a heart condition that both precluded strenuous exertion and turned her skin an unusual shade of blue, she drew on an immense reserve of strength during these fits and was a real challenge to subdue.

Occasionally her fits would adopt a less aggressive tone than the more common, Boris Karloff-inspired episodes: She would spin in circles for a few seconds before lurching into action, zipping along blindly in one random direction or another until hitting an obstacle, bouncing off of it and starting the whole process all over again exactly like one of those old battery-powered Radio Shack toys from the days when wireless remote control was available only to high-falutin' rich kids.

But Kim was also very critical and mean, constantly belittling people (to the best of her limited capabilities) in a squeaky, mewling voice. Which is why I didn't really blame Lou for not liking her. Kim certainly seemed to like me just fine, probably due to the time I was squatting down to grab a bucket of foul Burger King pickles and the crotch of my pants ripped from zipper to ass, displaying my dangling, underwear-less weiner and balls. Kim, the only witness to the incident, was delighted. She would talk about it with a faraway look in her eyes at every possible opportunity.

Anyway, Kim's job was to put frozen burger patties on the conveyor belt that fed the broiler. Nothing else. She didn't have to go in the walk-in freezer to get the burgers, or open the boxes that they came in, or sweep or do anything at all but load these frozen meat-discs into this giant, clanking robo-oven. But she was incompetent, and during busy periods it wasn't uncommon for the person working the burger station to have to dash back to the conveyor belt, shove Kim into a corner and throw handfuls of burgers into the machine in a frantic effort to ensure commuters would get their recommended daily dose of soybeans, horse meat and spider eggs (or whatever the hell it was Burger King put in those sumptuous, affordable patties).

One day when Lou, Kim and myself were the only employees on the clock, I was standing at the fry station trying to figure out a way to use ketchup and a hollowed-out French-toast stick left over from the breakfast rush to fake cutting off one of my fingers when I heard Lou curse and run back to Kim's station to feed the infernal machine. The lunch rush was just beginning, and he had run out of meat-stuff.

"Hey, Pat!" he barked. "Get me two cases of Whoppers and a case of burgers out of the walk-in! Now! Now!"

I liked the walk-in freezer. The walk-in freezer was nice. It was cool and dark and quiet, and one time this frisky heavy-metal girl who worked with us followed me in there and touched me on the po-po. It had felt good. So I knew Lou needed these burgers pronto, but I couldn't resist taking a few moments to breathe in that sweet, cold freezer air and enjoy the peace, the quiet and the memories.

When I emerged, Lou was locked in a death struggle with Kim. She was glassy-eyed, drooling and clearly having one of her fits. She also had a pair of metal burger tongs about three-quarters of an inch from Lou's face. Lou, a stocky and enormously strong guy who played varsity high-school football as a sophomore, had her by the wrists and was straining to control her. Every couple of seconds those tongs would clap shut like the jaws of a pit bull. Snap! Snap!

I dropped the burger boxes and rushed over to grab Kim.

"Make . . . the . . . burgers," Lou managed to squeeze out while fighting for his life.

"Hold on!" I said. "I'll help you!"

"MAKE THE BURGERS!" was Lou's answer. "HAAAYAARRRGH!"

That was Lou. A good soldier to the end. I ran to his station and started filling orders. From the back of the kitchen I could hear the continuing sounds of struggle. Kim was groaning low in her throat like Frankenstein with a hangover, Lou was grunting with the effort of battle, and those menacing tongs kept snapping shut every few seconds. Snap! Snap! I was pretty sure I heard punches being thrown, but I didn't look back. Just the thought of the desperate conflict happening back there was bad enough—I was afraid the actual sight of Lou beating up this poor old Be Capable while she had a seizure would scar me for life. I put my head down and concentrated on filling the orders that were pouring in.

After a few harrowing minutes of this, I heard the door to the walk-in freezer slam shut. Not long after, Lou returned to the burger-making station while I ran back to the fryers. He was sweating, breathing hard and his clothes were disheveled. I didn't like the look in his eyes.

Wordlessly, we worked nonstop for the next hour or so until the rush was over. As it slowed, the full weight of experience began to hit us, and shock set in. Was Kim dead? I looked over at Lou, but he wouldn't catch my eye. In fact, he wouldn't discuss the terrifying experience at all for months to come, and even then would only mumble something about being startled to look up and see Kim coming at him "like a *Dr. Who* monster" with those metal tongs. I don't blame Lou for being reluctant to talk about it. I mean, to this day I find the whole experience totally unsettling, and I'm not the one who had to engage in hand-to-tong conflict with a Be Capable.

We continued to work. A little while later Kim emerged from the walk-in freezer, a little more blue than usual but seemingly unharmed.

"You guys are mean to me," she said. She died a few months later, but not at work or because of anything Lou did.

UNCLE TOMMY, DAD AND VARIOUS FAMILY MEMBERS AT MY COUSIN'S WEDDING

2005

"I liked Bob Dole, but I didn't vote for him. I could never vote for a guy with one arm. What if they ask him to throw out the first pitch?"

"I can take any word and make it negative. Go ahead, try me."
"Okay . . . *Nice.*"
"You've got a nice big fat ass."

"So we ended up at this bar where a few of the go-go dancers were pregnant. It was disgusting. I wasn't having any fun, so I said we should play a game where we compete to try and steal the most interesting stuff out of the bathroom. One by one we'd go into the bathroom and steal something and bring it back and put it under the table. Towels, toilet paper, doorknobs . . . One guy brought out a toilet seat smuggled under his jacket. Anyway, it came around to my turn, and there was nothing left to steal. So I decided to rip the urinal off the wall. I got it about two feet off the wall, but couldn't break the pipes. The owner eventually went into the bathroom and saw all the damage and went nuts and called the cops. We snuck out the back when the state troopers showed up."

"I never mentioned the guy who parachuted into the parking lot?"
"No!"
"Yeah, I worked with a guy at IBM who was a former Green Beret. One day he parachuted into the IBM parking lot in full frogman gear."
"Holy crap, that's amazing! How did he do that? Where did he get the plane?"
"I dunno, but those guys can land on a dime. He got fired, though."
"For the parachuting stunt?"
"Yeah."
"That's totally worth getting fired for, though."
"Another time this same guy came into the bar with a deer he had just killed. He threw the deer on the bar, cut out its tongue and ate it raw in front of everybody."
"Oh man! That's incredible! I have to meet this guy!"
"Well, you can't. He went to prison after killing a guy in a bar fight."

"Why did they throw you out?"
"I didn't like the door guy's attitude, and I let him know it. He said something to me that pissed me off."
"What did he say that pissed you off so bad?"
"I don't remember, but it got me pretty mad."
"I remember what he said. He very politely said, 'Sir, you can't take your drink out in the street.'"
"Yeah, that was it. Asshole."

"Go ahead, give me another word. I'll make it negative."
"*Love.*"
"I love your big fat disgusting ass."
"You're not really making those words negative—you're just using them in a sentence with the word *ass!* And besides, 'I love your big fat disgusting ass' is positive. I mean, some people really like big fat disgusting asses. They'd really say that and mean it."
"Not if they were being sarcastic."

"Why did you think you were going to fight those guys?"

"They were jerks. They asked me if I was Amish."

"So he was a real cheapskate, and to get some extra money out of him she started giving him blowjobs every night. One night she was drunk and chewing gum and the gum got stuck in his pubic hair. They didn't notice—just went right to sleep. He wakes up in the morning and finds this pink lump near his dick and freaks out—he thought it was some kinda growth. But it was just the dried gum from the night before. They had to cut it out of his pubic hair."

"Tell the sequel to that story."

"The sequel?"

"Yeah, the sequel! With the cigarette."

"Oh, another time she was smoking a cigarette and giving him a blowjob and she dropped an ash and it caught his pubic hair on fire."

"Shit, I think I'd be giving her the extra money NOT to give me blowjobs."

"Look at him go! He's dancing his ass off. Oh man, now he's got a fire helmet on. Where did he get a fire helmet? He's going crazy. Can you imagine him doing this three years ago?"

"It finally happened. We unlocked his inner Hughes."

HELL-ROSE

1988

Siphoning gas is a lot harder than it looks on TV. On television shows or in the movies, you just throw that tube in the hole, suck on it real stylish and gentle for a few seconds and *voilà*—out comes the magic juice everyone loves. In this respect it's a lot like prom night.

But giving that shit a try in real life turns out to be problematic. You mouth that thing all awkward for a minute or two and nothing happens. Everyone stands around watching. Someone's keeping a lookout in case you get caught, a possibility which makes you nervous. You suck harder and harder. Then all of a sudden you're choking on a snootful of the worst, most toxic shit you can imagine while kneeling on the ground and coughing, eyes watering and trying to keep from barfing or crying. Your pals make fun of you and you want to die. In this respect it's a lot like . . . Shit, I don't know. Prison. Look, I already made one blowjob joke; cut me some slack.

Oh, one important difference—unlike prison or prom night, being drunk off your ass doesn't make it any easier.

Sometimes, though, like fellatio, an emergency makes siphoning gas necessary. Like, for example, maybe you've run out of beer and need to drive to Melrose to pick up some more before you sober up.

Melrose? It's a little rural place about forty-five minutes or so west of Gainesville. Snide college students and other uppity rich pricks think of it as a hick town. But it has one important cultural advantage over Gainesville (which is admittedly not a hard thing to accomplish): Melrose sells beer after 2 A.M.

I don't know if Gainesville punk rockers still make the late-night Melrose, or "Hell-rose," beer run anymore. I go to bed early, lead a quiet life. And I'm wise enough to know that if I'm going to be greeting the dawn with a refreshing cocktail, I need to stock up way before the nannies, party-poopers and Bible-thumpers start locking up the booze.

In years past, of course, I've made that trip plenty often. Too often. It's ghastly. Invariably the spirit of adventure wanes fifteen minutes into the trip. The mouth dries, the eyes turn bloodshot and the brain begins the crushing slide toward sobriety. You get sleepy without a drink or two to prop you up, and become a menace on the road. Also, there's invariably a cop sitting in front of the only open convenience store, and you have to park next to him and act all normal and try not to make eye contact and wonder if he can smell the alcohol on your breath or read your drunken thoughts. It's stressful. And by the time you score and make it back to town, everybody's asleep and the beer is warm. Fuck! The Melrose trip is terrible, IT'S TERRIBLE! Why the hell did I do it all those hundreds of times?!

God, and it's even worse when the gas fumes from your attempt at siphoning are making you sick. But, you know, it had to be done. Who wants to spend money on gas when you could be spending it on beer? There's plenty of gas in that frat boy's car, and I don't see any fuckin' beers handy, you know?

We had a full car on this particular run. Me, three or four genial skinheads and this weirdo named Bill. At least I think his name was Bill. Anyway, Bill was an odd guy. I'm not sure how he got involved with our little group of miscreants. I think you tend to be less discerning about company when you're a dirtbag, and back then I, at least, was a total dirtbag. This Bill character had just sort of attached himself to us for a few weeks, hanging around, and nobody objected. Despite the fact he was clearly nuts.

Bill looked like a cartoon hillbilly. He was small and scrawny and always wore denim overalls and a ratty straw farmer's hat. His face and head were covered in matted, black hair, and he had some kind of strange metal shit going on in his mouth, braces or wires or something. He rarely talked or blinked but occasionally laughed at random or inappropriate times. And he told us that he got kicked out of the Army because he went apeshit in Grenada. Apparently, the combat was too much for him.

Now, I'm the last guy to belittle the services of America's armed forces, really. But Grenada?! I'm sorry if this offends any veterans who might be reading, because I have so much respect for you, but going nuts from the traumatic experiences of Grenada is like going nuts because you really hated an episode of *Love Boat*.

Anyway, there we were, a car full of hoods coming back from Melrose at 3:30 A.M. The spirit of adventure had worn off long ago. We were all tired and mostly silent. I sat in the front passenger seat, high and nauseous from the gasoline and drink, nodding in and out of consciousness.

At some point we stopped and pulled off to the shoulder. I woke up a bit and looked around. It was a dark stretch of country road, no street lights or traffic. Life was painful.

"Hey Pat, we're going to get out and pee. Do you need to pee?" one of the skinheads asked.

"Fuhhh . . . Ehhh . . . Naw," I said.

This answer wasn't good enough. They tried again: "Umm, hey, Pat . . . DO YOU NEED TO PEE?"

"Fuck off." I went back to sleep.

Everyone got out of the car. I could hear them whispering outside. Then I felt a pressure from something metallic on the side of my neck. What the fuck?

"Drive."

"Huh?"

"Get in the driver's seat and drive! Now!" It was Bill. He was leaning forward from the back seat and holding something against the left side of my neck. Oh, a knife. How nice.

"Bill, I can't drive."

"Do it! Do it or I'll fuckin' kill you!"

"Bill! I can't drive!" I was getting exasperated.

"Do it! Do it! They're going to kill me!" He sounded desperate.

"Bill, I can't. I don't have a driver's license. I don't even really know how." All of a sudden it got very quiet.

The information began to process, I guess, and, confused, Bill relaxed the pressure. I jerked my head away and grabbed his wrist, then reached around the headrest and tried to punch him. I noticed that his knife was one of those dullish, serrated steak knives like they give you at Sizzler. Seeing the commotion, the skinheads ran over to the car, pulled Bill out and beat on him for a few minutes. Then everybody but Bill piled back in, noticeably agitated and disturbed. We sat there for a few seconds.

"Thanks guys. That was fucked up," I said.

"Why do you think we were trying to get you to come pee with us, asshole? He pulled out that knife ten minutes ago and had been sitting there, gripping it and muttering and acting all crazy," someone said.

The car started, and we swung around onto the road. Bill stood there, about fifteen feet away in the grass, staring at us. We were a good forty miles from where he lived. There was nothing around but woods for miles.

"Hey man, do you want a beer for the road?" someone in the back seat asked Bill.

"Sure, I guess so," he answered. He looked a little sad.

An unopened can of beer fired out of the car and hit Bill square in the chest. He looked startled and took a step back. We drove off.

We never saw him again.

I eventually got my license, the year I turned thirty-two.

DON'T EAT THE LASAGNA

2004

How do you know when the holiday season officially kicks off? Around here, it's when my little brother rings me up to tell me you can see a relative's mugshot online.

See, our other brother got ahold of some of the many aliases used by this chick his uncle married (I say "his" uncle because technically these two are my half-brothers but, seeing as we share a strong love for hijinx, we just dispense with the "half" formalities). Anyway, she needs those because she's a professional con artist.

In the process of looking her up in the offender databases provided online by the Florida Department of Corrections, he found—well, he found what I found, that she has about 219 convictions for petty theft and bouncy checks, but in addition he found a great photo of the guy I'll call Cousin Barry.

Cousin Barry is a family favorite. By "favorite," of course, I mean everyone hates him. Picture a cross between late-period Paul Lynde at his ass-searingly fruitiest and Gary Busey at his most terrifyingly unpredictable. Dress him in the grisliest, most Jurassic leisure suits not expressly forbidden by international law and drape him in cheap jewelry, and imagine him smelling like gin and standing real, real close and wanting to "tickle" you. That's Cousin Barry.

Sounds bad, right? Really, though, all that alone wouldn't distinguish him overmuch in our family. No, Cousin Barry's obnoxiousness alone isn't what generates ill will. There are other reasons, such as his propensity for holiday nudity. How many Christmases were spoiled by a sauced-up Cousin Barry, displaying his sixty-something-year-old ding-dong for all to see during his inevitable skinny-dip in my dad's pool? (The answer: all of them.)

But truth be told, while nobody was a big fan of Cousin Barry's annual "unwrapping of the gifts," it wasn't even his saggy moobs (*man + boobs*) that earned him his rep as the must-avoid sociopath in an extended family of sociopaths. His cooking, for example, didn't help his case.

Ah, his cooking. I remember cakes so dense, small dishes of candy would get sucked into their gravitational fields. Icing studded with generous dollops of cigarette ash. A lasagna that included a layer of whole cloves. Not garlic cloves, mind you. Cloves. It was totally inedible. The dog wouldn't eat it. I'm not making this up. Just think about it: a "lasagna" that included a layer of whole cloves. Fear this lasagna.

But you know, even potentially dangerous culinary monstrosities don't clinch your persona non grata status at the Hughes house. Croaking a guy, however . . . Well, it's a bit much, even by our standards. But not for Cousin Barry.

I do not know the details. I do not know the specifics. I do not know the method, though I suspect lasagna may have been involved. And I don't care to speculate. Don't ask. (He might hear you.) But Cousin Barry croaked a guy, back in the '50s. And he was sentenced to life. You don't get that shit for a little run-of-the-mill manslaughter or anything. First degree all the way for Cousin Barry.

Anyway, he was paroled when I was a kid and started showing up at Christmas, mincing around and making everyone uneasy and taking off his clothes and stuff. No killing, though. Not as far as we could tell.

I'm not sure when Cousin Barry started skipping the holiday gatherings at Pop's place. Probably when Dad told him to shut his damn mouth and Barry said something like, "Don't you tell me to shut my mouth. I can do things to you. I've done things you can't imagine." Not a smart move. Dad has at his disposal a daunting combination of red-faced Irish temper, an abnormally large dose of the fearsome Dad Strength and a general inclination toward all things whoop-ass. No geriatric Paul Lynde motherfucker can stand up to all that, murder-one rap sheet or not. So Cousin Barry doesn't come around any more.

But, thanks to his disdain for reporting to his parole officer, a recent traffic stop and the efforts of my intrepid brethren, we can now visit him online. And let me tell you, the picture is good. It's so, so good. He looks crazy . . . So crazy. Cuh-raaay-ay-zy.

Nope, I'm not going to show it to you. It might be in the public domain and all that, but somehow I suspect Cousin Barry might not want this info spread around too much. You think I want Cousin Barry paying me a visit? Uh-uh. Get your own convicted murderer.

TRUE LOVE? IT DEPENDS

1998

I had never really paid any attention to her. She was skinnier than I like 'em, and fucking wore these preposterous overalls every day. But when I saw her blow a smoke ring out of the gap in her smile that formerly had hosted a tooth, I fell in love with her. A little, anyway.

She was smart, and she knew it. She was witty, and quick, and she didn't put up with any shit. And she told me she planned to get a diamond-studded gold tooth to fill in that gap. Yeah, it was love.

She had her share of negative qualities, too, of course. She was a graduate of Florida's New College and shared the same unfounded elitism and sense of entitlement I've observed in everyone else who's ever set foot on that campus. Even more significant, though, was the fact she didn't love me back.

Oh, she liked me, I suppose. A strong like. Enough like to call me every day, but not enough to fuck me. I spent plenty of time with her, happy with what I could get. Which meant lots of great conversation, the occasional late-night adventure and a neverending stream of tiny, poignant heart-breaks, the kind that make your Joy Division and George Jones records sound that much sweeter. In this way it was pretty much exactly like the other 412,987 times I've found myself with a similar unrequited crush, and no doubt like all the others would've continued in the same vein until she moved out of town. Or until I instigated a total emotional meltdown by trying to yank forth some kind of emotional commitment, or acknowl-edgment, or something, out of our cozy little limbo.

But it didn't play out like all the others. Not this time.

We were at a party, standing in front of her apartment building. I was drunk. I was drunk a lot around this time—this all happened during Gin and Tonic Summer, a particularly successful binge undertaken by myself, Scott Adams and Todd Campisi. Gin and Tonic Summer featured plenty of good-natured mayhem involving firecrackers, 4 A.M. games of four-square and, of course, gallons of its namesake. In fact, Gin and Tonic Summer was such a success that it stretched well into winter. Hell, it might still be going on for all I know—go ask Todd.

Anyway, she had been out of town for a week or two. I was acting a bit aloof, little depth charges of sadness going off in my stomach every time the corner of my eye caught her laughing at some idiot dude's jokes. I think maybe I had just finished throwing a handful of bottle rockets into the mellow backyard bonfire, an immensely satisfying pastime I recom-mend to everyone.

I was fixin' to leave, and she sidled up to me and gave me a hug. "I missed you," she said. She was unusually subdued.

"I missed you, too," I said.

She pulled my head down and whispered in my ear. "You don't under-stand," she said. "I really missed you. I thought about you every day. I needed to see you." And she kissed me, softly.

This is the only time in my life this has happened, where someone I loved but that didn't love me back changed their mind, even a little.

"Hey cocksucker! We're leaving! Are you getting in the car?" It was Todd. Or maybe Scott.

She looked up at me and, arms around my waist, held my gaze. Not saying a word.

"I, uh . . . I think I'm staying," I said. And I did.

Later we went up to her room. I kissed her for the first time there, while lying on her bed. She took off her shoes, and took off those damn overalls.

She was wearing some kind of weird plastic diaper with a thick elastic waistband. Maybe a Depends? Were there some kind of . . . circus animals on it? What the fuck?

She kept kissing me. I was distracted. Was that really her underwear? Was it some sort of cover that went over her regular underwear? Do those overalls chafe or something? Is it a joke? An affectation? Evidence of some sort of disease? What . . . The . . . FUCK?!

"Don't you want to take your shoes off?" she said.

"I . . . I . . . I think I have to go," I said.

She looked surprised. I split.

The next day, Todd called and asked me what had happened. I told him I had left.

He was surprised, too. "I thought you really liked her, dude," Todd said.

"I did, or do," I said. "Todd . . . You fucked her once. Was she wearing some kind of diaper?"

"Whaaaa?"

"Some kind of diaper. She took her pants off and had on some kind of weird Depends thing. I freaked out and split."

"She didn't have a diaper on when I fucked her! Are you sure you weren't just drunk?"

"Well . . . Yeah. Dude, I'm telling you she had on some kind of diaper." I remembered their slick, plastic texture and being worried I'd take 'em off and find . . . poop.

"You're fuckin' nuts. She didn't have on a diaper. You should've fucked her."

We finished our conversation, and I thought about what Todd said. Had I just thrown away a chance at being with someone I loved? For nothing? For some imaginary diaper? It had seemed so real. Maybe it was a manifestation of my fear of intimacy? And maybe if I really loved her, the diaper shouldn't be a big deal. Sincere feelings should overcome a little petty incontinency, shouldn't they? Fuck. I screwed up.

I needed to find her. I needed to find her and fix things. Tell her that, whatever was up with that diaper business, we could work it out. She meant too much to me.

I hopped on my bike and went to the Utility House, a well known punk-rock hangout. She was on the porch, drinking a quart of beer. I sat down next to her and cracked one open myself. The previous night was not acknowledged. People came and went, drinking and smoking and telling stories and laughing.

Eventually, there was a moment where we were alone. I leaned in and started to whisper an apology in her ear . . .

"Ew! Dude! Get off of me!" she shouted. "What's wrong with you?! Why are you being so gross and romantic?! Have you lost your mind?!"

Then she sneered, shook her head and took a swig from her beer.

A MESSAGE FROM SEAN ATWATER

2003

Following is a transcript of the one phone message I received the entire month of July:

"Pat, I'm getting into a yelling match with these . . . idiots. I can't remember the fuckin' names of the British Bulldogs, both of 'em. Please call me back on my phone and tell me, because it's *very* important. I know you know the names of the British Bulldogs. I can only get one, I can't get the other, and it's pissing me off so fucking bad. So give me a call on my phone and tell me the names, and I'll rub it in their fuckin' faces . . . 'Cause they're claiming it's Jim 'The Anvil' Neidhart and fuckin' Bret Michaels, er, I mean Bret Hart . . . They're full of shit . . . Idiots. Okay, bye."

STRIDE NOT INTO YON LAKE OF POO WATER

2000

He woke up when I was spraying the shaving cream on his crotch, but he never noticed the swastika. I had drawn it on his forehead with a permanent black marker.

He was asking for it. I mean, he had passed out on our floor while we were still coherent enough to fuck with him. This wasn't Miami, you know? This wasn't even Nicaragua. This was Gainesville. Crackers play for keeps around here.

Really, we had no clue as to who the guy was, other than a Nicaraguan dude from Miami. He dressed kind of conservatively for a punk rocker, seemed to like late-'70s junkie bands a little more than the next guy. Mumbled a lot.

We didn't bear him any real animosity, mind you. Aside from a disconcerting resemblance to Billy Crystal, there was nothing about him that would make you want to draw a swastika on his head. He was just there, snoring away on our floor. An easy target. He had arrived with a mutual friend—who split after a few minutes, leaving him in our care—drank three or four beers and then just sacked out. We had to do something. Perhaps we wanted to teach him a lesson about trusting strangers too much. Or perhaps we were just dicks.

Anyway, he sat up, bleary-eyed and festooned with Nazi pride, looked around to see where he was, mumbled something, wiped the giant pyramid of shaving cream off the front of his jeans and a few seconds later stumbled out the door. Off into that dark night he went, swastika no doubt shining like a beacon, leading him through the fog to . . . to . . . ummm . . . Germany?

I've often imagined the moment when he discovered what I'd done. Did it come at a friend's house? A grocery store? Church? Did he try to pick up any girls or anything with that shit on his head? You know, I actually knew what happened, at some point in my life. But I've long since forgotten, the actual moment not being strong enough to hold up against the various scenarios I've manufactured. Which, as you might guess, involved grocery stores and churches and Jewish people. By the way, if you know the truth, keep it to yourself. I'll cling to my sweet falsehoods, thanks all the same.

Later, little Swastika Head would become Gainesville's unsung punk-rock MVP, enhancing any band he joined with gloriously caustic Johnny Ramone/Keith Richards/Johnny Thunders guitar and a deeply ingrained anger that manifested itself in yelling and swollen forehead veins. He would also become my roommate, and I take no small amount of pride in knowing that I helped stoke the rage that entertained us so much back in those days.

This should come as no surprise, but I'm impossible to live with—moody, irritable, mean, too big to easily beat up. I'll mock and deride your idiosyncrasies, and I did it to this guy. For example, he never wrapped up his cheese, and it would get all waxy in the refrigerator. I'd yell at him: "Dumbass! Wrap up your cheese! You're fucking ruining that cheese! How fucking old are you, dude?! You don't know to wrap up your cheese?! Didn't anyone ever instruct you in the proper care of cheese?!"

"Maybe I like it that way," he'd mumble. It was some weird, ass-backwards Third World Nicaraguan cheese, too, no doubt made from old soap or bat's milk and probably unsuitable for consumption now that he no longer lived in the jungle. God, you know what? Years later, I'm still getting pissed off thinking about that fucking waxy cheese.

What else? I also hate having people over, and I hate paying all the bills, even though I don't trust anyone else enough to delegate that responsibility. And I go to bed early and will totally flip out if I get woken up. And this guy would wake me up.

He liked to take showers, you see. Not excessively, by the standards of Obsessive Compulsive Disorder—just three or four a day. He'd go out drinking every single night and come home and shower at like 3 A.M before going to bed. The bathroom was next to my bedroom, and the sound of the water and his drunken smashing around would invariably wake me up. Oh, once or twice he skipped the shower, like when he passed out on the floor before getting to it. We found him the next day, a Wednesday morning or something, unconscious in front of the TV with a porno tape churning away onscreen and a couple of bagels charred to black in our malfunctioning toaster. Thank God he fell asleep before unsheathing his wiener.

We'd fight about those showers. He kind of needed them, you see. And I tried to be understanding about these things, I really did. I figure if he needed an extra two or three showers to make it through the day, it was a pretty harmless quirk, and who was I to judge? It wasn't like the cheese, sitting there unwrapped in the fridge, turning all fucking waxy. But the noise of those showers drove me crazy.

Eventually, this was resolved when he started dating a girl who lived a few houses down from us. Frankly, I suspect he was just using her for her bathroom. But again, who am I to judge? If she didn't mind, and he didn't want to use her for her vagina like a normal person, they had my blessing. They probably have different customs regarding relationships and stuff back in the Nicaragua, and I'm remarkably open-minded about primitive cultures.

He did other weird stuff in the bathroom, though. He'd go in there after work and wash his hands for about twenty minutes. If you didn't notice, this was fine. But if the sound of the faucet turning on and off registered on your consciousness, the noise was like torture: SHHEET-shoot. SHH-HEEEEET-shoot. SHEET-shoot. SHHHEEEEEEEEET-shoot. SHEET-shoot. SHEET-shoot. SHEET-shoot. SHEEEEET-shoot. SHHHHEEET-shoot. SHHEET-shoot. SHEET-shoot. SHEET-shoot. "AAAAAAGH, for the love of God, man, those things are clean enough! If you don't stop jacking off the fucking faucet I'm calling the INS! *Comprende?!* *La migra,* motherfucker! El deporto your ass-o!!!" I'd yell that in my mind.

He also went through a roll of toilet paper a day. This was weird, because he didn't seem to be wiping with it all. Just peeling it off and flushing it. Once we established that this practice meant he needed to buy the goddamn toilet paper for the house, nobody cared. Let him flush away, if that made him happy. Like I said, we were tolerant of his stupid foreign culture. Maybe it was some kind of sacrifice to one of his pagan gods. Better to flush the toilet paper down to his monkey jungle Aztec shit-god than our still-beating hearts.

One day I was fixing to go to class, and decided to check the mail before catching the city bus. A communal mailbox had been installed in our yard for the benefit of the mail carrier, and I hiked over to it. The ground seemed a little squishy to me, which was strange. It was sunny out, and hadn't rained for a day or two. Standing in front of the mailbox, I looked down, and noticed I was standing in a large puddle of bright blue water.

"That water's really goddamn blue," I thought. Then I noticed the shreds of filmy white paper strewn around the area. A sick realization began to creep up on me. I stared down at my feet, trying to place that color . . . Then a turd floated by, and I flipped out. Holy fucking mother of God, I was up to my ankles in a small lake of poo water.

Howling in rage and terror and flapping my arms with all of my might, I made it back to the house without touching the ground. I turned and looked. That poo lake was fucking huge. It took up like a third of the goddamn yard. Some kids were already messing with it, giggling and using a stick to poke at a stray turd out on the lake's periphery.

My stomach sank as I surveyed the scene. I couldn't just go back inside and pretend like I never saw the poo water. This was going to be my problem. I recognized that shade of blue, you see. It was the color of the disinfectant tablets I used in the tank of our toilet. While I didn't particularly care about ridding the bathroom of ass-germs, I found the blue water immensely cheerful. Anyway, there was no denying it. That poo water was our poo water.

Yelling a few words of encouragement at the kids, I kicked off my shoes and went inside. A few phone calls later, I was relieved to find out the city would take care of this problem. If no money had to come out of my pocket and the incident wouldn't put more than a two-hour cramp in our flushing, I could relax a little.

Until one of the workmen came and knocked on the door to let me know they were done. "A cap burst off the top of a pipe in your yard," he told me. "There was a giant clot of toilet paper out under the street that was causing your pipes to back up. Damnedest thing I've ever seen. Anyway, you're lucky it didn't come back into the house."

I thanked the guy, and turned toward the phone. Eyes wide and hands trembling, I dialed my roommate's work number. He answered. I began gibbering semi-coherent threats. "GOBBA HOBBA POO WATER!!! HOB-BA HOBA TOILET PAPER!!! GIBBA GOBBA NO MORE, MAN!!! NO MOOORRRE!!!"

That night he came home and quietly presented us with his solution: a second bathroom trash can, deployed specifically for toilet paper. Since he didn't actually wipe with the paper, but just yanked it off the roll by the yard, its presence would be unlikely to offend. We all agreed this was satisfactory.

In fact, it turned out fine. Better than fine. One day while using the bathroom, I glanced to my left and noticed the auxiliary trash can, filled to the brim with unused toilet paper. It was conveniently folded and loosely stacked in attractive, orderly rows. A few experimental swipes proved it had not lost any usefulness, and from that day on I no longer had to lean so far forward when practicing this particular form of personal hygiene.

AW, RON JEREMY NEVER FUCKED FRED FLINTSTONE

1975

Before my mom became a lesbian, she . . . she . . .

Okay, I think I need to go lie down. Feeling faint . . . Just typing the words "before my mom became a lesbian" has drained all the life right out of me . . . Seriously, all the mitochondria in my body just burst like so many rotten pomegranate seeds. Really. It sounded like bubble wrap.

. . . Alright, I'm back.

Anyway, before my mom became a lesbian, she dated a squat Puerto Rican dude named Ray who kind of looked like what would happen if Ron Jeremy fucked Fred Flintstone. And that's it, diary, that's your indignity for this week! "Before my mom became a lesbian, she dated a squat Puerto Rican dude named Ray who kind of looked like what would happen if Ron Jeremy fucked Fred Flintstone." Enjoy, and please don't forget to tip your bartenders.

Ha ha, not really.

During this time, my interests were focused toward stealing other people's stuff (like fifty dollars in collectible silver dollars) and burying it in the yard, peeing in weird spots (like behind my bedroom door or in the clothes hamper) and trying to convince my Lite Brite to come to life as a murderous, subservient robot. Occasionally I'd also take mail out of the neighbors' mailboxes and tear it into little shreds, but during an unsuccessful interrogation regarding this little hobby the phrase "federal offense" was made known to me, so I did my best to rein in *that* urge, at least. Also, one of the neighbors I targeted for this practice had a teenage daughter with a nubbin for an arm, and she scared me.

A lot of stuff scared me, actually. Lightning was about the worst. This isn't a good phobia to have when you live in Gainesville, as seven months out of the year there's a gnarly thunderstorm at 4 P.M.

Once, after imagining I saw a bolt of that stuff strike our driveway during an intense storm (who knows, maybe it even happened), I totally freaked out. Budding antisocial tendencies and pathological cries for help aside, I mostly tried to avoid the adults in my life, a sound practice that to this day I recommend to children of any age. But this time I really wigged: hyperventilating, screaming, running around in circles, crying, flapping my arms, the works. I was completely hysterical.

I remember everyone thinking it was pretty funny at the time, which is understandable. I certainly didn't think the coming of Ragnarok was so funny, but then at age six I wasn't taking as many drugs as my mom and her friends.

It was after this pathetic little display that Ray decided to toughen me up a bit. This was to be accomplished with chores, discipline and beatings. First step: get me to make my bed in the morning. This was no easy task; even at six I knew that I was just going to fucking mess it up again that night, so why bother? Then, as now, I wasn't so much a fan of wasted motion.

Ray, however, didn't view bed-making as useless effort. The discipline of it mattered to him, the symbolism . . . Yes, the symbolism. I think it symbolized him being a big, fat, Puerto Rican douche-bag bed-Nazi.

As you might imagine, I didn't put a lot of work into the bed. This really chapped Ray's ass. We went back and forth on the issue a lot. And one morning he just hauled off and whacked me.

This was surprising. I stood there, stunned, and considered this new negotiating tactic. This wasn't the response Ray had hoped for—no doubt he figured a good smack would instantly turn me into an efficient, obedient bed-making machine. Or maybe he was just a prick? Anyway, he doled out a second one. This just started me bawling. Frustrated, he busted me a third time. This caused me to cough up a huge wad of snot, which flew out of my nose and landed on Ray's arm.

Both of us stared for a second, amazed by the size of the glob. Then, the pause over, an enraged Ray started yelling incoherently and smacking me in earnest.

I fell back on the unmade bed as he whaled away. I looked down at that huge, green goober smeared all over Ray's arm and felt a warm glow deep down inside. The blows didn't hurt me, not one bit. It was all totally worth it.

Some time later, Ray would drag me to a meeting for devotees of some yogi or maharishi or other fake-ass rip-off artist. Ray was a big fan of that mystical guru kook shit. At the meeting everyone was all hugs and good vibes. Incense was burning and they sang devotional folk songs and banged tambourines and played sitar records.

"Alright," Ray said, beaming, as we walked inside. "It smells like people in here."

People smell like armpits and dirt, I thought.

I surveyed the scene and experienced my own kind of enlightenment, one likely quite different from the common goal of the assembled attendees. But it was enlightenment nonetheless: I suddenly knew my destiny, my purpose in life. Why hadn't I noticed it before? It was all so clear . . . I was put on this planet to fucking hate hippies, hate them with an intensity that would melt diamonds.

Hey, what's the statute of limitations on fucking up people's mail, anyway?

YET MORE ADVICE FOR CHILDREN

An important rule of thumb for fishing: the shallower the water, the closer you are to the top of the food chain.

I don't care if it's Burger King or Ritzy McShittington's—if you're a dick to the help, you're going to be eating a loogie.

Conversely, nobody gives a shit how busy you are or how the shift manager fucked up your schedule. If you can't handle the job, get another one. Don't take it out on us. In the meantime, your tip will be one shiny penny.

A little lotion never hurt. Yes, I'm talking about what you do with your ding-dong, Chappy.

Dolphins are all smiley and frolic-y and shit on TV, where they solve problems, rescue kittens and do flips. In the wild, they're as big as Volkswagens and twice as fast. Not to mention totally evil and smart enough to really fuck with you.

For that matter, no other wild animal ever acts like it does on TV, or in a Disney movie. Unless that Disney movie is *Claw Claw the Bear Feasts on Your Entrails*. Those cute squirrels with the fluffy tails? Tree rats. They bite.

There's a big difference between being bitter or cynical and just being flat-out mean.

Quick—what's the worst job in the world? Wrong! It's picking watermelons. Big-ass twenty-pound "jubilee" watermelons, out in the hot Florida sun all day. This is the worst job in the world. Now, while no honest work should ever be beneath you, you really should try to avoid this job. Well, unless you're part of a gang of big muscle-bound redneck gorillas who think it'll just be hi-fucking-larious to throw those things overhand as hard as you can at that skinny punk-rocker dude with the gay haircut who has to catch 'em and put 'em in the truck. Haw haw haw, ain't we having some watermelon fun now, motherfucker! Shit.

All the tradition, bowing, belts and *ki* in the world won't keep your ass from getting whooped.

The discovery of an afro puff down there can be daunting, sure, but think about this—a little too much topiary sculpting might mean she's showing it off to a larger audience than you've been led to believe.

For fuck's sake, just go ahead and pop that disgusting blister. It won't get infected, and you know the damn thing is going to bust open sometime anyway.

Try to not believe in things. Most people frankly aren't qualified to have a belief, and when they go ahead and do it anyway it almost always makes the world a shittier place.

Look here, Spooky. You're not really a vampire.

You are also not really a ninja.

Really tough guys do not have orange-y tanning-booth tans and six-pack ab muscles. They look like Harley Race.

And, by the way, wrestling was a whole lot better when it was fat guys in underpants pretending to fight. It was called "wrasslin," and it was real.

Don't use *energy* as a synonym for "every fucking stupid made-up tarot-card bullshit scam of which my foolish hippie brain can conceive."

Now that you've got yourself a handful of that lotion, take some time with the whole thing. Pour yourself a glass of wine. Light a candle. Pace yourself—the Internet isn't going anywhere.

Contrary to popular belief, you don't become a geek because you're smarter than everyone else. You become a geek because your social skills are retarded. While you're off administering a Linux system, the rest of us are kissing girls. So the tech-support guys can be as snide as they want. The minute the clock strikes five, we win.

Tofu is okay. Just don't make it a cause.

Neither your iPod nor your cell phone is impressing anyone. Well, anyone who counts. My cell phone, on the other hand, has Galaga. Top that, peasant.

The rest of the country can make fun of Florida all they want, but if air conditioning had never been invented all that shit would still be their problem.

There's a little-known law that says if you wear one of those tennis visors when you're not playing tennis, the rest of us get to hit you with rocks.

That stripper doesn't really like you.

All the local bands are terrible. If they were any good, they wouldn't be begging everyone for "support."

Curiosity is good, but remember—there are a lot of things out there that, if you go research them, will stick in your brain. Forever. Like *bukkake*. So be cautious. Once some shit like *bukkake* gets in there, it ain't never coming out. You could be in the middle of a job interview or something, and your brain might start whispering, *"Bukkake. Bukkake. Bukkake."*

A wise man once said, "If she can take the occasional punch without running off and crying to the cops, she's probably worth keeping around." Hmmm . . . Wait a minute . . . Did I type that out right? Shit, who the hell told me that, Ike Turner? Christ, that's terrible. Kids, maybe you ought to hold off on this one until further notice.

Boozing and drugs and all that is okay, for a while anyway, when you're young. But when it comes to getting involved with that stuff, remember two very important words: diminishing returns.

Planning to put that funny buttplug story on the Internet? Or the thing about your drunken, failed high-school threesome? Be forewarned—even if you don't use her name and haven't seen her in a decade or more, she's going to read it.

Say you find yourself drinking with George Rebelo, the drummer for Hot Water Music, and a couple of sexy, giggly, tattooed punk-rock girls. And say—this is just total conjecture here, by the way—these girls promise you guys a few hours of naughty fun if you'll kiss George right on the mouth. Now, if you're sitting there and everyone's taking turns shaving your left leg and this far-fetched situation does come to pass, I recommend going ahead and kissing George, even if you're not especially inclined.

Because you know that horndog George won't object, and it'll be over soon, and you can be more or less sure George's tongue slipping in there for a second is accidental—or, wait, even better, a hallucination—and then you'll get to see two sexy punk-rock girls naked and touch their boobies and stuff and it'll totally be worth it. But if for some crazy reason this unlikely scenario occurs, maybe you should skip peeing in that big ceramic bowl by the couch as a prank, even if nobody will see you. Maybe a cat sleeps there. Cats get all weirded out and territorial about pee. Anyway, this is all hypothetical.

It takes longer than you might expect for leg hair to grow back. Wearing long pants all through the hot Gainesville summer can be mighty uncomfortable.

By the way, learn from George's mistake—if you get busted having sex with Skinhead Katrina around the side of the house during a party and some outraged girl wanting to know if you had a condom asks if you "used anything," do not grin and say, "Yup! I grabbed a tree branch for support!" Actually, now that I think about it . . . What the fuck. I take it back. That's exactly what you should say.

Oh, I almost forgot—you probably shouldn't have sex with Skinhead Katrina.

If you do have sex with Skinhead Katrina, and you do it around the side of the house during a party, know that you will never live it down. Your asshole friends will be putting that shit on the Internet ten years later. You didn't even know the Internet was going to be invented, did you? Ha ha! Should've kept it in your pants, Caligula.

Plan for the future. For example, if you live in an abandoned house and you get pissed off and kick through the wall, or take a bunch of drugs and shoot out a few windows, that shit will be really, really cold come winter.

Also, if the hot water heater quits working during this time, you might look and see if it has a breaker switch that can be flipped before you freeze your ass off all winter trying to take showers in a room with a hole in the wall.

Unless wolves raised you, having to deal with the dirty dishes by moving them out of the kitchen sink and into the bathtub should be looked upon as a personal failure. If you leave them in the tub for a month because it's too damn cold to take a shower with that wind blowing through the hole in the wall . . . Well, you just managed to erase about ten thousand years of civilization. Good going, Chaka.

Last, but certainly not least: Things will go better for you during periods when you listen to Thin Lizzy at least once a week.

CRYPTIC SIGNALS FROM THE PUNK-ROCK MOTHERSHIP

1982

After visiting my dad for the summer, I decide that I don't want to return to Gainesville. I move in with him and my stepmother in suburban Palm Harbor and prepare to start high school.

It was in Palm Harbor I discovered the redemptive possibilities of personal reinvention. Freed from the baggage of going to school with kids I had known for years and the attendant threat of having my current actions judged in relation to my past, I threw away my Led Zeppelin records and began slowly transforming myself into the 100% hardcore punk kid I had secretly wanted to be.

In a nice dovetail, I also discovered the widespread moral bankruptcy of life in the subdivisions. For example, the first kid I met there would eventually get sent off to prison for rape and attempted murder. (It would've been proper murder, except the chosen method involved tying a cement block to the victim's feet and throwing her off a bridge, and the rope he used was longer than the actual depth of the water, so she just swam to shore dragging that thing. He was really good at Defender, though.)

Another example of this troubling suburban amorality was the Tom phenomenon. My first day on the bus, the other kids seemed excited. "Hey, we've got a new Tom!" someone yelled.

I took my seat as they began chanting: "Tom! Tom! Tom! Tom!" The bus driver smiled. After a minute or two, it dawned on me that I was actually Tom. Weird. The other kids seemed so happy, chanting away. Maybe this was some kind of special honor, or greeting for new kids? I smiled and waved, acknowledging the attention.

Turns out Tom was an actual person, a guy who lived in the subdivision. Despite having a wife and kids, he'd cruise around the neighborhood in his car with a cooler full of beer that he'd use to try and lure teenage boys into make-out sessions.

Later, my dad and stepmom would ask me how the first day of school went for me. "Eh, not so good," I said. "They call me Tom." I explained the situation and was surprised to learn they already knew about Tom. Turns out everybody knew about Tom. Fuck, they chanted his name on the bus: "Tom! Tom! Tom! Tom!"

This experience is somewhat mitigated a full year later, when Morakis (who might still be in eleventh grade for all I know) takes pity on me and decides a kid named Pudgy is the "new Tom." I chant along with the rest.

This sort of dark-underbelly shit found a kind of focal point for me in the music of a hardcore punk band called the Dead Kennedys. At their early best, the Dead Kennedys played short blasts of furious, psychedelic thrash that specialized in satirizing the hypocrisies of a society that lived in pristine houses with well-kept lawns and went to church every Sunday while simultaneously raising psychopaths and turning a blind eye to the Toms of the world.

Back in seventh grade, I had scored a copy of the Dead Kennedys seven-inch single "Nazi Punks Fuck Off" from a taciturn, gangly pothead kid named Clyde. The record just blew me away. I was a fan of groups like the Clash, the B-52s and Devo, and in comparison "Nazi Punks Fuck Off" sounded like getting sucked into the engine of an airplane. It was so fast and so loud that it was flat-out disorienting. Today, of course, with all the new advances in musical velocity they have, it just sounds kind of quaint.

Not long after my first semester in high school, I snuck this prize over to Lou Ricardo's house, where me and my buddy Mike Maresca were planning to sleep over and play some D&D. My plan was to convert them to the punk-rock cause. Late that night, after Lou's folks had gone to sleep, we put the record on and spontaneously started beating the shit out of each other. It seemed like it was over before it started. Then we did it again. And again. Half hanging off Lou's bed, my lip swollen and my legs tangled underneath my sweaty friends, I ~~knew for the first time that I was totally gay~~ was as happy as I had ever been.

I just saw Mike this past weekend, the first time we had hung out in more than a decade. He still plays in punk bands. "If you hadn't brought that record over to Lou's, and I had heard Slayer or something instead, I would've ended up being a metal head instead of a punk rocker," he told me. I was proud.

Of course, it's tricky to be a hardcore punk kid when there isn't actually any hardcore punk scene. We were isolated and only picking up partial, cryptic signals from the punk-rock mothership. We knew, for example, that punks were into anarchy and that the symbol for anarchy was an A with a circle around it. I had enjoyed some exposure to Gainesville's hardcore scene before my move, and with the authority this bestowed I explained that true punks drew this symbol on a shirt.

So one day Mike showed up to school with a two-tone blue terrycloth shirt, a nappy one with a collar. He had taken glue and gold glitter and made a giant, shiny anarchy symbol on it. It looked like he spent some time on this little craft project, too—the circle A was careful and symmetrical.

I was aghast. "Dude, you look like a poseur," I said. "You're supposed to get a white T-shirt and scrawl it on there all messy. That shit isn't *punk*." Mike just frowned and walked away. I sighed and shook my head. We'd never get a real hardcore scene going if the punks couldn't even make anarchy shirts the right way.

Mike, I'm here to tell you that today I'm ashamed. A blue terrycloth shirt with a giant, glittery gold anarchy symbol on it is, in fact, the punkest thing in the entire universe. Please accept my apologies. I was as wrong as wrong can be and should've never belittled you. I should have run home and painted a giant pink pentagram on the V-neck velour sweater in the back of my closet and joined you, you marvelous, rebellious, forward-thinking and brave man.

That time you told me Bauhaus was more punk than Black Flag was gay, though, and I don't mean gay in the good way, where two guys like each other and kiss. And gluing that M&M to your ear and telling people it was an earring was pretty wack too.

CHATTING WITH TODD CAMPISI, PART 2

2006

Is your daughter there?

Yeah.

Send her away, because I want to talk about the fish-tank story. Do you want to talk about the fish-tank story?

Yeah, I'll talk about the fish-tank story.

Well you gotta go hide your daughter. Or put some earplugs in. So you can tell it to me.

Okay. Wait a second . . . What's that, honey? No names? Why not? Honey, it's too late. No, you can't sue Pat. Honey, I've already told this story in front of other people! What do you mean, it's different?

I could just call you "Todd C."

Aw, I don't care.

It's going to be in libraries. Your daughter could grow up and read it.

Aw, how the hell are you going to Dewey Decimal this one? Anyway, let's see . . . I think it was a Thursday night. It was after the bar was closing. The lights came on, and my ex-girlfriend was there. We had broken up, but there was that lingering spark . . . Plus, we were loaded.

An attractive girl, but Mike Clifton used to describe her as having hairy monkey arms.

Yeah, I think she did. She was pretty lanky. Anyway, we went back to her house. We were all loaded and screwing around, and I was all nuzzling around in, like, the area, and she's like, "You might want to be careful, because it's that time of the month." I was like, "That's just great." But then I thought about it and decided, "Aww, I don't care."

What do you care? You had plenty of drinks in you. You were fortified. Fortified against the red tide.

That's right. The crimson tide. So yeah, we were screwing around and we passed out.

Wait, that's not what happened. You told me you were trying to get her to have an orgasm, and it was taking you forever. You were humping and it wasn't getting anywhere, so you got your hands in there and were rubbing away . . .

Yeah, I was all spelunking and exploring, and I passed out. The next day I woke up, and she had to work. And the sunlight was making me all like, "Bleeargh." And she was gone. And I was looking around the room and surveying the situation and . . .

No, you said there were people over.

That was it! Her best friend came over.

And your ex-girlfriend went to go answer the door, and was like, "You gotta be quiet, don't let her know you're here."

You know it better than I do! She was out there having coffee or whatever with her friend, and I was trapped in the bedroom. Anyway, I look down and there was all this red crust all over my hands and I was like, "Did I hurt myself? Did I cut myself? I'm looking at my arms, my legs . . . " And then I remembered last night, and I go, "Ohhhhhh nooooo."

And you threw back the covers and, remarkably, there was no blood on your weiner.

That's right. Anyway, my ex-girlfriend had told me to stay in the room, because her friend would give her shit about us getting back together. And they're out there talking and having coffee, and I'm thinking, how the hell do I wash this off? So I'm looking around the room again, and there's her fish tank. So I just dunked my hands in her fish tank, and then rubbed 'em and wiped 'em of on my clothes. Then I just waited it out, and after her friend left I got out of there.

And then!

Yeah, and then a couple months later I'm walking home from the bar with the guy who was dating my ex-girlfriend's roommate. It was all awkward, and I was like, "What the hell do I say to this guy?" So I told him the fish-tank story, because he knew the girl and everything. I told him the whole story, the whole thing. And there's like ten seconds of quiet, and we're just walking. And he says, "You know what the best part is, dude? The fish died the next day."

AH HA HAH HA HA HAH! That's the best *part, that you killed her pet fish!*

HA HA HA HAH HA!

Oh . . . Oh man . . . So did she ever find out?

No.

MMM, DID SOMEONE SAY CAKE?

1988

A year or so after high school I was living in a semi-abandoned old house with two skinheads and my buddy Kalpesh. I say "semi-abandoned" because it *technically* had an owner—the University of Florida, in fact. We had kind of inherited the house from its previous renters, the family of Kalpesh's buddy Christian, after they moved away to put Christian in some kind of asylum or home. Anyway, I think we paid rent once. We were kind of late with the second check and noticed that nobody came to fuck with us, so we just quit paying, and that was pretty much that.

It was a pretty surreal time, and me and Kalpesh and the skinheads made for a pretty surreal sight. Because this was the era of skinheads spouting goofy racist rhetoric on daytime talk shows, and Kalpesh had really long, curly hair, not to mention a pleasing dark brown color to his skin (something that, unlike the hair, he thankfully retains to this day).

Seeing us all together confused people.

But we liked confusing people. And, sometimes, beating them up.

Since we resembled a cross between the Munsters and some kind of post-apocalyptic *Road Warrior* gang, this shitty old house suited us. It was ugly, decrepit and hidden from the surrounding neighborhood by a dense thatch of thick bushes and huge trees. It was also rumored to be haunted. Well, rumored by Christian, who told us he was occasionally possessed by its ghosts, one of whom made him shoot an arrow into his brother's back. But Christian also claimed to be a vampire and, frankly, I suspect he might've been inclined to get his spectral presences and assorted supernatural hoo-hah all intermingled and confused, so take that for what it's worth.

I don't know if those stupid ghosts were ever hard-up enough to possess one of us but, fratricidal impulses aside, it probably would've been an improvement, at least from the point of view of society. We were constantly fighting, drinking, taking awful drugs, blasting thrash metal at ear-melting volumes, burning things, humping girls who really should've known better, kicking holes in the walls and shooting out windows while all high out of our minds on LSD. The only time it was quiet was when we were hiding from police. We were terrible people, and thinking back today, a malignant ghost seems like Mr. Rogers in comparison.

There were moments of tenderness, though. One freezing-ass cold night, this giant, grizzled, feral housecat crawled through one of the empty panes in my bedroom and befriended me. We named it Outside Kitty. Outside Kitty would sink its gnarly yellow claws into my shoulder and perch there for hours, riding around, baring its one huge fang and growling at anyone who came too close. I thought this was great—it made me feel like a pirate.

Yes, sociopathic tendencies aside, we had a lot of fun there. Drugs, violence, Outside Kitty, sex, a guy who claimed to be the son of George Clinton sleeping on our couch for a week and barfing on the floor . . . There was even a movie made at the house, a delightful twenty-minute film by the name of *I Spit On Your Chick,* which featured Kalpesh as a pimp and our pal Bob Chicken as a prostitute named Queefy Butterfinger. The climactic scene, where I, the skinheads and Chuck From Hell took turns pretending to cornhole Bob Chicken—passed out for real and wearing a totally unconvincing drag get-up—on my hot-pink weight bench was a real crowd-pleaser. (In lieu of a traditional porn-style money shot, we ended the scene by spitting loogies all over Bob's bare ass, something he had no idea even took place until watching the film days later.)

Of course, thinking back today it's all fond memories of ass-spit *bukkake* and hitting each other over the head with pieces of PVC pipe, but it was even fun just doing nothing with those guys. Andy, who slept on my floor, was as friendly and jovial a skinhead as you'd ever want to meet, not that you'd really want to meet any skinheads. And, unlike the skinheads of the day you could see breaking Geraldo's nose on the television, Andy really liked black people.

In fact, at his rural Florida high school, Andy had been a part of what he called a "Negro shirt gang," something anyone who attended high school in north Florida or south Georgia in the early '80s will instantly recognize. This was when four or five black kids would go to the mall and get matching T-shirts with slogans like "Chill Dog Sagittarius—Fresh for '84" airbrushed or ironed on with those old-school felt letters. Negro shirt gangs were fucking cool, and Andy was the only white guy we had ever even heard of who had been invited to join a Negro shirt gang. Thus, he had a lot of credibility with us.

Occasionally, when I wanted to eat solid food, I'd go with Andy out to his mom's place, located in a small rural town about an hour outside of Gainesville. This was usually pretty interesting.

Once, while staying over at Christmas, we were trying to sleep while Andy's older brother (who was housebound after being busted for DUI— he'd rigged his windshield-wiper fluid dispenser to squirt whiskey through a little hose in his dashboard, making it easy to freshen his drink without pulling over) kept babbling and mumbling crazy shit at us until Andy told him to shut up. "I can't," his brother slurred. "I, um, ate some speed." Andy just sighed.

Driving around his hometown, we'd pass some guy drinking a beer in his front yard, and Andy would wave and yell out, "Hey Barry!" Then he'd invariably say something like, "Barry stabbed his grandma in the face with a shish-kebab skewer, but they couldn't keep him in jail because his brother dropped a brick on him when he was a baby and he's not right in the head. Plus his mother's cousin is the police chief." I got to hear hundreds of variations on this general theme. And if I was really lucky, I'd get to hear the story of how Andy's mom busted their next-door neighbor kid bare-ass naked on the front lawn at noon, down on all fours, letting a dog fuck him up the butt.

Andy had all *kinds* of good stories about murderers and perverts. One of our favorites besides the dog-fucker was Chef Henry. Chef Henry was an elderly pedophile who hung around downtown Gainesville, leering at kids and creeping everyone out. Andy would run afoul of Chef Henry while skateboarding around downtown, waiting for his mom to finish running errands or whatever, but it seems he and the other kids regarded

Chef Henry as little more than a nuisance. He was old, squat and slow, both physically and mentally. And he couldn't see too well, as one of his eyes was all swoll up and gooey and rolled up back in his head. So he was pretty easy to evade.

Chef Henry even had a couple of catchphrases, which Andy would mimic in an exaggerated drawl: "Heeeey, little boy, c'mere. Ah'm gone bake you a cake and fill it full uh creeeeeamy ice cream," or, "How'd you like a cake, little boy? Ah'll give yuh plenty uh creeeamy icing." Apparently these were Chef Henry's pick-up lines. Hence, "Chef."

Me and Kalpesh and the other skinhead liked it when Andy would do Chef Henry. "C'mere if you want some creeeamy ice cream," he'd say, and we'd run. "Noooo, Chef Henry, you won't get us! Yaaaaah!" we'd yell, laughing. Andy would roll his eyes up all funny and lurch around like Frankenstein. "Creeeeeeamy icing! Creeeeamy ice cream!" Sometimes he'd throw in a little of this one eerie dude who'd come through the line at the campus cafeteria where he worked: "Saaaalty biscuit. Soooo saa-aaalty. That biscuit was the saaaaaaltiest thing I've had down my throat in months."

Yes, Andy worked. He was the only one out of us who had anything resembling a regular job. For a little while Kalpesh and I sold tickets over the phone for a ramshackle local community theater that pretended to put on plays for kids in burn wards and shit, but one day we decided we didn't feel like going in. So we didn't. And that feeling just kind of . . . stuck. After that, when we were really desperate for ~~cigarettes and beer~~ groceries, we'd work the occasional odd job for Kalpesh's handyman buddy, Roy.

Much like Kalpesh and the skinheads, or Andy and the shirt gang, Kalpesh and Roy made for an unlikely pairing. Roy was a seventy-some-thing old-timey, unreconstructed Florida cracker who worked on Kalpesh's car, which was a green, spectacularly raggedy 1970 Buick Wildcat the size of a battleship. In a typically odd twist, Roy's very real affection for Kalpesh led him to saying some obscenely racist stuff when I was around.

"Kalpesh, now, you watch out when you boys go fishing," I once heard him say. "You're dark, now, almost dark like the blacks, so you might have some of that smell on you that gets the alligators hungry."

"Dude, seriously, what the fuck?" I later asked Kalpesh. I mean, I've been exposed to all kinds of racist bullshit, both passive and overt, and I've heard old cracker types pontificate forth with all kinds of idiotic country homilies and lame folk wisdom, but that took the cake. But Kalpesh just grinned and shrugged. Roy meant well, I guess. And I suspect Kalpesh kind of liked hearing some of that crap, just because it was so goddamn weird to think anyone who survived past the Mesozoic Age actually believed it.

Once Roy sent us over to a house in Gainesville's Duck Pond neighborhood. The Duck Pond is near downtown and is full of cool two-story houses that are all restored and historical and stuff. This nice old lady met us there and put us to work in the yard, spreading mulch and cleaning out the gutters and shit. I can't say for sure that at some point she brought us out a couple of cold glasses of old-fashioned homemade lemonade, but it was definitely that kind of scene.

After a little while we noticed some guy sitting on the porch, watching us. We figured it was the lady's husband. I looked over and nodded. He gave us a little wave and kind of . . . gurgled.

"Dude," I said to Kalpesh. "I think he's retarded."

He kept watching us as we worked. So much that it started giving me the heebie-jeebies. No matter where we were in the yard, he'd be sitting on a nearby porch or set of steps, just staring. I couldn't really tell, but it seemed like he might even be muttering to himself.

Kalpesh and I were up in this tree, ripping Spanish moss off the branches as per the lady's request, when she came outside to see how we were doing. She was standing under us giving us some directions when the guy on the porch made a weird noise, halfway between a laugh and a croak. Reflexively, I glanced over.

"Oh, don't you all mind Henry," she said. "He's a little slow, but he doesn't mean anyone any harm." Then she went back inside.

"Henry . . . Henry . . . Hmmm." For some reason this kind of bounced around in my mind. Then, slowly, a sick realization began to bloom . . . I looked over, and the guy gave me a big, toothless leer. For the first time I noticed one of his eyes was all fucked up and weepy, dripping some kind of macabre goo.

"Fuck!" I whispered to Kalpesh. "It's Chef Henry!"

"Whuh?" he said, looking over. "Chef Henry?"

Then it hit him. His eyes got very big.

"Oh! Oh! Chef Henry!" he whispered. "Shit! What do we do?!"

"We gotta get out of here!" I said. "Fuck!" We were seriously in a panic.

So we split. Didn't wait around to get paid or tell the lady or nuthin'. Just bailed. Jumped out of the tree, hauled ass to the Wildcat and tore out of there as fast as we could go. It just wasn't worth it. Shit, we were just relieved that we didn't get any of that creamy icing on us. Brrrr.

So, ummm . . . A close call.

FUCK TOUGH LOVE

1986

Apparently, my mother and grandmother didn't get along. I saw plenty of evidence of this while growing up, as anything having anything to do with Grandma elicited expressions that ranged between exasperation and hostility from Mom. I didn't place too much stock in it, as sunshine and flowers elicited pretty much the same deal, and Grandma, somewhat notoriously, happily embraced her own essential crabbiness as well.

But after Grandma died, I found out that she was pretty harsh with Mom when Mom was a child. Harsher than she was with Mom's sisters. As Mom grew into her teens, the fights they had increased in intensity, making everyone else in the family thoroughly miserable.

When I was old enough for my beloved aunts to be frank with me about dark ookie family stuff, hearing about the turbulence between Mom and Grandma didn't really surprise me, aside from one detail: when Mom flew the coop and split for college, Grandma was so distraught she couldn't get out of bed for weeks. She was crushed. Yet they hated each other and fought nonstop. It's like . . . Uhh . . . What do you call it . . . What's the word for that? Oh, yes—*crazy.*

Mom, despite frequently stated proclamations to the contrary, grew up to be just like Grandma in a lot of ways. As my sister and I got older, a disturbing kind of sadism manifested itself in Mom. Okay, well, maybe it wasn't sadism, per se, but it sometimes felt like it. Panic was a daily occurrence for my sister and me, as we'd become frantic as Mom pulled into the driveway after work. We'd race around wringing our hands and double-checking the house. Were the chores sufficiently done? Was the carpet as clean as it should be?

Whatever, it was never enough. Invariably, Mom would enter the house with a scowl, slam the door and start yelling at us within minutes. A whole pathological drama would play itself out over the next several hours, complete with raw-throat screaming, tears, begging, punishments, declarations of explicit hatred and the occasional bout of physical violence. My sister was hardly spared but, generally, I'd get the worst of it.

Who knows why all this happened. Maybe Mom was so bitter at the state of her life at the time that she just couldn't help taking it out on us. Maybe she grew up immersed in such similar heightened emotional states that she had no perspective, and it was the only way she knew to communicate. Maybe she was cursed by the fearsome spirit of Grandma, like something out of an awesome King Diamond song. Except Grandma wasn't dead yet. Regardless, this was what my life was like for years, night after night. I really envied kids who, instead, got to watch cable TV.

Eventually I got fed up with it and requested to move in with my father and stepmother. I didn't learn until much later that my move crushed Mom, much the same as Mom going to college devastated Grandma. If I knew how much it hurt Mom at the time, it would've mystified me. I would've assumed she'd have been happy to have me out of there.

Living with my father brought about a different set of tensions. He wanted to instill in me the values he thought would serve me throughout life but, by his own admission, didn't really know how to do it, so any efforts to reach me came off heavy-handed or emotionally detached. And my poor stepmother was suddenly faced out of nowhere with raising a teenage boy. And a spectacularly creepy and weird teenage boy at that, even by teenage-boy standards.

Stifled, suffering from suburbia-induced culture shock and just as confused by the situation as everyone else, I retreated from Dad's family and spent lots of time at other kids' houses, basically vacillating between Dungeons and Dragons and mild drug use. I became increasingly disconnected. Eventually I felt so alien and confined that returning to Mom's seemed like a pretty good deal. It was psychotic there, yes, but it promised a certain freedom of self-expression that was downright appealing to an arty little goblin like myself.

I distinctly remember the thing that got me to jump back into Mom's world. It's so pathetic and absurd that as an adult, or at least a semblance of one, I can barely believe it. Dad wanted me to get a normal haircut, you see. And Mom promised that if I returned I could do whatever I liked with my hair, dye it crazy colors or whatever. That was it—that was enough to sway me.

But there was a catch: the first day I moved back in with Mom I received a list of colors I was allowed to dye my hair. While not entirely forbidden to dye it like I was at Dad's, I could only dye it colors Mom liked.

Now, all things considered, this in itself was hardly what you'd call a Draconian measure. But the lack of logic behind it bothered me. At Dad's, you could anticipate the things that would generate disapproval, all the usual disapproval-of-teenagers stuff like punk rock and smoking weed and denouncing America. With Mom, it was subject to whim. And if you violated one of those whims it'd trigger yet another hours-long screamfest, replete with generous helpings of tears and punishment. There was significantly more freedom living with bohemian Mom, but in some ways it was the freedom to run around in a minefield.

But I took a chance and moved back in. Things went downhill fast. In retrospect I'd guess Mom's deep sadness at my having left in the first place had transmuted itself to white-hot anger. Her expectations and boundaries shifted and reversed themselves at the speed of thought, seemingly designed more to provoke than instruct. The fights were more intense than ever. I felt like I had burned my bridges with Dad. I felt trapped. And I responded accordingly. My favorite was punching lamps. Sometimes they'd explode in a shower of dramatic sparks, and Mom always had like forty-nine crazy-looking ones around the living room, all kooky and old and scavenged from yard sales.

Never one to shy away from a support group—in fact, they completely defined her social life—Mom joined a group called Tough Love. Started by a man named Hitler, Tough Love teaches parents that the best way to deal with rebellious or weird kids is to do things like forbid them to have posters and take their bedroom door off its hinges. I swear, if I ever meet this Hitler guy I'm going to haul off and smack him one square in his stupid little mustache. I would've done it back then, too, but I had to make do with the lamps.

One night I got out of the shower, wrapped myself in a towel and walked into the living room, on my way to my bedroom to get dressed. I was surprised to find about twenty-five or so adults standing around, waiting for me. Whatever this was, it looked like no fun. I needed a plan! Whipping off my towel before they could surround me, I briefly hypnotized the group with a sensuous, naked dance before diving off the balcony and making my exciting escape!

Actually, they surrounded me pretty easily while I instead chose to keep the towel on and stand there slack-jawed and amazed. "We're Tough Love, and we're here to force you to bow to Hitler's evil plan," someone said. They closed in, arms outstretched and eyes shining, chanting, "Hitler! Hitler! Hitler!"

"Excuse me, but I was just heading to my bedroom to get dressed," I explained. Have you ever run across one of those no-good smart-ass kids who suddenly gets all articulate and Eddie Haskell when faced with an authority-figure showdown he knows he can't win? I totally pulled that same shit.

"Patrick, we're here tonight to show you that your mother has the support of a community, that you can't circumvent her authority over this household," someone said. I looked at the spokesman. He didn't have a Hitler-style mustache, but a different one I still didn't like. One that still reeked of petty tyranny. The mustache of an assistant manager. The Compensation Mustache.

I whipped off my towel and began to dance! No, not really. "May we continue this after I get dressed?" I said, and made a move toward my room. Two nervous guys stepped in to close the ring and block me. I noticed I was the biggest one there.

"Patrick, we're going to discuss this now. It's important for you to know that you don't call the shots here," the spokesman said. I looked around the room for Mom. She was off to the side, crying and being consoled by two women. She wouldn't make eye contact with me.

"I'm going to get dressed now," I said. I lowered my shoulder and walked through the two men barring my way. As soon as I touched them, the entire place went totally apeshit.

"Violence! Violence! He's using violence!" someone was yelling. While getting dressed, I could hear crying, screaming, requests for the police. Usually I threw myself into our little family dramas, working myself up and getting just as hysterical as everyone else, but for some reason I was very, very calm.

I finished dressing and returned to a scene that resembled the aftermath of someone kicking over an anthill . . . a stupid, pathetic anthill full of hapless drama-queen ants. The Tough Love Ring of Cowardly Might had dissolved, revealing the witless mob beneath. Faces pushed into mine, spitting and snarling. Fingers pointed and voices were raised. I was told that my mother could put me up for adoption. I was told that I should have been aborted. A crying woman screamed half-understood threats at me, calling me by the wrong name. I assumed it was the name of her son. I just stood there, waiting for everyone to exhaust themselves. At one point I caught the eye of the man who had acted as their spokesman. I like to think what I saw there was shame.

Eventually everyone left, trickling out a few at a time, spent, and leaving me and Mom alone. She had collapsed into herself, weeping and weeping. I stood in the room for a while, expressionless, before returning to my room. I lay in bed all night fully clothed and facing the wall, sleepless, wondering what was going to happen next.

The next day at school I sat in class, totally removed from everything around me. I was borderline catatonic, moving through the day as if through water. In math class, my teacher singled me out for a question, but all I could do was sit at my desk, staring. I was aware she was talking to me, but she sounded very, very far away, and responding just wasn't a priority.

Sitting next to me was the school's star basketball player, on the mend from an ankle injury. Along with the rest of the students in the class, he watched me, seeing if I would respond as the teacher called my name and waved her hand in front of my face. I just sat there, staring straight ahead. After a few minutes, the teacher gave up and returned to the front of the room to lecture. The attention of the class followed her, except for the basketball player, who continued to scrutinize me, thinking.

After a minute or two, he reached into his backpack without saying a word and pulled out a small bottle of pills. He opened the bottle, shook out six tablets and leaned over, carefully placing them on the desk in front of me, one by one. The teacher stopped her lecture, silently regarding us, and the rest of the class once again followed suit.

The pills suddenly presented themselves to me in sharp focus. I saw they were Tylenol 3, a prescription medication that includes codeine. I looked over at the basketball player. He smiled. I started swallowing the pills, one by one, and smiled back.

FUN WITH SCIENCE, PART 2

1993

Girls are different from boys. First of all, there are the boobies and the hoo-hah. Also, in my general experience, girls seem to be a lot smarter than boys, if significantly crazier. Finally, there's the whole masturbation thing.

Girls, assuming some of you actually read this crap, here's the lowdown on male masturbation: for boys, beating off is the same as taking care of any other biological function. It's no different to us than having a bowel movement or breathing. It's one more chore hardwired into our anatomy, one of the parameters that defines our gender—hell, our existence. Just something we need to do to function. Shit, as some of you may have noticed, the minute we have fifteen free minutes in our schedule and access to a locked door, we're rubbing one out. And if we're not, we're at least contemplating it.

I only point this out because girls I know occasionally find themselves dismayed upon discovering their pet boy furtively knocking off a batch by hand. Or, even worse, uncover the dreaded porno stash (the modern equivalent of which might be the uncleared Internet Explorer History folder). These things can trigger strong reactions—moral disapproval, worry that a partner's sexual needs aren't fulfilled, etc.

To these women, I say: Fret no more! Your boyfriend, son or husband is too inarticulate to say it, but the simple truth is that masturbation is not a sexual act. So relax, don't be so uptight. You wouldn't get upset or morally outraged at finding a roll of toilet paper in the bathroom, would you? Well, unless that porno is really grisly stuff (the police can help you decide—you should always take all porno you find to your local police department so they can take a look and decide if it meets community and erotic standards), just lay off. We're not crazy about tampons, you know? But we don't make a big fuss unless one ends up in our box of Wheaties or something.

Frequency, though, is another matter. Much like pooping, male masturbation is generally performed once or twice a day. You'll always find anomalies within any sample set, of course. Some dudes only whack it every few days, some four or five times a day. This is probably no surprise, but at certain times of my life (such as from puberty until, oh, about twenty minutes ago) I've tended to fall near the higher range of masturbatory frequency.

About twelve years ago, I was sitting around with a couple of girls, when one of them asked me if I was gay. Note that this was a long time before I may or may not have drunkenly tongue-kissed George Rebelo, drummer for Hot Water Music, in exchange for sexual favors from really hot punk-rock girls, a one-time act that he enjoyed waaaay more than me, I'll have you know, not that I'm at all insecure about that, or anything else, and shutthefuckupwhythehellarewestilltalkingaboutthisanyway?!

"Nope," I said. "Why do you ask?"

"Well, unlike the other guys I know, you're not always trying to sleep with me, and I never hear you comment on the tits of every slut that walks by," she said.

"That's because, unlike a lot of insecure guys, I honestly like and respect women," I said.

Which was, and is, true. Of course, what was also true was that I was working part-time, the owner of a giant stack of porno mags and living in a house where my roommates were often gone for weeks on end and, therefore, beating off about nine times a day. So on the rare days I actually made it out of the house, my sex drive was somewhat dissipated.

The question got me thinking, though. I was always kind of a loner (and by that I mean "wholly unattractive to women"), but maybe if I wasn't constantly jacking off all the damn time I'd take more of an interest in girls and relationships and that kind of shit.

Right around this time, my friends in the band Spoke were preparing for a month-long tour. At its culmination, the group was to record its first full-length album. Spoke's guitarist and singer, Jon Resh, told me he was planning on abstaining from self-pleasure for as much time as possible before recording, perhaps even through the entire tour, with the idea that it would help his voice boom forth with stored-up masculine authority.

Hmmm. Who couldn't use a little more masculine authority? And maybe I was missing out on that girlfriend stuff, too. There was only one way to tell, and that was to invoke our old friend, magic! Er, I mean science! And undertake an illuminating, educational experiment!

So I determined to last a week without playing with myself. If successful, it would be the longest I'd gone without stimulation since I discovered I had a damn ding-a-ling.

The first day or two produced no noticeable physical effects. I did notice that I had more free time than usual, especially in the mornings and at bedtime. And I had a little trouble falling asleep at night. But it wasn't like my testes swoll all up with unused man-goo or anything, and I figured I had this thing licked easy. Did someone say licked? That reminds me of a picture I have lying around here somewhere . . . Licked . . . Licked . . . Eaaasyyy . . . Lick it easy, so easy . . . Huh? Oh, sorry. Lost my train of thought.

On days three and four I started observing some distinct changes in my behavior. I took a shower and got a haircut. Primarily, though, I noticed that I was suddenly very interested in what girls had to say. I would even call them on the phone and stuff. We'd talk and talk and laugh. Just go on and on about nothing, really. Weird.

Also, occasionally I'd be struck by the nagging impression that there was something I was forgetting to do, like pay a bill or water the plants or something . . . Once I found myself trying to sort out this feeling while absentmindedly stroking an uncooked hot dog, and some teenagers laughed at me.

Days five and six were kind of a blur. My breathing was shallow and I was hopelessly distracted. I couldn't tell if my voice had more manly authority than usual, but I did sport a perpetual hard-on that I sort of had to tuck down in my jeans, making me walk kind of stiff-legged. Girls would talk to me, and I'd mutter and drool in response. I was excited by their exposed ankles, their rounded shoulders, their fingernail clippings, canes and wheelchairs. I found myself gazing wide-eyed and longing at a knothole in my fence that I had never noticed before. On day six, a slight breeze blew across the front of my pants, and I shuddered.

Day seven came, and so did I. Vivid thoughts of sex were playing endlessly in my tortured mind. I was home, knowing my presence was unfit for civilized contact. Any contact with my body was unbearably overstimulating, so I was naked, restlessly pacing while mumbling and twisting my hands into strange shapes. I was sobbing and hyperventilating. It was rough going, friends, but my commitment to science was absolute, and I was determined to see the experiment through and last until the next morning.

Still naked, I lay on the futon in my living room, and turned on the TV. I was hoping I would find something, anything to distract me. Images of supple, glistening Jell-O caressed the television screen, taunting me. I noticed that Oprah had a set of big ol' titties, and started imagining them free, bouncing unfettered in all their round, brown glory . . . It was real, so real. I could almost smell her womanly musk and . . .

"Okay," I thought. "This is seriously getting out of hand. I need to get a grip on myself—er, maybe that was a bad choice of words—and settle the fuck down." I changed the channel to something with nonsexy stuff like dudes and news and took a few deep, cleansing breaths.

"I am a man, not a base animal," I said to myself. "Yogis and monks and fakirs and shit practice self-control and rise above their urges. You don't even believe in any of that metaphysical nonsense—you're not going to let those mystical types top you, are you?"

Hell no. I hate those magical dickheads. I composed myself, reached down (hmm, bad choice of words again) and discovered an untapped well of self-control. Soon I found myself disassociated from the corporeal, almost floating on a plane that was . . . well, I had always derided the word, but it was almost *spiritual*. I lay like that, naked and priapic, yet calm, for an undetermined amount of time. I felt enlightened, empowered and strong.

Then, absentmindedly, I reached down and scratched my crotch area. My wrist brushed against my boner, and I had an orgasm I was afraid would kill me.

I'm not kidding. I saw spots, started to black out and seriously thought I might be having a massive heart attack. My entire body spasmed, each taut nerve humming and crackling with liquid electric fire. My eyes rolled up into my head. Digging my fingers into the futon mattress and gasping to catch my breath, my hips thrust forward uncontrollably again and again, while a thick stream of pearly untapped potential arced several feet over my head, landing on the floor with an audible glop. I screamed out in joy and terror while becoming one with all creation; all knowledge and life and the stars and planets whirled and hummed through each of my cells . . . I glimpsed the indescribable face of God. This lasted for only a few moments, but it seemed like hours.

The jerks and involuntary contractions racking my body finally began to ebb. My breathing became deep and regular, and I was covered in a thin sheen of warm sweat. I couldn't believe what I had just experienced—in a lifetime of adventure and mayhem, this was the most amazing thing I'd ever felt. You could rodeo-ride a nuclear-powered shark on the moon while eating a deep-fried Twinkie and getting a backrub from Molly Ringwald and it wouldn't compare to the force, the passion, the . . . the . . . majesty. No words can possibly do it justice.

I made up my mind right there—I was going to masturbate just once a week from then on out. It was just too good, too intense. I was exhilarated. New vistas of pleasure stretched before me, and for the first time in a very long time I actually looked forward to what forthcoming days would bring. I was going to change.

I beat off again a few hours later, of course. It wasn't the same. And the next morning, I whacked off first thing. I think I may have jacked off around lunchtime that day, too, and definitely sent myself riding off to dreamland on that reliable, sturdy ol' steed of hand lotion and moist tissue. Pretty much the same as I've done every day since.

ASS-KICKING YOGA FOR FIGHTS

2006

I reckon any discussion of shame in this diary is going to ring pretty false, what with me always using it to flaunt my pee-hole and such.

But while it's true that I'm not exactly wallowing in the stuff, I do feel shame. Sometimes. Of a sort. Etc. Even though my good friend Anatol Blass, a bona fide smarty-pants if there ever was one, once told me, "Shame just gets in the way of a good time." Or maybe he said self-esteem? You get the picture. Anyway, Anatol has a real-life Ph.D. in physics and somehow landed a wife who is so far out of his league in the hotness department that people stop on the street, point and stare when they walk by, so you should listen to him and not sweat that shame business.

Of course, Anatol did light his penis on fire during a high-spirited moment gone slightly awry at Caryn and Sean's wedding and had to douse it with toilet water to avoid injury . . . I really need to tell that story sometime. But, for now at least, I feel like it's important that you just be made aware of this event when considering Anatol's advice. Seek balance in everything.

Wait a minute, what did I just say? "Seek balance in everything?" Where the hell did that come from?! Is that one of those goddamn *Free to Be You and Me* songs? No . . . Wait. I know where it came from. Fuck, this is exactly the sort of thing I was worried about.

See, I was feeling a little shame yesterday, skulking around with an armload of VHS cassettes like a dungeon master trying to sneak a batch of Sybil Danning movies past Mommy. But it wasn't low-grade soft-porn I was hiding—no, my collection of that enjoys a prominent display in my house, on the shelf right next to Godzilla humping Barbie and . . . What? No, not there, around the corner past the meth lab. Yes, there. No, you can't borrow them. And those are action figures, not "dolls," thankyou-verymuch.

Anyway, my shame was born of yoga.

Look, I don't want to hear it. Flexibility, of which I have exactly none, is a key part of effective kickboxing. Yeah, that's right, smart-ass—I said kickboxing. So if you don't want me to yoga my shin up your ass, you'll clam up, and pronto.

To tell the truth, I've been intrigued by yoga for a while now. When I was younger, it seemed like yoga advocates were all either doughy hippies who smelled like patchouli, or wiry but impenetrably foreign guys who smelled like turmeric. There was this one beardy dude who always did yoga in this one open courtyard at the university, and he seemed like he was in good shape, but he also lived in a field and never wore a damn shirt, and one time he was doing some kind of complicated upside-down thing and I looked over and one of his nuts had flopped out of his jean shorts, right there in front of God and everybody. Ugh.

Nowadays I know a couple of broads who teach yoga and do that shit all the time, and you know what? They're hot. So hot that I don't even care that they're total hippies who smoke weed and everything. I'm telling you—hot. If their nuts flopped out you'd totally look, I just know it. They're all lean and muscley, but in a cool, flexible way, and let me tell you, if there are four words nobody's using to describe me, they're *lean, muscley, flexible* and *cool*. So I figured I could use a little of that action.

I got me that *Yoga For Dummies* off Netflix and also hoofed it over to my beloved downtown library, where I navigated through the bums, poked through the VHS tapes and skittishly darted over to the fishing videos every time I heard someone approaching.

I thought about going to a class or something to learn that shit but was a little worried about making my hippie debut in public. Also, I wasn't sure what the boner etiquette was for yoga class, and chances are I'd be sporting one of those before long, and I kind of didn't want to, you know, call up and ask.

There is a place down the street from me called—not making this up, cousin—Big Ron's Yoga College, which is a fucking awesome name for a yoga place and very reassuring to a guy like me, who's a little wary of all those places named shit like Meadow Leaf's Incense Grotto of Ayurvedic Serenity and the All-Seeing White Light Temple of Scientology Indoctrination. The hippie joints might be chock-full of hot babes like my friends, or I might even end up in one of their classes. And boner or not, you just know that shit is going to eventually get me into some kind of trouble. Chances are, though, watching someone named Big Ron bend over isn't going to give you a hard-on. But I bet if it did he'd be really cool and understanding and non-judgmental about it. Maybe you'd go out with Big Ron after class and get a pitcher and some wings and talk about it, have a few laughs and then be friends forever.

The deal-breaker for Big Ron, though, was the fact that he costs money, and the library tapes are free. Browsing through the selection there just reinforced my impression that I'm a statistical outlier in the world of yoga demographics. Everything was either insufferably cosmic (serene photos on the cover, vaguely Sanskrit-looking font, lots of earth tones) or hosted by Kathie Lee and intended for the elderly (day-glo and cheery, like David Lee Roth's pants or a 1985 Trapper Keeper folder after chugging half a two-liter of Jolt). I chose a few from some series called *Power Yoga* because, well, they had *power* in the title, and that was the closest any of 'em came to *fighting* or *ass-kicking*. Hey! If there are any yoga creeps reading this, you should cobble together a tape called *Ass-Kicking Yoga for Fights*. There's definitely some untapped market potential there, at least around my house.

I ran by the gym on the way home and did some leg-presses and a few sets of squats, hoping none of the gym dudes could detect the yoga taint, and then went home and threw in *Yoga For Dummies*. It started out demonstrating some basic stuff. I followed along and did it, and noticed that it really stretched your shit out and definitely took a lot of effort to do 'em right, and mostly didn't seem quite as, um, made-up as all that other hippie stuff, like astrology and peace and wheat grass.

I did, however, skip the somewhat traumatic cat pose. (Way back on prom night I swore I'd never find myself in that position again.) But it all went pretty well. For the most part, the chick demonstrating everything skipped preposterous claims, and though I found her kind of patronizing in tone I relaxed after remembering that it was, after all, designed for use by dummies.

I finished that, and a-flush with enthusiasm decided to fire up some *Power Yoga* and really get down. The tape began and some mostly naked Asian dude named Rodney gazed out of the TV, radiating so much peacefulness and mystical insight at me that I started getting a tan. Somehow, I suddenly found myself even more embarrassed than I was at the library, where I hid my tapes behind the biggest book with guns on the cover that I could find in case someone I knew saw me. I got up and closed the curtains, and I don't even bother to do that when I'm watching porno.

Soon Rodney, who if you ask me could've used a little more loin coverage in the fabric department, was sitting next to a rock and a cactus or two and going on about listening to the wisdom of the universe and letting go of childhood trauma in a way that projected just a little too much personal intimacy for me. A minute or two later, Rodney got started, stretching his man-parts up into the camera and I shut him off, just cutting my losses before I got too into it and had to drastically rethink my lifestyle. I kind of wanted to hang onto my beloved childhood traumas, too. And not necessarily add any new ones, at least any that involved watching a magical naked Asian dude on my TV.

Today, despite the *Power Yoga* leaving me feeling a little queasy, I got up and did my poses. I even paid attention to my breathing. It was alright, too. I think I'm going to keep it up. Though I might have to start just calling them "stretches."

Oh, and you know what? Last night I said fuck it and ate some tabbouleh for supper, too. Had a little yogurt, of all things, for dessert. *Namaste,* bitch.

KEEP PARTYING

1995

Some people found it disconcerting, Frog's trick. He did it when I first met him—pulled out his top row of teeth and grinned this huge grin, squinting, tilting his head back a bit and letting a leash of thick, clear drool sag between his hand and his mouth.

I could understand why some found it off-putting. It was a strange kind of intimacy, being suddenly faced with all those shiny pink gums. I mean, it wasn't like were you were suddenly looking up his butthole or anything but, dentists aside, how often do you get confronted with a view like that? It was downright biological.

I thought it was kind of endearing. Maybe a little more on the gooey side than I usually prefer my tricks to be, but whatever. Turned out his original set of chompers had been knocked out in an unfortunate golfing accident, just in case you were curious.

Eventually, Frog had some permanent teeth put in. I didn't blame him. It had hit the point where people weren't shocked by it anymore. Hell, they expected it. They would run up to Frog and ask him to whip 'em out. Leeched some of the fun out of it for him, I could tell. It was in danger of becoming routine. Plus, having teeth that were actually anchored to his mouth in some fashion probably made it a lot easier to eat.

This was back in the '80s. I've known Frog for going on about twenty years now. During that time, I've heard a lot of peculiar stuff about him. For example, an ex-girlfriend of mine once told me about how he had decorated a room with pictures of . . . of . . . Shit, what was it? I can't remember exactly, but I think it was either dirty shots of lactating women or dirty shots of ejaculating women. And—I might be getting this wrong, I admit—he was allegedly going around the room and whackin' off on, like, every spot in it. Just methodically shellacking the joint in his DNA over the course of a few months.

Jesus, now that I've typed that out, I'm sitting here thinking, "There's no way. That can't be right." But I seem to recall her saying something about the smell. Oh god, the smell. Can you imagine? I can't be remembering this right. That's about the damnedest thing I ever heard.

Well, whatever. I reckon this illustrates an important point regarding Frog: just like the night I got food poisoning with Dan Aykroyd, you can't take shit for granted with that guy.

Uh, I mean Frog, not Dan Aykroyd. All I know about Dan Aykroyd is that he smokes a little weed now and then. Hmm, can I get in trouble for saying that? Okay, he *allegedly* smokes a little weed now and then.

About ten years ago I lived upstairs from Frog for a few months. He was a good neighbor, friendly and considerate. Every so often he'd rope you into some scheme, like when he recorded me hollering random holiday stuff for some kind of avant-garde Christmas tape he was making. I want to say I helped him put a bunch of dirt on his kitchen floor too, but, to be honest, I could just be making that up. I swear at one point he had like six inches of dirt packed down in the kitchen, though. Anyway, even with those types of hijinx going on, he was surprisingly quiet. Mostly.

During the time I lived above Frog, my buddy Woogie and I had a little record store, right around the corner from my apartment. Basically, Woogie (who, unlike me, had marketable skills, responsibility and a steady income) threw a chunk of dough my way to open the place, and for a few years my life turned into *High Fidelity*. Almost exactly.

Seriously. The first time I saw the book, I read the shit on the back, screamed in horror and flung it across the room. It summed up my life accurately enough to give me a grim, week-long case of the heebie-jeebies. You know, if you watch the movie, the only difference between it and about six years of my life is that I was the obnoxious Jack Black guy, the mousy little weiner dude and the loserish John Cusack cad all rolled up into one. One big, not-very-appealing *High Fidelity*–ass package.

The store, which was called Shaft in tribute to the excellent film (there was already a pet-food shop in town named Citizen Kane, thanks for asking), shared a large, cluttered space with a used bookstore run by my pal Bob. He was a sweet, sort of nervous guy who preferred hiding behind stacks of unsorted books with bottles of whisky to actually selling anything. I, of course, was inclined toward bellowing, smashing things and challenging large skinheads to wrestling matches, and so often drove poor Bob into eye-crossing bouts of consternation. But we both liked Joy Division and The Cure a lot, and he didn't mind a little free jazz, so we struck a balance.

One thing Bob and I shared was a dedicated clientele. This was nice, and unexpected, considering our combined business acumen wouldn't have clogged a gnat's butthole. But we had the goods. There were plenty of shiny, organized places in town to go if you wanted a paperback bestseller or CD of whatever was on the radio, but Bob and I sold the serious shit, the shit you can't get just anywhere. And while staff members at the shiny places were certainly better groomed than us, if not significantly more emotionally stable, they didn't know or care a damn thing about what they sold. Me and Bob, we knew our shit. Hell, it was all we knew, but we knew it.

So when we'd have bands play in the store or have an art show or something, we'd always get a big turnout. The biggest crowd we ever had numbered in the hundreds. We had teamed up with a well-known local artist named Celino, who builds awesome lamps and sculptures out of all kinds of crazy junk. Yeah, Celino knew how to pack 'em in—gallons of booze.

The storefront looked out on University Avenue, which is what passes for a main drag here in Gainesville. We had big windows, and even with all the people crammed in, we couldn't help but notice when traffic started to back up the night of Celino's show. Gainesville's pretty goddamn sleepy, so this was unusual.

A quick investigation showed police had blocked off the road at the corner, maybe twenty feet down from our door, and traffic was slowly being diverted down a side street. "Huh, what's that all about," we wondered. "Perhaps another glass of wine will help us sort it out."

We had cut off the main lights to better display Celino's lamps, which mixed with the flashing lights from the police cars and fire trucks, lending the affair a nice ambience. Kind of a gritty authenticity, really. Anyway, it wasn't too long before a handful of cops and a fireman or two popped in, standing in the doorway looking confused in the dim light as they scanned the crowd. I pushed my way over.

"Can I help you guys?" I asked, shouting over the noise.

"Yeah. Do you have a bathroom we can use?" one said.

"Sure. Hey, uhhh . . . If you don't mind me asking, what's going on out there?"

"Ah, we got a bomb or something in this lady's car. Which way is the bathroom?"

"A bomb? Shit, do we need to clear out?"

"Nah, y'all are good. Keep partying." The cop grinned.

I was a little taken aback. Bombs always seemed kind of serious to me, even when I was the one manufacturing and detonating them. And, frankly, I never know what to do on those rare occasions when police are nice to me. I always feel like I'm getting set up, like any minute they're going to yell "Gotcha!" and shoot me. But there he was with his cop buddies, grinning and waiting to pee just as friendly as you please.

"Ladies and gentlemen!" I announced, leading the officials through the crowd to our tiny bathroom. "There is a bomb, but the officials are just here to pee! We are instructed to keep partying!" A small cheer went up.

And so people kept drinking and yapping, music was played. Every so often a friendly officer or fireman would come in to use the bathroom and maybe sneak a drink. It was all very exciting.

At one point I grabbed a passing cop. "Hey, what's up with that bomb?"

"They just brought out a machine that's gonna shake the car to try and set it off," he said.

Man, that seemed like a really bad idea to me. But who was I? No expert. Bombs were never more than a hobby for me, so I said fuck it and had another drink. Leave that shit to the professionals—if they want to go around shaking bombs, let 'em. They know what they're doing.

Word started spreading through the crowd about the whole bomb-shaking thing happening down the street. Ripples of concern made their way around the room, but a fireman had suggested it'd be best if we stayed put while they did this, so nobody left. A lot of people couldn't really get to their cars anyway, and traffic looked like it was backed up for miles while they continued to send people down the side street. There wasn't much else to do except keep drinking and looking at art or whatever.

Now, the scene was a bit chaotic, so I'm not really sure exactly when the firemen threw open the door and started screaming. "Out! Out! Everybody out! Evacuate! Evacuate the building! Now! NOW!"

Sensibly, everyone started to panic. There was a drunken crush near the front as people made for the door. Toward the back, where I was stuck, rumor was the firemen had found a bomb in the building. I got a little antsy. Somehow in the melee I found Bob, who had a trickle of blood running down from his forehead. He was good and well drunk.

"Bob! Are you okay?"

"I hit my head," he slurred

"What the fuck! Are we fixin' to get blown up?"

"No, no. They found a gas leak in the restaurant next door. The building is filling with gas."

Fuck, bombs and gas. Everything was going apeshit.

This was the best art show ever.

Somehow we managed to get everybody outside. Hundreds of people spilled out around the building, trying to get to their cars, while dozens of cops and firemen stood around with megaphones, issuing directives and urging everyone to get out of the area as fast as they could. We secured the shop, and I walked to my apartment, which wasn't even a block away.

Once home, I cracked open a beer with my friend Jill, yet another stunningly beautiful girl I hung around who never let me see her without any clothes on, and we watched all the action from my upstairs porch. It was nuts—lights, sirens, cops yelling, people running through bushes and down streets, horns honking. Just total mayhem.

I thought it couldn't get any better until the voice started booming forth, drowning out everything else.

"PEOPLE OF EARTH-RTH-RTH! YOUR DEMISE IS UPON YOU-OU-OU! THE APOCALYPSE HAS ARRIVED-IVED-IVED!"

Holy shit, it was loud. And it was coming from downstairs.

"THIS IS YOUR FINAL JUDGMENT! THE END OF DAYS-AYS-AYS! THE END OF EVERYTHING-ING-ING! YOU ARE ALL GOING TO DIE! DIE! DIEEEEEEERRRRAAAAARRRRRRGGGHHHH!!!!!"

A good couple hundred people were still straggling out from the art show, and they started scrambling, frantic. People stuck in traffic were just leaning on their horns. Jill and I looked at each other. "It's Frog," she said.

"PEOPLE OF EARTH-RTH-RTH! SMELL YOUR FINAL DOOM-OOM-OOM! EMBRACE THE VOID-OID-OID! THIS IS THE APOCALYPSE HEEEEEYAAAAARRRRRGGHH!"

Goddamn, he wasn't just broadcasting that crazy shit. He had put some feedback and delay effects on it, too.

"I AM YOUR GOD BLLLEEEEEEEEYAAAAAARRRRGHH! SCRE-EEEE! SCREEEE! SHEEEEEHAAAAAHHHH! GRRRRRRAAAAAAW-WWWLLLL!!!"

Fuck, now he was just screeching and growling wordlessly. It was echoing off all the buildings in the neighborhood, as loud as anything you ever heard. I could see police running up and down the streets, waving flashlights and barking into walkie-talkies. "You better go stop him," Jill said.

I ran downstairs, right into a squad of five or six wild-eyed, confused cops. "What the fuck are you doing?!" one yelled.

"It's not me! It's not me!" I yelled, "It's Frog!"

I jumped the backyard fence before they could grab me, and ran around back there for a minute or two in the dark, completely discombobulated, screaming for Frog and bumping into all manner of sculptures and obstacles. Frog continued his amplified gibbering: "GROO HOO HAH HA! SKWEEEEYAAAAAAARRRRGH! KKKKKKSSSSSHHH!!!" There was no way he could hear me.

Eventually I found the giant amplifier Frog had set up, towering over me like the obelisk in *2001*. Shit was burly. All that malignant electro-powered glossolalia was forming a physical barrier, but I leaned into it like you would a strong wind, eventually forcing my way forward and getting my hands around a power cord. Breathless, I yanked it from its socket. The noise stopped.

My ears were ringing, but I could hear Frog, who was standing in a nearby window, and barely make out his silhouette.

"Hey Pat," he said, "Why'd you do that?"

"Dude, the cops are here," I whispered. "You better hide."

"Oh," was all he said. He stepped back from the window, disappearing inside.

I came back around to the side of the house, where Jill was standing on the stairs, talking to the one police officer who was still there. He was pounding on Frog's door and shouting. Walking up, I waved to get his attention.

"Sir! Sir! I couldn't find him," I lied, "But I did manage to shut it off. I don't even know if he's in there."

He banged on the door a few more times.

"What do you mean, 'not in there?'" he said.

"Maybe he had a tape or something set up? To be honest, I just don't know."

He gave the door a few more half-hearted knocks, then looked at Jill, who shrugged. He looked over at me, staring me right in the eye. He didn't seem as angry as he did genuinely confused. I shrugged too.

"Why? Why would anybody do that?" he asked.

I thought about it for a second or two before answering. Meeting his gaze, I decided to go with the truth.

"He's an artist," I said.

He looked at me for a few moments, then nodded his head. He glanced at the door a last time and took a deep breath. Then, slowly exhaling, he walked off into the night.

Later, we were disappointed to find out there was no bomb. Some lady's dying car battery was making a clicking noise, and she called the cops.

MY ASS IS THE WORST PLACE ON EARTH

2005

So a couple of months ago I squirted some blood out of my ass.

Unlike most of the blood that drips or sprays out of the various parts of my abused or perhaps just fragile body, this particular emission sent me on an exciting, magical adventure, one in which I ventured far and wide to seek the counsel of wise sages while navigating the tricky, treacherous mazes of the dread behemoth spoken of in whispers and curses as "the HMO."

I have emerged from this odyssey a changed man. I have gazed upon things not many see, and with good reason, because these things are really kind of gross. And I now know things about myself, things borne of intimacy and insight so brutal they'd give the most intrepid, navel-gazing Tibetan monk pause . . . Self-knowledge so fiercely honest it'd positively cauterize the gray matter of a lesser man, reducing him to a bespectacled goofball trapped in endless adolescence, one pimping out half-assed, embarrassing stories and mocking his family on the Internet in order to get the positive reinforcement denied him in his dead-end career or train-wreck social life . . . Yes, the things I've experienced would take a normal human and reduce him to a bald, self-loathing creep who hunches over a sticky keyboard, typing foul-mouthed inanities into the void while real life continues just outside the crumbling shards of his . . . Wait, what?

You know, it wasn't even that much blood. Maybe a tablespoon's worth. Shoot, I've lost more than that during haircuts or vigorous nose-picking. But you have to go get shit like ass blood checked out. I mean, a variety of mundane things such as hemorrhoids or small elves can make blood come out of your ass. But sometimes ass blood is a symptom of something serious, like cancer, or large elves.

So I called the doctor. I'm not a big fan of going to the doctor. I'd much rather conflate any symptoms I have into something potentially fatal, so I can walk around grumbling and hating everything and putting off paying bills and imagining all the awesome things I'm going to do to my enemies the day before I finally kick the bucket. But ass blood . . . You can't really conflate ass blood.

Now, usually it takes a few weeks to see the doctor. At least. I reckon they want that cough or twinge to really work itself up into something good, something expensive and chronic and debilitating, before you go bothering them. I know if I was a doctor I'd get pretty pissed every time Grandma Dustpussy hobbled in with some phantom complaint like a broken hip, just because there was a mix-up with Social Security and her cable got cut off and she can't talk to the TV during *Matlock* and needs a little attention with her stupid hip, a boo hoo hoo. No, Granny better get, like, tuberculosis in her eyes or spine worms or something awesome before she goes stinking up my waiting room. And, oh shit—if I was a doctor I'd totally be up to something nefarious, too, like making a Frankenstein in the back room or inventing a ray that gives you the plague. So I totally understand the delay, and don't begrudge those guys anything.

But it turns out that when you have ass blood it kind of moves you to the head of the line. At first, I was like, "Shit, only two days? That's awesome." But then I started thinking, "Man, they wouldn't rush you in there if they didn't think you were gonna, you know . . . die."

I mulled that shit over for a bit, and then did the only sensible thing: look up ass blood on the Internet.

Most of the time, punching any sort of symptom into Google is fuel for an instant, brain-shattering panic attack. This time, though, it was actually a little reassuring. Like I said, just about everything can give you ass blood. I had no idea. Sure, my psoriasis sometimes causes a little streak or two to show up on a sheet of buttwipe, but I swear . . . Just sneeze more than four times in a row or eat a big glob of peanuts or something and wait and see if your ass doesn't barf up a little hemoglobin in response.

Still, the few serious things that'll give you ass blood tend to be really, really, really serious, so I did manage to work myself up a bit, just out of habit as much as anything. But my Internet investigations seemed to point at something called an anal fissure as the cause. Not serious. Just . . . delightful!

A few days later I stroll into the doc's. I'm not really insane or anything, because I'm fairly sure my ass is okay, but I am a little on edge. Partially because there's always the chance I have something terrible lurking up my pooper, or I reckon I should say something more terrible than usual, which is pretty damn terrible. But also because I know what's going to happen to me in there: a man is going to put his finger in my butt. A man who doesn't even love me.

I'm keeping my composure, though. My butthole is scrubbed nice and clean, so as to make the experience pleasant for at least one of us.

But there's a problem. My employer has switched from something called a PPO to something called an HMO, and I discover up at the check-in that my doctor apparently doesn't play nice with the HMO.

"Mr. Hughes, I'm sorry, but you're no longer our patient," says the nice lady at the counter.

I stand there for a few seconds, stunned and not sure what to do. There doesn't really seem to be anything I can do, at least there at the little doctor window, so I shrug and head back out to my truck. But I can feel my anxiety and anger rising—I mean, I have ass blood. I need to get that shit checked out. They move you up to the front of the line for ass blood.

"Who?" I think, sitting in my truck. "Where? Where can I get a man to finger my ass? Why does it have to be so . . . damn . . . hard . . . to simply get a goddamn man to finger me up in my ass?"

Fuming, I head back to the office and start asking fellow employees for recommendations and manning the phone. Seems like most of the doctors in the fucking HMO aren't taking new patients. And you can't go directly to an ass specialist—the dickhole HMO makes you get routed through some family doctor or whatever. After a few calls, I'm frankly starting to freak out. I can feel the giant elves in my ass dancing around with glee and mining gallons of my precious ass blood, knowing the stupid HMO has bought them a reprieve.

I take out my insurance card and contemplate using it to just get it all over with and sever my damn jugular vein right there at my desk, and notice I already have a family doctor. His last name is the same as my original doctor—looks like some genius over there at HMO central just swapped the dude out when they noticed my original physician didn't want shit to do with the HMO. I'm impressed with the simplicity of such a move—someday, when I become a faceless, paper-pushing cocksucker, safely insulated from culpability by several thick layers of beige bureaucracy, I hope to employ the same uncomplicated grace in resolving any conflicts I may come across. Anyway, I fight off a bout of facial tics and decide to ring up this new doctor and see if they'll finger my ass for me, or what.

Turns out they will see me and on that very same day! Ass blood can really open doors.

A few hours later, I'm in another office, filling out form after form and staggering under the deluge of pamphlets informing me that federal HIPAA regulations insure that no pictures of the inside of my ass nor accounts of me getting all ass-fingered will turn up on the Internet, plus if I die they're just going to chuck me in the back dumpster and not tell my family, and everyone who's going to be fingering my ass that day will be wearing a blindfold, which come to think of it is probably just as much for their protection as mine, morning scrub or not.

A nurse takes my blood pressure.

"Whoa," she says.

I'm a little concerned. "What?"

"Let's try this again," she says. "Hmmm . . . Wow."

Now I'm really concerned. "What?!"

"Shit, dude, how are you even alive?" she says. Apparently, my blood pressure is like 160 over 110.

She goes to fetch the doctor while I wonder if this is somehow related to my ass blood. Maybe it's the cause? Like, my pressure is so high that I'm just going to occasionally shoot a little out of my ass, so I don't blow an eyeball gasket or something?

Six hours later the doc comes in and takes my blood pressure again. It's a little lower, 150 over 100. Apparently this isn't good.

"When's the last time you had a checkup, Patrick?" he says.

"Man, I don't know . . . I had my appendix out last summer. I reckon they had a pretty good look around then," I say. "Am I just falling to pieces here?"

He fixes me with a blank look. "I don't know," he says. That's reassuring. "Let's schedule you for a physical next Tuesday. Now, what's the problem today?"

"Well, doc, I got ass blood," I say. "I need you to check it out, finger me in the ass or whatever. I scrubbed it, but frankly I don't envy you much. Oh, I'm pretty sure it's a fissure. I had a strangely big poop last week and felt a tearing sensation, right about at six o'clock."

He gets all perky when I mention the location.

"Why, that's the classic location! Six o'clock and twelve o'clock. Yes sir!"

Mustache bristling with excitement, he starts sketching out a little diagram for me, one reminiscent of a mushed spider.

He points to the six and says, "Yup, you'll see the fissure about here, and of course the taint and scrotum are right below it, down here, and . . . "

"Whoa, whoa, whoa, doc," I say. "My taint and scrotum are up at twelve o'clock." Doesn't this guy know his anatomy?

We look at his drawing for a minute or two and try to sort it out before it hits him.

"Oh, here's the problem. we're just turned around a bit. I'm usually looking at it from the opposite side, you see," he says.

Oh . . . Ah yes. That reminds me.

He takes my hand and gives it a reassuring squeeze. "I think it's time," he says, gazing into my eyes. I sigh and nod.

I drop my trousers and underpants, put my hands on his table, bend over and stare straight ahead. My eyes are only inches from his office wall, but all I see are faraway clouds and blue, blue sky.

"Oh yeah . . . I see it," he says. His voice echoes, distant. "Yup . . . Oh, it's a classic, right where you said it was. It even has a little lip on it . . . Right . . . THERE."

And he pokes me. Fucking pokes me, right in my fucking fissure. Hard.

It hurt.

"Alright, ramrod, you found the damn thing," I say. "There's no need to see how deep our love goes."

Sheepishly, he removes his finger with an audible pop. I pull my pants on and glare at him for a few seconds. After a deep, soulful tongue kiss, I gather up my battered shreds of dignity and head out.

"I'll . . . I'll . . . I'll see you Tuesday," he says. "I'll be thinking about you."

Yeah yeah, that's what they all say, I think.

Meanwhile, I have several days until Tuesday, time which I can use to further explore the various ailments and conditions related to the ass and ass blood. I'm relieved that my fissure was so quickly and easily identifiable, but can't shake the feeling something abnormal is brewing down in my shitter, something even more foul and unusual than the time I drank an entire bottle of Evan Williams and ate an entire bag of Oreos and shit a daunting volume of black, dusty pudding that filled the toilet to its rim.

You see, along with ass blood, one of the symptoms for colon cancer is narrow bowel movements, and I have those. At least sometimes. Frankly, I'm not much for examining the diameter of my poo, so I'm not sure. And it's not like I have a baseline to measure turds against or anything.

Fuck it, I thought. I'll just bring it up to the doctor during my physical. I've had a few friends who recently had colonoscopies and stuff done, even a few who've had surgery for growths and treatment for tumors and stuff. You never know.

I watch my poops closely for the next few days, though, and sure enough, a few of them come out long and flat, like someone jammed that damn Playdoh toy up my ass.

Tuesday rolls around and my new doctor sleepwalks through my physical. At least my blood pressure is normal—they figure all that nonsense from before was just me freaking out about my ass and the HMO and stuff.

"There is one thing I need to ask you about, doc. I read that narrow bowel movements can sometimes mean something serious, and I've been having pretty damn narrow movements."

He looks up, uninterested. "You have a fissure. I saw it," he says.

Yeah, and you poked it really hard too, I think, glowering. "Well, I'm worried about it."

"Frankly, if you have anything in your colon big enough to narrow your bowel movements, you'll probably show some signs of anemia, and we'll see that in your blood tests," he says, sighing. "But if it'll make you feel better, we'll send you home with a fecal blood test."

Oh yeah, nothing will make me feel better than smearing my own filth on a card for three days and sending it through the mail and . . . Actually, you know, the mail thing is kind of appealing.

Doc Pokey wraps up his cursory physical, and I head back to the office feeling like he kind of rushed me out of there. Guess I'm not that interesting when I'm not putting out, hmph.

I spend the next week obsessively watching my poops for variation in width and asking everybody I see, "Do I look anemic?"

But my blood tests and all come back alright. Still, those narrow poops are giving me the creeps. I feel a deep but fleeting sense of relief on days when I take a normal poop, and days when I take a big poop are cause for celebration. Unfortunately, the narrow poops persist.

I wait a few weeks until that damn fissure heals and start doing the test. Figures, though—I pop another ass seam a day into it, not like the last one, but enough to get a little blood on the toilet paper. That test is supposedly super sensitive and can detect, like, a molecule of ass blood, so it's all queered up now.

I fret over my situation for a week or so. It seems like every time I turn on the TV, there's some shit on the news like, "He seemed to be in perfect health, but a pernicious and hidden ass cancer took his life at the young age of thirty-six," or a commercial for the Florida Ass Cancer Treatment Hut, where state-of-the-art medical technology can extend your painful, miserable life for three months, or that one Coldplay video that goes, "You're gonna die, yeah yeah, from ass cancer, shoulda got that ass blood checked out and now you're gonna croak, yeah yeah, or maybe shit in a bag for the rest of your life, whoa whoa."

Finally, I call my doctor's office and request to see a specialist. I get put on hold, explain the situation with the fecal smear thingy to four or five people and eventually leave a message on someone's voice mail. A week goes by, and nothing. I do it again. Another week, and I get a message that they've set something up for me, in about a month.

So after a month of staring at my poop every morning and gobbling fiber pills like Wilford Brimley I go to the ass specialist. Everybody in the waiting room is a thousand years old, and they all stare at me, no doubt thinking, "He seems to be in perfect health, but a pernicious and hidden ass cancer will take his life at the young age of thirty-six, how sad. Not even the Florida Ass Cancer Treatment Hut will be able to help, I can tell just from looking."

The specialist is a pleasant Indian man who chats with me about my paltry excuse for a career for a few minutes. He's just pretending to be interested so I'll be distracted and he can slip me the ass finger, I think. But no—will wonders never cease, I am spared the fissure poke of doom this day.

"I'm fairly certain that there's nothing serious going on with you, Mr. Hughes, but we'll schedule a colonoscopy, just for peace of mind," he says.

Peace of mind . . . Peace of mind . . . That sounds nice. I wonder what that's like?

I fill out a billion forms, and they schedule my procedure for a month later. They also give me pages of preparations I have to follow before they Roto-Rooter that camera up there: food I need to avoid and pills I need to eat and there's something called phosphate soda I need to drink.

Ah, phosphate soda. Yes, after another month of obsessive poop-gazing, the week of my procedure rolls around, and I start my low-residue diet. This isn't too bad—I switch from whole-grain bread to cheap white bread and eat peanut butter sandwiches all day long, plus boil up the occasional plate of spaghetti, dressed only with plenty of butter. Considering how strict my diet is most of the time (not that you could tell by looking at me), this part of the prep is actually kind of fun. Not so much the restriction to clear liquids the day before the "journey to the center of the earth," and certainly not that goddamn foul-ass phosphate soda. Man, that shit is rank. Imagine if seawater could go spoiled and you'll be in the ballpark.

On the label for that diabolical phosphate soda stuff it says "bowel cleanser," and there's some truth to that, I tell you what. You start shitting about ten minutes after you chug that stuff, and you don't stop. I was rumbling and gurgling and spewing and running to the goddamn toilet all fucking day long until nothing but a thin yellow foam sprayed out of my ass.

The next day I hobbled over to the Ass Center so I could get violated and inspected some more. I filled out four billion forms, got a blood test, the usual. They threw me on a gurney and wheeled me into a tiny little room where the ass-specialist and a few of his minions were waiting. The camera things they snake up your ass were hanging on a rack, and were pretty cool looking, all black and techno with numbers marking off every foot so they can place bets on how deep your ass goes and laugh at you and stuff.

I asked if I was going to get a copy of the video in this dealie, thinking it'd be a hit at Christmas, and they didn't even answer, just sneered and zapped me unconscious with a Taser and went to work.

I woke up all woozy from the roofies some point later. A nurse was watching over me.

"So what's the deal?" I asked.

"Well, your symptoms are the result of hemorrhoids, Mr. Hughes. And there's nothing serious. But they did find and remove a polyp."

Those camera snakes apparently have nail clippers or something on the ends and they can just snip that shit right out of there while they're tooling and rooting around in your pooper. Cool, huh?

I wasn't too upset by the revelation that there was in fact a little something extra a-growing up in my colon, because I knew from my Internet research that polyps were common and not too much to worry about. The nurse started explaining what they were going to do with my little ass nubbin and such, and pulled out a report. I caught a glimpse of my polyp on one of the pages.

"OOOOH!!! OOOOH!!! Can I get a copy of that?!"

She seemed a little startled by my enthusiasm, but complied. Staring at the photo, I decided to name her Polly.

She was a cute little sessile nub, measuring about 4 mm. Tests confirm that she was technically precancerous (most are), but benign. Hell, I could have told them that. Just look at that sweet little juicy face, I thought. Would a polyp that adorable cause me any harm? C'mon.

PUPPET SHOW OR INTERPRETIVE DANCE, YOUR CHOICE

1991

Remember when I was foolin' around with that girl, using the flavored condom that made my weiner all minty and limp? I forgot—earlier that night, before the pathetic attempt at fucking, I had cooked supper for us and booted my roommate out of the apartment. I made some sort of pasta thing and had candles and stuff; the whole works, as best as someone as retarded as me could muster.

At one point during the evening I dipped out into the kitchen to get us a second bottle of wine. I wasn't able to peel off the wrapper on the neck of the bottle with just my hands, and grabbed a huge butcher knife for assistance. Somehow during the removal process I managed to put a three-inch slit in the middle finger of my right hand.

Blood was squirting everywhere, and I panicked. Not because of the blood—if there was one thing in life I was used to, it was blood squirting everywhere, so that didn't faze me. But I was reluctant to ruin the atmosphere of our dinner, as well as really, really horny.

I improvised a dressing for my wound as best I could using electrical tape and several handfuls of paper towel. The blood was seeping through, but I had confidence that it would stop. I returned to the supper table (a four-legged folding card table with a blue sheet thrown over it) and with the help of the dim light offered by the candles managed to hide my injury. I kept my hand under the table and commenced to romancin', with her none the wiser.

A few more glasses of wine, though, and I became careless. She was making some point about art or politics or life or something and I leaned forward to feign interest and get a better look at her sumptuous titties. Forgetting myself, I rested my jaw on my hurt hand, placing my sliced-up finger along my chin in what I thought was a thoughtful pose.

From her perspective, of course, it seemed more like I had suddenly whipped out a giant blob of blood-soaked paper from under the table, perhaps to begin some sort of ghoulish after-dinner puppet show.

She screamed.

DON'T USE THE MICROWAVE

1994

No man! No man, I say! No man should have to endure the stench, the stinging! The choking, the burning! As sweet air turns to foulest poison!

I speak, of course, of the time Jeff fried a human turd.

It turns out you don't want to take a human turd and put it on a stove in a pan of hot grease. Bad things ensue. I'm happy to clear that up. Just in case you were wondering.

So don't do it. And it doesn't matter if the turd is your own, you won't be immune. For does not even the mighty asp sicken and wither should the fang and venom he wields pierce his own flesh?! Verily, even your own turds will cause your eyes to water and your gorge to rise should you take them and fry them up hot and fresh and stinking and crisp! And . . . Wait, did I just say "verily"? What the fuck, who do I think I am, Thor?

You know what else? Sometimes people say unkind things about drinkers.

I understand why. It's not like I, personally, never got all liquored up and kicked all the slats out of a fence or threw a small man into some bushes or helped Eric Gilmore huck a frozen turkey through a window with such force that it actually crashed through a corresponding window in the house next door, like six feet away, and we had to run outside and pretend we knew nothing about it, a ruse that worked because everyone was preoccupied with water squirting from the bathroom pipes I had burst moments before by firing a large firework into the toilet and holy shit that was one of the best parties I've ever been to and I often like to think it was our partnership that night that helped Eric overcome some of his dislike for white people.

You never want to wholly overcome your dislike for white people.

Anyway, I can't speak for Eric, but I'm willing to accept some of the blame for the unkind things some people say about drinkers. I've had drinks, I've been naughty.

But then, the people who say unkind things about drinkers, who are they? They sit at home, gray and shriveled souls sipping tea and gnawing at cardboard and using the bitter resentment only borne from a life without joy to criticize and castigate those of us who occasionally take in a draught or two of spirits to loosen the shoulders, sharpen the mind and googly up the eyes. A practice that—as you and I know—puts a little sparkle on the Twinkie, just like Grandpa used to say. So fuck those guys.

I feel like a good drunk does for the soul about like what four or five bowls of raisin bran do for the bowel. I even enjoy the hangover, as long as there's nothing too taxing on the schedule and I can swagger through the day with a refreshing minimum of forebrain activity, just as pleasantly retarded as Coldplay fans, Democrats, Buddhists and people who maintain that Harry Potter books can be enjoyed by adults. (You know, the simpleminded everyday common folk whose scorched bones will one day adorn the walls of my temples.)

Even if I'm a little sensitive to sound and light and motion, I always feel happy and dopey and carefree the day after a good drunkie-wunkie. Why, on hangover days I sometimes even whistle! Or rather try, because really I can't. And then I start laughing to myself when I remember I can't, and people stare because I'm stumbling down the street laughing, but I can't help it because it comes out all like, "Fwoooo! Fwoo!" And sometimes there's a little drool and ah ha hah ha hah, I'm laughing right now, thinking about it, ah hah ha hah ha ha! Fwoooo, fwoo, fwoooo!

Oh, and you know what else? I don't want to get all blah blah blah about society and gender roles and certainly people should be free to define masculinity in any way that makes them happy, but there's this thing, right, with men, this lowest common denominator, and it's that on some level we all measure our manliness by the level of menace we present to polite society. Like, even the most law-abiding and square of us take pride in, for example, how bad our feet stink or that we shat out an abnormally large poo or that we did a cannonball into the pool that ruined a nearby wedding ceremony.

We'll brag about it. Sometimes under the guise of regret, but make no mistake—it's still bragging. Look for the gleam in our eyes as we apologize. Somewhere, deep down in our hypothalamus, that apology is being transmuted into a humorous tale shared with our brother warriors around the campfire.

Don't try and change this. Don't try and dim that gleam. Recognize that it's there for, like, evolutionary reasons, because back in ye olden times disputes were settled by the size of poo and men of the tribe often had to drive away saber-toothed tigers with their terrible, terrible feet.

Now, with our new-fangled modern ways, we're not often called upon to poo into the scales of justice and such, so we need to express ourselves by watching Rodney Dangerfield movies and occasionally becoming a drunken nuisance for a few hours. This is as much a law of science as the law that states a dog will vigorously lick at some peanut butter no matter where you put it, or the fact that channels are changed by an elf that lives inside your TV and, hey kids, why not pour a Coke down there because he sure is thirsty?

Sadly, not every man heeds the call of drunken menace. Some who turn their back on the natural order—most, even—get all pinched and gummed up inside and eventually grow a mustache and become an assistant manager.

In some, though, that menace just builds and builds, growing in strength and permeating every cell until they become a diabolical volcano of horror, capable of spectacular, inhuman feats of botherment. Like frying a turd.

Now, I don't want to get into all the details, but at one point in my life I had developed something of a reputation for lively hijinx. And like I said earlier, I can't deny that in my life there have been periods marked by the generous, perhaps irresponsible use of Evan Williams and underwear and fire.

But I never saw anything like the trouble Jeff and his crew generated. Hell, screw modesty, I'll just go ahead and say it—I was the king of trouble 'round these parts before they came along, the fucking king.

I can't fry a turd, though. Mine or anyone else's. Just can't do it. As I've said many times before, unless there's blood or gold doubloons coming out of my ass, I'm just going to pretend like the place doesn't even exist, much less monkey around with it. And Jeff monkeyed around with his ass and its vile progeny, frying up turds and the like, while sober. Sober! It's astonishing.

Jeff lived in a small apartment with several other sober guys, in conditions that even I, veteran maker of hijinx and squalor that I was, positively feared and envied. They called it Dick House. It was filthy, of course. The front door was studded with uncooked rice, embedded there during an experiment with black powder and a homemade cannon. It was this sort of experiment, as I understand it, that triggered some kind of disagreement between landlord and tenants, one that resulted in a police investigation into possible terrorist activities and a redecoration effort involving painted insults that referred to the landlord by name as well as many, many explicit images taken from pornographic magazines of the spectacularly gay variety.

Terrorism, ha! The cops had no idea. I'd rather have a thousand little rice-sized holes poked in me than put up with one—one!—of the indignities those guys inflicted on each other just to pass the time. These . . . these . . . sober people were just too goddamn comfortable with their own bodies. A little repression is not a bad thing, especially if it prevents you from posing for photographs naked in the shower with a carrot shoved up your rear end, like Jeff did. Or, God forbid, taking a shit into a pickle jar. Which someone there did, as a friendly prank.

Instead of disposing of the befouled pickle jar, as one might be expected to do when striving to remain inside the boundaries of modern civilization, those little goblins kept it around. And they'd offer you a pickle when you came over, then clap and dance and laugh and caper around with glee after you saw that damn turd-pickle swirling around in the brine. Gah! How?! Why?!

The worst was the time someone shat into a hot dog bun, slathered it with mayo, relish and all your favorite condiments and then stuck it in the microwave. They set the power on high and the cook time for the longest possible duration, and then left. I often think about this incident, mulling over the possible motivation for such an act and contemplating the potential presence of supernatural intervention, like maybe demonic possession was the cause or, verily, perhaps even the influence of Loki.

As the story goes, various roommates kind of drifted in, wondering where the turd smell was coming from, but it took hours for them to discover it, like a satanic treasure hunt where the treasure has about the same effect on your sinuses, and perhaps will to live, as the Ark did on those Nazis.

You'd think girls would have nothing to do with this kind of behavior, but no. You'd go over there, maybe mention a girl you liked, one that caught your attention with her quiet intelligence, wholesome good looks and demure personal style, and Jason or Eric or one of those fuckers would go, "Aw, dude! I fucked her last week! I got her to lick my butthole!" And then they'd produce a photo or two, taken by whoever else happened to be in the room. And then they'd start skipping around and clapping and laughing, full of joy and life and ass-carrots, while your vision dimmed and everything that was right and true in the universe unraveled at your feet. Your sad, sad feet.

Girls liked them. A lot. A lot more than they liked me, anyway. Or you. Probably.

Not that they needed girls—they had the Party Melon! Oh wait, maybe this is the worst thing, not the hot dog turd. Aw, who can tell? Anyway, Jason and Eric had a small watermelon that they kept on their coffee table and called the Party Melon. It had many holes cut in it, holes Jason and Eric would use for humping. They wouldn't even take it into the bathroom or anything, just spread out a porno mag on one end of the table, get on their hands and knees and mount up. They didn't even, like, lay down a tarp.

I like to think that, should I ever sink to depths of such casual depravity, I'd have the decency to hide my Party Melon from company or at least swap it out with a new one once in a while. Shit, any self-respecting drunken melon-baller would. Not Jason or Eric, though—they were proud of it, with their values all warped by sobriety. It sat there for weeks. "Ooh, look, look at all the holes," they'd say, obviously quite pleased with their efforts.

I shudder.

Why did I hang around them, you must be wondering? It's a fair question. A lot of it had to do with fear. You simply don't want to cross the wielder of the Party Melon—it's too fearsome a weapon. Members of Dick House were constantly battling with various Gainesville cliques, and the results were terrifying. Nobody could stand against them. Would you want to go to war against an enemy who deploys a hot dog turd against his allies? They used to crap into plastic sandwich bags and freeze it, saving their waste for those times when a rival faction planned to move against them. They'd thaw their shit and sneak out, stealthy under the cover of night, and pack it into the empty spaces under the door handles of their enemies' cars. A few wipes with a towel to the surface of the handle and nothing would seem amiss, but, ah, the next day . . . Unsuspecting fingers would sink into warm, soft offal and terror would sweep across the land. Why hang around them? I wanted to keep an eye on them! I wanted to know where their poo was at all times!

I wasn't there the day Jeff fried that poo, though, thank God. Seriously, witnesses have told me they had to leave the house. It wasn't just the revolting smell. Apparently during the cooking process it gave off some caustic gas. Everybody had to run outside, coughing and choking. Not Jeff, of course. He just stood there, eyes watering, cooking away and laughing.

They had to throw out that frying pan.

Jeff went on to become a schoolteacher.

But they all drink now, for the most part, and in the last decade have drastically reduced the level of danger they pose to society. Which totally proves my point.

MY TAINT IS ALSO THE WORST PLACE ON EARTH

2002

What do you call that stuff, like talking to girls and voting and getting out of bed? Like, when things are futile, but you do them anyway? There's a word. Oh yeah—*symbolic*.

Sometimes it surprises my friends when they find out I enthusiastically buy and read magazines such as *GQ* and *Esquire*. But I do. I get them every month and marvel at all the swank, expensive clothes, dreaming of a day when I'll be able to afford them. I also dream of a day when I'll be able to swap out my grubby, surprised friends for a social circle featuring sailboats, dinner parties and fancy hotels, not to mention single-malt whiskies, serious conversation and maybe sunshine, so I'll have places to wear all that swank, expensive stuff without feeling like a giant dickhead. Although I suppose there is some appeal in sporting the latest fashions around the poor, just to rub it in their dirty faces. Ha ha, take that, poor! Tally ho!

Until my dream comes true, of course, I'm consigned to enthusiastic grooming, putting forth that extra little effort that distinguishes me from all my Neanderthal friends. Doing so helps me pretend I live in a civilized society. I wash myself with dedication, regularly mow the little patch between my eyebrows, apply a spritz of manly smell-good before leaving the apartment and coordinate my inexpensive, but clean, outfits. If I had an ounce of intelligence or wit, or perhaps an erect penis in my mouth, I could almost pass for gay. Ah, sweet fantasy.

Grooming, though, is more than just a ticket to fly on the back of a candy unicorn named Sparkles across a rainbow bridge to Santa's shimmering kingdom of make-believe. It's symbolic. And it's symbolic because it's essentially futile. Every drop of moisturizer applied, every nostril hair plucked—these are Sisyphean tasks. Does not my face drink yon moisturizer and spit up but pimples? Does not the plucked nostril hair yield but a mighty sneeze that causeth two new hairs to sprout forth from my earhole? Well, yes.

As with many futile tasks, solace and meaning can be found when you look to the philosophical. I'll never win any beauty contests (despite doing surprisingly well in the bikini competitions). Children will never stop running from me, screaming. I'll never be able to go to the mall without first donning my government-mandated Hood of Shame. But still I persist, because grooming is symbolic of my overall struggle for personal betterment. I'll never settle for my sad destiny, but instead rail against the cruel machinations of fate and—ooh! I'm like the Elephant Man! Totally. There's a certain fucking nobility in my fucking situation, you know? Class all the way.

Sometimes taking care of your appearance requires more than habitual trips to the salon or holding a line against the introduction of pleats, those terrible pleats that summon forth the hideous visage, or at least pants, of MC Hammer. Sometimes taking care of your appearance requires attending to a spot or two that doesn't really, well, even *appear* that often, although this might depend on your line of work. I'm reminded of the time I required the services of a physician to freeze a giant wart off my taint. Seriously, that thing was enormous. Like an enormous, wobbly thumb.

The taint? It's, ummm . . . You know. Down below. From the Latin, *taint neither here nor there*? Commonly known as "no man's land"? Yes, that's it! The Vikings had six different names for it, including "perineum," and Abraham Lincoln is credited with popularizing the colloquialism "grundle." Just a little trivia, something to share over a single-malt with your expensive sailboat friends at the next sunshine dinner party. Oh, and did you know that area is also where we get the expression "tainted food?" Because you really don't want to eat anything that's been rubbin' on it. Especially if it's been, you know, worked into a lather.

Anyway, a few years ago a desire to better myself caused me to bring my taint forth out of the darkness and expose it to my beleaguered dermatologist. And I was apprehensive about it, much more so than all the other times I brought the accursed thing forth, which is incidentally the habit that led to me getting a damn wart on it in the first place. I don't want to talk about it.

With the dermatologist, though, I *had* to talk about it.

"Before we get started, I need to ask you a question," he said. "Have you notified your sexual partner?"

"All my sexual partners have long since faded into the misty hazes of time," I replied. "Really I'm just doing this because it's symbolic of my aspirations for self-betterment. Sparkles suggested it."

"Very well, then. Let us begin," he said.

I took off my pants and drawers and climbed up on his doctor table, which was covered with a fresh sheet of that ass paper. I crinkled and scooched until I was comfortable, then reclined, opened my legs and let my taint unfurl before the harsh gaze of science.

"Those aren't warts," he said. I looked down to where, alarmingly, he was grinning up from between my thighs. "Those are skin tags."

"No, there's a wart down there," I said. "You're just gonna have to go exploring around a bit."

"Are you sure, Mr. Hughes?" He started fumbling and poking around. "Because I don't—Whoa, what the fudge! Are you growing a damn tail?!" He had found it.

"Look, I just want to get it off of there. What's it gonna be, doc? Lasers? Freeze ray? Pistols at dawn?"

"For this procedure, we use a bitter-ass, freezing-cold chemical generated by a malicious arctic elf kept in this here canister," he said. Good enough. I gathered up all my genitals in my hands for protection, and he began blasting away.

"The wart has grown rather thick, so I'm going to wait a few minutes after the first application, do a scraping, and then reapply the chemical," he said. "Oh, you know what? I might as well go ahead and clean up these skin tags while I'm down here. Regardless, this is going to take a while, and you should expect a fair amount of discomfort."

That's fair, I thought. Discomfort is a small price to pay for a shiny, pink new taint and crotch. Spray and scrape away, intrepid dispatcher of warts.

He continued his work, occasionally glancing up at my stoic expression. "You're taking this rather well," he said. "It's common that patients undergoing this procedure request I stop, to recover from the extreme pain."

"My sense of the absurd serves as a buffer," I said. "Besides, the spray is actually somewhat of a refreshing, morning-time wake-up. Bracing."

He didn't laugh. Sometimes I think my dermatologist is something of a fucknut.

Some time later, my taint had been effectively converted to a wintry, wart-free tundra, a barren landscape where, hopefully, any potential new growths would find no purchase.

"These things typically grow back, so I'll need to see you again in a month," he said. Great. He explained I should expect my grundle to painfully blister, and that for the next few days I should vigorously scrub it during showers to slough off all the dead wart-skin. He made it a point to mention I should throw away the loofah or spatula or whatever used for the scrubbing when finished. Yeah, like I need a memento.

I left his office, driving off into a sunny day filled with promise. Promise and a weepy, blistered taint. That someday would no longer bloom with thumb-sized warts. My taint and crotch stung, but I knew I could parlay this experience into some substantial symbolism. I was not the kind of man to let these things just grow, or at least not the kind of man who'd ignore them after they'd grown to a somewhat unwieldy size. No, I was about self-betterment.

So, let's review: skin tags, that polyp, a huge wart, your everyday poop, blisters, psoriasis, 'roids, fissures and the occasional pimple or fungus. Like the title says, the worst place on Earth. What horror will it birth next? How do I even live with it? Denial, mostly. And drinking. Sparkles, fly me away.

STILL YET MORE VARIOUS HISTORICAL TALES OF INDIGNITY

Age twelve: I grew up nominally religious, mostly because being raised by a psychopath makes the possibility that some benevolent, all-powerful force exists seem really, really appealing. But I still hadn't found a church in which I felt comfortable—Mom practiced some kookified form of that Wicca nonsense and Dad is Catholic, and neither faith held much appeal for me. Too complicated, too ritualistic, too many weird outfits involved, etc.

My friend Randy, who at the time was devoutly religious, was attending a Christian church he described as non-denominational. Supposedly, the aim of this church was to cut out a lot of the hoo-hah and just get down to the straightforward Bible-y stuff. I liked the sound of that. And I relied on Randy for spiritual guidance, even though he once admitted that he thought babies were made by kissing until he was twelve or thirteen.

So I accompany Randy to a church "lock-in," where we're to have fun and socialize, potentially with girls. And who knows, maybe this church will be the house of worship I've been seeking.

We're there for a few minutes when the youth pastor starts discussing science-fiction movies, another passion Randy and I share. Excited, I mention how much I enjoyed my recent viewing of *Time Bandits*.

"You shouldn't be watching Satanic movies like that, Patrick," the pastor says. "It contains a blasphemous portrayal of a supreme being."

My face flushes. It's very quiet. Everyone stares at me like I'm wearing a hat made of dogshit. I think about being "locked in" with these people for the rest of the night, and a cold feeling forms deep in the pit of my stomach.

I give up on all that Jesus stuff once and for all.

Age thirteen: I go to school without first taking a shower. This is not uncommon, because I am a dirty greaseball, but in this instance turns out to be significant.

You see, the day before, in an effort to join the madcap antics of the cool kids, I had thrown an egg out of the window of my schoolbus. Though it was intended for a passing schoolbus transporting kids from another school, it did not find its mark.

Instead, the universe, sensing that an uncool kid was attempting to perform actions outside of his designated scope, threw a little physics into the mix and used some sort of compressed air cushion to slam my egg back into the edge of my own window. Thus, like an Icarus of social acceptance, my temerity was punished and the cosmic balance of life was once again set right.

Well, really, it was more of a warning than a punishment—I barely got gooed at all, though the other kids, whose eggs all hit our rivals with no major complications, found it remarkable that I was unable to successfully deploy my egg at such close range and at such a large target. And they let me know this in ways that, if memory serves, included improvising special songs and chants. I sat for the rest of the trip wondering why I even tried to be popular, or regular, or accepted or liked at all, and cleaned up when I got home.

The next day, though, I show up at the bus stop and it's quickly pointed out that I have shell fragments in my hair, as well as a faint eggy smell, and it is in this way I announce to the world my spectacular lack of hygiene.

I SAT IN SOME GUM

2000

I have this friend, okay, and I'm going to call him Anatol. Because that's his name.

Anatol doesn't drink, or didn't use to, and for a while lived with all those sober fried-poo guys in Dick House. Anatol's also, like, a genius. A bona fide smart guy with a Ph.D. in physics to prove it. For all his fancy book-learnin', though, Anatol hasn't always made such wise choices when deciding how to use his penis.

Taken as detail, the Ph.D./penis dichotomy is a mystery, to be sure, but then Anatol himself is a bit of an enigma. For example, the man is a shambles. He has remarkably shapely calves, but aside from that is just sort of doughy and nondescript in a poorly groomed kind of way. Personal style? He looks like he fell asleep in a pile of someone else's clothes and left the house that morning just wearing whatever stuck to him. Hairdo? That same low-maintenance cut they give to small children, people fresh off the boat from China and folks with Down Syndrome. Yet Anatol always dated extremely attractive young women, smart and fit and well dressed to the last, and eventually even married one. Her name's Jill. I'm still a little pissed off about it. She's even Asian! Or, uh, half Asian! Or something!

Several years ago I was dog-sitting for this guy who—well, let's just say the guy was a douche, and the way he conducted himself lent a lot of weight to my friend Kyle's credo, Don't Trust Anyone Who Uses an Initial in Place of a Proper First Name. (And the first initial followed by full use of the middle name doesn't exempt anybody. Hell, Kyle's first name is Buddy, but he just goes by Kyle, not B. Kyle or something equally douchey.)

This guy with the dog and the initial was always getting fucked up on cocaine and testing me, acting all tough and trying to start a fight, even though he was reedy and sallow-chested and any normal well-fed American man could've broken him in two with half an ass cheek. I wanted nothing more than to use this fellow to test my theory that punching someone really, really hard on the balls can potentially flip their breaker switch, ideally resetting their personality to something more manageable. Despite this urge, I had to be nice to him, because ~~he was a powerful wizard who kept my soul in an enchanted jar~~ he was an editor at a magazine where I worked, and I needed the dough. I liked that dog of his pretty well, too.

One morning D. Ouchebag was out of town, and I was staying at his apartment, passive-aggressively blasting the air conditioning and leaving all the lights on while taking care of that dog. The dog needed a lot of attention, because Editor Boy was in the process of switching his personality from coked-up unconvincing gangsta dude to hippied-up unconvincing deeply spiritual dude without the assistance of a ball-punch, and he insisted on taking the poor beast to this holistic fuckin' shaman instead of a real veterinarian.

This medicine man was all, "Ooh, look at me, I'm mystical, I think Western culture is bad," and he wouldn't give the dog antibiotics, even after he performed some kind of ball surgery on him, so of course the dog developed an infection in his ball sack and would mope around dripping blood and pus out of his balls and dick and I'd have to wipe that shit up and feed the dog, like, a special root. I saved a small vial of that disgusting, infected ball juice, and if I ever run across that magical quack I'm going to put him in a headlock and make him drink it.

Anyway, it was early in the morning, and I fed the dog his phony-ass holistic ball root and took him for his morning walk. I left my glasses behind in the apartment, because I was half asleep and didn't think about it, and also because I didn't like seeing all that dog doo in crystalline detail, but while walking along I nevertheless managed to spot an attractive female a few streets away. I could only make out her general shape, but even with poor eyesight I knew she was fine. A minute or two of squinting and I also noticed she was holding hands with some terrible-looking blob. "Jesus, look at that fat bastard," I thought. "How does a heap like him score a girl like that?! What's his secret? He doesn't even have a good haircut."

I walked another block or so toward them, the whole time thinking, "I'm a shambles, but I'm only half the shambles that guy is, and my weiner's been as dry as the Sahara for months! I should kick his ass, just for having the temerity to date so far above his station, not to mention going all public with it and rubbing it in my face."

A half block closer and the couple waved and called out my name. It was Anatol and Jill, of course. "Hey guys," I said, all cheerful. "What's up!" In my brain, though, I was like, "I should kill him. Or at least get shapely calf implants. Maybe both?"

God, you know, I lived with Anatol for a while, and it was amazing. I swear his room was decorated by a hobo, socks and garbage everywhere. And he didn't have a cover or sheet or anything on his dirty futon, which subsequently was so covered in skeet marks it looked like someone hid behind it during a doughnut fight. No pillowcase, either, and his one pillow was all threadbare and ratty and dark with head-grease in the indention where your head goes, and it smelled like rancid hair from several feet away, ugh. Disgusting! No shortage of slender, bright-eyed young ladies lured in by Anatol's calves to wallow in all that filth, of course, humping around and making noise while in the next room it was just a two-hundred-pound, wood-paneled VCR from 1978 that runs on steam and a fourth-generation tape of *Young Lady Chatterly* keeping me and my dusty ol' dry-ass penis company.

It was during this era that I first witnessed Anatol—remember, a guy with a Ph.D. in physics—do something really fuckin' stupid with his man-bits.

It was inspired by something I showed Anatol, a maneuver called the Minnesota wristwatch. At its core, it's simply one of the many things you can do with your penis to make other people deeply unhappy.

Somehow, in my life, and God knows how, really, I've become acquainted with a number of these disagreeable exercises. For years, at least in my social circles, it was common on festive occasions for someone at some point in the evening to simply pull their scrotum through their fly and start bellowing, "I SAT IN SOME GUM! I SAT IN SOME GUM!" And lo, the hilarity would never fail to doth commence, I swear.

In my occasional sober moments, though, I wondered about the arrangement of I SAT IN SOME GUM. While certainly funny, it didn't seem conceptually sound. I mean, I understood that the pink, wrinkly skin of the scrotum symbolized a wad of used chewing gum, of course, but how did it get to the lap area? Was the gum supposed to have been placed on the underside of a desk or table? Was the initiator of I SAT IN SOME GUM using the gum chair in some novel, lap-oriented way? Did they encounter a wad so mighty that it smooshed up through the taint area and into the frontal crotch region? I'd mull over this for hours.

Years later, I witnessed a more methodical prankster bust out with the move in a way that made it all come together. See, you're supposed to take out the scrotum while sitting, then—this is key—pin it to the seat of your chair with your thumb. Taking advantage of natural ball-sack elasticity, you then rise to a half crouch and exclaim, "I think I sat in some gum!" Voilà! Everyone will look at your awful stretchy balls and be bummed, filling your heart with pure whirling smiles of delight. When I finally saw this feat performed by a qualified professional, it resolved years of questioning for me.

How this trick degenerated among my friends to simply pulling out your balls and hollering is a mystery, but I'm sure there's a sad commentary on the state of society in there somewhere.

But the Minnesota wristwatch operates on the same basic premise. First of all, though, Minnesota doesn't have anything to do with it. It's just an arbitrary kind of appellation, something to divert the attention of your potential victim. I like the rhythms of "Minnesota" and feel a regional prefix adds zest and hearkens back to a time before the homogenization of American culture, when different areas of the country still had their own distinctive cultural flavors. Some, however, prefer a textile approach and favor the title "snakeskin wristwatch." The important thing here is just to distract the section of the brain in the hapless recipient that's always on the lookout for intrusive penises or balls.

The first step in physically performing the Minnesota wristwatch is to extract the penis through the fly hole with the right hand. Next, firmly grasp the mushroom head between thumb and forefinger while moving the left arm toward the crotch, keeping it low. The left wrist should be held against the body, palm down, as close to the fly as possible. Using the dickhead for guidance, you next wrap the penis, moving from right to left across the back of the left wrist. Performed correctly, the veiny and unpleasant shaft will stretch across the outside of the wrist, presenting a smooth expanse of weiner tissue to any unfortunate onlookers.

To complete the trick, you carefully—very carefully, you're not going to be too mobile here—sidle up to someone you want to freak out and say, "Hey, have you seen my new Minnesota wristwatch?"

The great thing about this gag is that ~~children enjoy it so~~ it's difficult to discern the exact nature of the strange, fleshy mass on first glance. Inevitably, the recipient of the Minnesota wristwatch will spend seconds, minutes or even hours staring at it, trying to figure it all out: If it was really a wristwatch it would have a dial, a digital readout . . . It's bizarre looking, yet somehow familiar . . . Perhaps a little too *organic* . . . Is that suede? Leather? Say, why is he holding his arms in such a weird way, so low and close to his crotch and aaaaAAAAARRRRRGGGGHHHH NOOOOOO!!!

The victim, having necessarily stared at the ghastly thing for longer than anyone would want to while working through the clever wristwatch disguise, will have had a good dose of weiner molecules fly right into their eyes by the time they figure it out, significantly intensifying their shame and disgust. Self-immolation or seppuku are frequent reactions, and if you love pranks and lively high jinks, that's really about the highest praise you can get.

So, one time Anatol and the other roommates were clustered on a couch, watching TV, and I crab-walked in and pulled the Minnesota wristwatch. Everyone was grossed out for about four seconds before getting re-hypnotized by the TV (they were also generally blasé about things most respectable members of society find repellant), except for Anatol. It was his first encounter with the trick.

"It's amazing," he said. "How do you do it?"

"Just wrap it, dude," I said.

"But . . . how? I don't think I could do it. You must be very well-endowed."

"Yes, my whole family's very proud."

"I have to try this," Anatol said, and went into the hall. For the next few minutes we could hear him out there, making strange grunting noises.

"I can't do it!" Anatol yelled.

"Keep trying!" We didn't want to discourage him.

"It hurts!"

"Stretch it!"

Anatol yelled, obviously in legitimate pain. "It's not working!"

"I gotta go see what he's doing," I thought, and joined Anatol in the hall. Turns out Mr. Ph.D. had overlooked the obvious and was trying to wrap his scrotum and balls around his wrist instead of his penis. Jesus. I wince just thinking about it.

Even that remarkable lapse of good judgment was but a warm-up to Anatol's grandest achievement. Now, this is something I didn't personally witness—I've just heard secondhand accounts and am fairly certain that what I'm about to write is not strictly 100% accurate. Frankly, though, I don't care about the truth and figure if my take gets repeated often enough it'll supplant reality and enter public record as the definitive version.

It takes place at an informal wedding reception for my friends Sean Bonner and Caryn Coleman, something held at an unbelievably dirty and sleazy punk-rock club called the Hardback. The Hardback was much beloved by Gainesville dirtbags and hipsters for years and years, as it hosted many good bands and pretty much let you get away with damn near anything. In return, you occasionally had to pay a small cover charge and, should you need to pee, brave the club's awful restrooms.

Now, despite sobriety, Anatol encouraged other people's drinking habits (like they needed it) and around this time was known for his Flaming Dr. Peppers. He carried around a backpack with all the various elixirs and potions you need to make this refreshing drink and would gladly fix you one up upon request, carefully measuring the amounts and calibrating the ratios before delivering the coup de grace—fire! Yes, the last step to making this cocktail was to float some kind of combustible substance on top and set it aflame. Yay!

So Anatol is at the party, making his Flaming Dr. Peppers and giving best wishes to the happy couple, when inspiration strikes. They have those disposable cameras everywhere, like they do at weddings and such, so guests can snap photos. Anatol figures it'd be fun to go into the bathroom with a camera and some of that Flaming Dr. Pepper mix and secretly snap a pic of his penis on fire. Imagine the wonder on Sean's and Caryn's faces when they develop their reception photographs and come across this!

Jill, still totally bewitched by the calves, agrees to assist Anatol, and they head to the restroom. Like I said, the Hardback was filthy, but the bathrooms were positively toxic. Really, people would jog a quarter mile to Subway to take a poop rather than get their butt cheeks anywhere near a Hardback toilet. Hell, even when peeing you'd stand as far back as you could from that gaping, demonic maw, lest a germ fly up from the seat and light upon your ding-dong.

Inside, Jill gets the camera positioned while Anatol drops his pants and douses his penis in Pepper mix. Once alight, Anatol figures the alcohol will burn for a few seconds, giving them plenty of time to take a picture before his weiner becomes seriously endangered. I guess in physics class they don't teach you about the nature of pubic hair, though, because after everything's set up and Anatol flicks the lighter, his man-bush immediately bursts into a giant fireball, shooting hot flame up into his face.

Anatol screams. Jill screams and, sensibly, runs out of the restroom. Frantic, Anatol pats out his pubic flames as best as he can without mashing up his balls. A minute or two later, Jill reenters, and finds Anatol standing there, terrified, with his hands covering his crotch.

Anatol turns accusatory. "You left me!" he says.

"I'm sorry," Jill says. "I was scared."

"I'm scared, too," he says.

"Are you hurt?"

"I don't know. I'm afraid to look."

"We have to, baby," Jill whispers. "If you're burned, we're going to have to get you to a hospital."

Anatol is absolutely mortified. The last thing he wants to consider is serious penis burns. But he has to look. Slowly, ever so slowly, he moves his hands away from his crotch . . .

Nothing! No burns, no blistering . . . It seems Anatol has somehow escaped injury. They both breathe a sigh of relief.

Problem is, Anatol's crotch is still doused in flammable liquid. A second or two after removing his hands, the inrush of oxygen reignites a hidden pube ember, surprising Anatol and Jill with another gigantic fireball.

Anatol screams. This time, though, Jill just laughs, and snaps a picture.

Anatol rushes over to the toilet, splashing the water there onto his crotch to douse the flames. Me, I would've opted for the fire, given the choice. Those bathrooms were seriously gross.

Later, Sean and Caryn develop the pictures. Something about the flash on those cameras rendered the flames invisible, so all you see is Anatol's tiny penis, shriveled in pain from an attack by an unseen enemy.

I wonder how that works, those flames turning invisible in the photo. You reckon a physicist could explain it?

WE WILL
BE GOOD
PENISHEIMERS

1980

I spent a year as a Webelo, which is the pupal stage of American scouting . . .
Yes, the transitional period between wormy, larval Cub Scout and the splendid, colorful butterfly-dom that is, uh, Boy Scouts and . . . Jeez, never mind.

If I remember correctly, I think *Webelo* is supposed to be some kind of
fuckin' anagram or euphemism or something for "We will be good Scouts,"
although frankly the connection there strikes me as tenuous, at best. And,
frankly, I wasn't really paying a lot of attention there, back in the day.

Regardless, it's clear to me that whoever thought that shit up was a fucking dumbass, because in addition to not really doing a very good job of
evoking that little "good scouts" mantra, "Webelo" is the most awkward
and stupid name for an organization this side of my grandfather's beloved
Penisheimers, a popular American social club that as I'm sure you know was
founded by West Coast community leaders in 1887 to oppress the Chinese.

Man, I was a shitty Webelo and . . . Webelo . . . Webelo . . . Weeee-be-looo . . . Wheee-buh-looow . . . Wheeee-blow . . . Ah hah ha ha, "We blow." I just noticed that.

Anyway, I was a shitty Webelo. Perhaps the shittiest. I had long, greasy hair and had been raised to hate America and not care about the Bible. All the clean-cut churchy dudes who had blossomed into full Boy Scout status were supposed to be mentoring us Webelos, but they could totally tell I was a degenerate and didn't even talk to me. My mom was too cheap to spring for a proper uniform, so I had to wear a faded, ancient Webelo getup scrounged from some garage sale, and it was all fucked-up looking and unstylish and made out of, like, stained pantaloons and ripped lederhosen.

Pretty much the only people in my troop who acknowledged my presence, and really the main reasons why I signed up in the first place, were my buddies Chip Coldwell and Alex Stein. By getting on board with all that Webelo shit we could all go camping together, which was super appealing, since my mom had up and converted to lesbianism by that point and the only camping we did as a family anymore involved the female softball team. Joining the Webelos gave me my only real opportunity to go fool around in the woods without being subjected to shit like Sapphic tribunals tasked with deciding whether me and my eleven-year-old weiner should be sequestered away from all the womyn-folk, lest they stray too close to my crotch and get raped by the pre-tumescent man-vibes emanating from my ding-dong, and I swear to God I'm not even making that last part up, and if you say I am I'm going to punch you in the brain.

This should come as no big surprise, since I've already informed you that they were my friends, but Chip and Alex were almost as socially awkward as I was. Oh, and dirty Jews to boot, so the Bible-y guys and various squad leaders and troop chiefs (or whatever they had, I can't fuckin' remember) were more than happy to ignore them, too. The three of us often found ourselves left to our own devices on camping trips, squatting in the leaves, discussing the latest episode of *Dr. Who* while everyone else was running around tying knots and praying and learning CPR and being wholesome.

Well, mostly wholesome. The older scouts occasionally made a stab at bad-kid-ism, but their frame of reference was just too white-bread and they could never pull it off. One trip, I think to the Big-Ass Scout and Webelo Good-Timey Jubilee, saw our troop meet up in the woods with a rival bunch of squares for a planned gang rumble, but everyone just ended up comparing merit badges and reciting the Pledge of Allegiance or selling each other *Grit* or whatever, and shit never threw down. I had a D battery in a sock that I was fixin' to use to conk somebody on the head, so you can imagine my disappointment.

That same trip I came 'round a tent near the edges of our site and spooked three or four of the older scouts. Turns out they were all jumpy because they were smoking—get this—dried pine needles in a rolled-up piece of brown paper grocery sack and didn't want to get busted. They told me I was too young and naïve to cop some of their fine pine-needle buzz, and I kind of laughed, because despite my young age I had already smoked several cigarettes made from marijuana at that point. Informing them of this just reinforced my dirtbag rep.

Hey, when you're a kid, how often are you supposed to get scoliosis tests? Because I just remembered—the head troopie guy was also my middle school P.E. coach, and he administered a damn scoliosis test every other week. Everybody dreaded it—you had to march into his office and close the door, and he'd be sitting there wearing mirrored aviator sunglasses, smiling a tight little smile. Nobody would speak—you knew the drill. Take off your shirt and bend over toward him and he'd kind of feel and press around on your spine and ribs, looking for abnormalities and no doubt enjoying his massive boner. As best as I can remember he never stuck anything up my butt or anything, but those tests were still pretty traumatic, and I wasn't exactly jumping at the chance to share my tent with the guy on camping trips, you know?

Oh! Man! One Webelo camping trip traumatized me even worse than those scoliosis tests. It was pretty much the second scariest experience of my life, an incident involving a kid named Carsten Vala. Remember the first scariest thing in my life, the time when I was just a little kid and went to go make a pee-pee in the big-boy toilet for the first time and I got up on my tippy-toes and rested my ding-dong on the rim of the seat to make a tinkle and the lid fell and clamped down on my lil' nubbin like a giant clam on an old-timey diver's leg? And I stood there screaming in horror until Dad came running to pry me loose? Well, the Carsten Vala episode was just like that, except without nubbin, thankfully.

Hmmm . . . No, actually, come to think of it, it really wasn't like the toilet-clamp at all. And, to be totally honest, I don't know for sure if it was, like, even officially the second scariest thing or not. I haven't been in the habit of ranking that sort of thing, and the more I think about it now the more it seems the scoliosis tests might actually come in at number two. Frankly, though, I kind of don't give a shit.

But it was scary.

We were camping and doing the traditional thing where you tell scary stories around the fire, and it all seems like good squirmy fun until you hump your ass back to that dark fuckin' isolated tent and have to lie there for nine hours quivering every time a nearby squirrel bumps into a goddamn acorn, because somehow the removal of that warm, fiery glow makes the existence of the Moss Man suddenly seem all too possible and—what the fuck was that?! Shhhh! Shhhhhh!! What the fuck was that rustling sound?!

. . . And, shit, Carsten? You think a kid named Carsten Vala is going to protect you from the fuckin' Moss Man? Carsten was Danish or some shit and wore those terrible little Umbro shorts all the time. What the fuck is he going to do? You can't whoop the Moss Man's ass in Umbros. You can't whoop anybody's ass in Umbros. The best you could hope for with Carsten is that he'd whip out a soccer ball and challenge the Moss Man to a scrimmage. And maybe you could book on out of there while the Moss Man dined on his flesh.

Oh, the Moss Man, yeah. Supposedly he was a crazy murderer that got all bit by dogs and cut up by barbed wire escaping from a local prison. As the story goes, he was on the run through the swamps around the clock for a solid week before finally shaking Smokey and the dogs off his trail and collapsing into a big wad of Spanish moss, where he slept for like four days. When he woke up, he found the moss had taken root and grown into the deep cuts and gashes all over his face and body, and this turned him extra double crazy, and ever since he roamed the Florida woods all hideous and mossy, just killing the fuck out of everybody in a most grisly fashion and—wait, wait, shhh! Did you just hear something?! Oh, fuck this. That better not be no goddamn Moss Man rustling around out there. Shit.

Laugh all you want, sure. We'll see how hard you laugh the next time you're out in the dark-ass woods all surrounded by spooky moss and you hear kind of a murder-y noise in the bushes.

Anyway, the older scouts filled us full of campfire dread and then ex-pelled us from warmth and communal protection, sending us on a Bataan Death March through acres of moss back to our tents where we were to cower away the night. I was sharing a tent with Carsten on this trip, and while this was certainly preferable to bunking down with Coach Fondles, it didn't exactly settle my nerves in regards to fighting off forest haints. But we made it there okay and mumbled a few consoling words to each other as we got in our sleeping bags and hunkered down, hoping for a few minutes of shuteye before daybreak. Surprisingly, I managed to suppress thoughts of the Moss Man and drift off fairly quickly.

At some point, though, I was woken up by a noise. A rustle.

I was in the thick of dreamland and struggling to swim back to consciousness when I heard the noise again. Totally disoriented, I just kind of lay there. Where was I? Why was I all cold and unhappy? And why is that sound significant?

Then I heard it again. And close. And it hit me: Moss Man.

The thought jolted me awake. I lay there in the darkness, still as I could be, still woozy but with all senses on overdrive. And the rustling sounded again, loud.

This time, though, it was accompanied by a frantic, wordless moaning. Whoah.

The initial shock lasted less than a second, quickly giving way to a handful of dueling lightspeed rationalizations. Raccoon? No, raccoons don't moan. Wounded raccoon? No, no, too small.

Then it happened again. It was loud. And close. And it was accompanied again by that terrible, desperate moaning.

Cougar, maybe? Cougars don't moan, unless . . . Cougar in heat? Bear? Dare I even consider it, like for real? . . . Moss Man?

Ah, no—it was probably some of those douche bag older scouts.

When they bothered to notice me at all, it was usually to try and pull typical lightweight hazing shit that only fooled their fellow Baptists—sending kids out to go get left-handed steak knives or thirty feet of shoreline, rounding up dupes for a snipe hunt, that kind of thing. Lame. That kind of shit never worked on me, probably because I once read, like, an Encyclopedia Brown book from 1912 or something that wised me up, and I knew they were resentful that I never fell for any of their antics. The noise was probably just them thinking they were going to Moss Man me into some kind of candy-ass frenzy. Well, fuck them. I had survived the fearsome Tribunal of Separatist Lesbos, had I not? I'd show them!

Suddenly, the rustling turned into a bona fide thrashing. And this time it didn't stop. And that moan started up again, and I realized just how close it was—it wasn't in the bushes! It was right up against the side of the tent! I could feel it bumping against my leg!

I turned wholly candy-ass and started kicking and squealing. The moan transformed into a terrifying, bestial grunt: NNNGH! NNNGH! NNNN-NNNNNGGGGGHHH!! Holy shit, it was loud, and right outside!

No! Wait! It was there—it was in the tent with me! AAAAAGH! I could see something spazzing around on the other side of the tent—it had Carsten! It was . . . Eating him alive! Or . . . or . . . Humping his face! Or something!

Frantic, I grabbed my flashlight. The terrible noise and commotion reached a crescendo, becoming unbearable. Every nerve in my body threatened to shatter as I clicked on the light, fully prepared to come face to face with what I expected to be endless horror, rivers of gore that moments ago were my fellow Webelo Carsten . . . I could only hope my death would be swift, that the Moss Man's infernal powers met their limit at the edge of the physical world and I would escape his hellish grasp as my soul escaped the constraints of my earthly body . . .

The light came on. I trembled. I saw Carsten's eyes, shining in the beam, but starting to dim as he succumbed to . . . to . . . the grasp of . . . a big wad of nylon? What the hell?

Turns out Carsten's complicated dental headgear had snagged on his sleeping bag. He rolled over five or six times after sacking out, pulling the bag tight around his shoulders and head. His arms were pinned and he seriously couldn't breathe.

I got him out of there before he died and we went back to sleep.

. . . Oh, wait! Shit! Just now I remembered the worst thing!

There, was this movie, right, *Dressed to Kill,* directed by Brian De Palma. And my mom got together with a pack of lesbians and went to go protest this movie, because it was supposedly misogynistic and promoted violence against women and stuff, though your guess is as good as mine how they figured that out, because I'm pretty sure none of them had actually seen it.

Anyway, Mom knew TV reporters and all were going to be there, so she made me dress up in my ramshackle Webelo costume and join the protest. I was forced under pain of endless grounding to wave a placard and march around in a circle in front of the movie theater, because Mom thought it lent their stupid thing credibility to have a Boy Scout out there chanting "Hey hey! Ho ho! Bad ol' movie has got to go!" or whatever with all the commies and killjoys and hateful rug munchers.

So I did. I muttered their dumb rhymes and marched around and carried my sign, and the people waiting in line stared at me like I was a giant douche, and Mom of course made a giant fuss over everything. She got some news dude to come over and interview me, and they had a TV camera and a light on me and asked me why I was out there. "Violence against women is bad," I mumbled. And it is. I believed it.

In the back of my mind, though, the Moss Man was stabbing them all, the lesbians and the movie people and the TV guys and everyone else, just stabbing and stabbing them over and over and over again. With his penis.